About the Author

I began writing after retiring from teaching in the Humanities Department of Vanier College in Montreal. Two of my comedies were produced at Montreal's Fringe Festival. "Behind the Masks" is my first novel. I am working on a second thriller. Tentative title — "Best Served Cold".

BEHIND THE MASKS

Irene Saharov

BEHIND THE MASKS

Vanguard Press

VANGUARD PAPERBACK

© Copyright 2023
Irene Saharov

The right of Irene Saharov to be identified as author of
this work has been asserted by her in accordance with the
Copyright, Designs and Patents Act 1988.

All Rights Reserved

No reproduction, copy or transmission of this publication
may be made without written permission.
No paragraph of this publication may be reproduced,
copied or transmitted save with the written permission of the publisher, or in accordance
with the provisions
of the Copyright Act 1956 (as amended).

Any person who commits any unauthorised act in relation to
this publication may be liable to criminal
prosecution and civil claims for damages.

A CIP catalogue record for this title is
available from the British Library.

ISBN 978 1 80016 629 5

Vanguard Press is an imprint of
Pegasus Elliot Mackenzie Publishers Ltd.
www.pegasuspublishers.com

This is a work of fiction. Names, characters, businesses, places, events and incidents are either the product of the author's imagination or are used in a fictitious manner. Any resemblance to actual persons, living or dead, or actual events is purely coincidental.

First Published in 2023

Vanguard Press
Sheraton House Castle Park
Cambridge England

Printed & Bound in Great Britain

Dedication

Dedicated to my son, Robert Saharov (1969–2022)

Chapter 1

A little yellow bird flew out of the thick green canopy of Bangkok's sprawling Lumphini Park. It flew over the gleaming chrome of the elevated Skytrain, over the clogged, blaring traffic on Rama IV Road, and past the Abdul Rahim Palace with its glittering crown for a roof. The little bird landed on the edge of a fountain under a sprawling banyan tree in the courtyard of the ochre-walled compound of the International High School. Having quenched its thirst, it flew across to the building that housed teachers from abroad and landed on the third-floor window ledge.

"Hi, birdie, hot enough for ya?" asked Elizabeth. With one bare, suntanned knee on the windowsill, she turned the air conditioning unit on high. Elizabeth was slim and curvaceous, with translucent skin and short copper locks. People always noticed her eyes. They were turquoise and remarkably beautiful.

The bedroom was tiny — two narrow beds separated by a white night table. Both Elizabeth and Marie-France were barefoot, in shorts and tank tops. Marie-France, her short black curls bent over the piles of clothes on her bed, dropped a stack of underwear into her suitcase. "My brother said that Mother's surgery went well, but I don't believe him! I can always tell by his voice. He was lying."

"They do wonders with hearts nowadays." Elizabeth patted her friend's shoulder. "You'll see. It will be all right! The principal was so nice to let you go before the end of the term. I'll see you in September, if not before," said Elizabeth, and sat down on her narrow bed.

Elizabeth did not tell her friend how sorry she was to be left alone. All their lives Elizabeth and Marie-France had been inseparable. They lived next door to each other in the Notre Dame de Grace district of Montreal. Both were children of single mothers. Both graduated from Concordia University with Bachelor of Arts degrees. Marie-France suggested they also acquire English as a Second Language certificates before stepping across the threshold of adulthood and embracing the adventure of life. Marie-France found the International School in Bangkok, where they were hired to teach both English and French. It was Marie-France who planned their tour of India and a trip to Angkor Wat. Elizabeth admired her friend's energy and organizational skills. She called her 'Wonder Woman', though in reality Marie-France was no Amazon. She was short and a little pudgy, with a round face, big blue eyes, and rosy cheeks. Her lips were usually smiling. But not today.

"And thanks again for taking over my private French lessons at the embassy," said Marie-France, while deciding which clothes to leave behind. "I know it's a chore."

"I really don't like embassy types. At that Friday night happy hour, the only guy our age was such a self-important little twerp! Your Stephen Turner, isn't he one of the top guys?"

"He's the head honcho for trade, but he's really, really nice! His only problem is that he misses classes all the time. The government, bless its big generous heart, pays me whether I actually teach or not. Remember, you'll have to go to his office in the Abdul Rahim building. And be prepared — he's absolutely gorgeous."

"Really? He must be old. Probably over forty! How's his French?"

"Pathetic. He needs to pass the Level A proficiency test if he wants to be posted to some place sexy like Paris. Look, I feel guilty. This gig will spoil your summer travel, but you can still take long weekend trips."

"What are friends for?"

When Elizabeth went to the Canadian Embassy on the fifteenth floor of the Abdul Rahim Palace for the scheduled French lesson, she sat in the waiting room for half an hour before Stephen Turner's personal assistant, Mrs O'Donnell, told her that he was still on the telephone with Tokyo. Elizabeth waited another fifteen minutes before Mrs O'Donnell said, "Sorry, dear, now he's been called to the ambassador's office. He may be there for a long time."

The two women chatted as they walked to the elevator.

"Does Mr Turner always work late in the evenings?"

"No, not always. We're part of a working group for the upcoming SEATO conference; it's a busy time."

"Have you worked with Mr Turner for a long time?"

"Two years now. But this is my last month. I'm retiring. Ottawa is sending a new Global Affairs Staff recruit. She's a Thai-Canadian — actually speaks the language." Mrs O'Donnell also told Elizabeth that Stephen's wife, Laura, was a professional artist, and Christine, their daughter, was away at some posh school in England. "Mrs Turner is so beautiful! She's British, you know. They're both tall, thin, and so very good looking. They always make a splash at embassy cocktail parties."

Before the next scheduled French lesson, Mrs O'Donnell called Elizabeth and said that Mr Turner was cancelling. Elizabeth finally met Stephen on her third visit to the embassy. It was five fifteen, and Mrs O'Donnell informed her boss that Elizabeth was waiting.

"He said he will come and get you in a minute or so," she said, and left.

The door to Stephen's office remained closed — five, then ten minutes went by. *He knows I'm here, damn it! Am I some sort of a court lackey? This is such a waste of time! OK, that's it! I'll walk in and tell him I quit on the spot!*

"Mr Turner."

He was at his desk, staring intently into his computer.

I must be invisible. "Mr Turner," she repeated, hoping he would not hear the trembling in her voice.

He looked up. "Oh," he gasped. "Oh, yes... You are the new Marie-France."

"My name is Elizabeth!"

"Sorry, I mean Elizabeth. I forgot! I simply forgot," he said, as he rose from his chair and walked towards her.

Elizabeth, her irritation rising after his frank admission that he had forgotten her very existence, stood biting her lower lip. "It's a little late for a lesson, Mr Turner. I came to tell you that I'm going home."

"I do apologise," he said, following her out of the office. "We've been so swamped this week..." The elevator door closed before he could finish the sentence.

Elizabeth was still upset when she walked into her apartment. Impulsively, she sent off an email.

"Dear Mrs O'Donnell, I waited forty-five minutes only to find that Mr Turner had forgotten about me. I am very sorry, but I cannot work like this." As soon as the email was gone, Elizabeth shuddered. What about her promise to Marie-France? What would she have done? She'd tell me not to be so impulsive, to look before you leap, etc. etc. *I'll call Mrs O'Donnell tomorrow and apologise.*

At lunchtime on the following day, her cell phone rang. "Elizabeth, Mr Turner asked me to call you. He is sorry about the misunderstanding. He will be ready for next Tuesday. You do understand that he is a busy man. Marie-France assured us of your reliability."

Elizabeth felt chastened. She arrived at precisely five fifteen. An unsmiling Mrs O'Donnell ushered her into Stephen Turner's office and left for the day. Elizabeth was apprehensive. Turner was glued to his computer screen. Elizabeth was uneasy, not sure what Mrs O'Donnell had told him about her email.

He looked up with an ironic smile and said, "Sorry about last week, Miss Burgess. It was sheer hell around here." He stood up and motioned to a brown leatherette couch in the corner of the office. "You can put your stuff on the coffee table." Then he opened the door of a wooden cabinet behind his desk to reveal a bar with a mini refrigerator.

"I find it difficult to switch off work right away. Do you mind if I have a drink?" Stephen asked, and poured himself a scotch and soda. "Marie-France never did join me, but perhaps I can get you something?"

"No, thank you." Elizabeth tried to assume an all-business tone. "I will follow Marie-France's lesson plans. Mr Turner, did you prepare the exercises she assigned?"

"No," he said, and sank down on the armchair across from the couch.

"Have you been practising with the audiotapes? They really help with pronunciation."

"I have been a bad boy," he said with a disarming smile. She noticed the slight gap between his front teeth. Elizabeth switched to French. "Tell me about your first posting. Just talk, don't dwell on grammar."

Stephen's French was basic, and he often injected English words. He managed to give a schoolboy-level description of Buenos Aires, where he served as the third secretary. He spoke with enthusiasm about the sophistication of the city he called 'the Paris of South America'.

"Did you know that couples dance the tango on street corners? My first Argentinian girlfriend was a tango teacher," he volunteered, and got up to make himself another scotch and soda. "The women in Argentina are so lovely," he said, and looked at Elizabeth with frank appreciation.

Their eyes met, and Elizabeth felt her cheeks flare. As she listened to Stephen talk, she could not help but notice his long, thin fingers. She made an effort not to stare. Her gaze wandered to his face. *High cheekbones. Wide mouth. The lower lip is a lot fuller than the top lip. Not totally unattractive. I wonder what it would feel like...* She winced, shocked by the onset of an inappropriate thought.

At the end of the hour, Elizabeth looked at her watch. "I hope this wasn't too painful."

"I really enjoyed it. I got more out of this conversation than all those dreary grammar drills. Can I expect you on Thursday?"

"Yes." She pushed some papers across the coffee table. "Do try to squeeze in these exercises. Marie-France said you have the audiotapes."

For the rest of May, the French lessons took place twice a week, on Tuesday and Thursday. Elizabeth selected articles on economics or politics from French-language newspapers for discussion. In the beginning, she was a little intimidated by this high-ranking diplomat, but Stephen, particularly after his second scotch and soda, was unpretentious and charming. Even in his bad French, he was an engaging raconteur, with stories about his experiences in various posts. Some time during that month, they switched from Miss Burgess and Mr Turner to Elizabeth and Stephen.

Once, while Stephen was talking about his posting to Mexico, Elizabeth asked, "What was the name of your girlfriend in Mexico City?" In the next instant, she froze. *Lizzie! That is an inappropriate question!*

"Margarita," he said. "I almost married her."

"I'm sorry, I should not ask personal questions. Where did you meet your wife? Sorry, that's also a personal question."

"I was working in Ottawa, and Laura came from England on some sort of exchange. We met at an art exhibition. It was love at first sight."

"Love at first sight. Does it really happen?"

"Yes. Often, in my case," he said with a wry smile. "Come now, you must know. You must have broken a few hearts with your beautiful eyes."

"Please, you are making me feel uncomfortable." Elizabeth blushed.

"Why? You know that you have beautiful eyes! The women in Argentina, at least at the time I lived there, accepted compliments graciously. My mother was half Spanish, you know. Her father, my grandfather, was such an old-school Spanish gentleman. I remember he used to kiss ladies' hands, open doors, and was always profuse with compliments. That kind of behaviour used to be considered gallantry."

"Times have changed," said Elizabeth. "Now, let's discuss this article from *Le Monde*."

By early June, Elizabeth had to admit that she looked forward to the French lessons. She showered and changed into fresh clothes before each meeting. She took the time to add a little eye shadow to show off her turquoise eyes. When she was not working, she found that her thoughts, like a relentless tide, always rolled back to Stephen. Life seemed drab and uninteresting between lessons. *You have to snap out of this, Lizzie!*

In late June, as she stepped out of the elevator on the fifteenth floor, she saw a throng of employees waiting to go down. Once inside the Canadian Embassy, there stood Stephen closing his office door. The back of his sky-blue shirt was wet.

"I hoped they'd fix the air conditioning by now. We can't stay here."

They were the only two people in the next elevator. They both pushed the down button at the same time. Their fingers touched, and they both pulled back as if scorched. The elevator was stifling, but Elizabeth felt a cold frisson rise up her arm. She dared not look at him, lest he notice her sudden discomposure. On the eighth floor, a mass of people crowded in. Elizabeth and Stephen were pushed up against the back wall of the elevator. Her right arm was glued to his. She felt a burning heat spread from her arm through her entire body. They were the last out of the elevator. They did not look at each other as they stood on the sidewalk of Rama IV Road.

"Which way are you going?"

"I live right here," she said, and pointed to the ochre walls of the school compound. He followed her down the street.

"I know you work here."

"I live here, too."

They stopped at the main entrance to the compound. Elizabeth did not invite him to follow her onto the grounds. Nor did she say goodbye. They sat on a white wrought-iron bench under the banyan tree. She felt wound up like a tight spring — every muscle rigid and tense.

"Let me give you your assignments."

Stephen did not respond. He sat silently, looking across the school grounds.

"We could discuss this article," she offered, and took a printed sheet from her briefcase. "Why don't you read it out loud?"

Their discussion of the article was stilted. He spoke without looking at her. Stephen's French seemed to have deteriorated.

"I can't seem to concentrate," he said. "Where do you live?" He looked across at the three buildings that edged the grounds.

"The top floor over there." She pointed to a three-storey structure that abutted the Abdul Rahim Building. "It's mainly for teachers from abroad. My apartment is the one with the air conditioning unit in the window." She felt as if she had just said something inappropriate.

Stephen rose abruptly. "See you on Thursday," he said, and walked away.

Elizabeth was taken aback by his sudden departure. She remained sitting on the bench until the knot in her diaphragm relaxed, then she went home.

On Thursday, Mrs O'Donnell phoned just as Elizabeth stepped out of the shower. She told Elizabeth that Stephen would be delayed. It was best to cancel. Elizabeth's pleasant buzz of nervous anticipation vanished. She trudged to the bedroom and put on a pair of shorts and an old T-shirt. Feeling deflated, she sat on the rattan couch in the corner of the main room, which served as a living room, dining room and kitchen. For a long time, she stared into the coffee table, until she felt her stomach rumble. The refrigerator was empty except for a few cans of beer and a plastic bag of wilting iceberg lettuce. She remembered the glass jar of Bolognaise sauce at the back of the cupboard and was about to place a large pot of water to boil when the doorbell rang. Elizabeth assumed it was one of her neighbours and opened the door. It was Stephen. Elizabeth felt a surge of panic. Her first thought was that she was barefoot. Without her flip-flops, she felt naked. Wide-eyed, she stood and stared at Stephen. He looked deflated, as if his confidence and self-assurance had vanished.

"I brought the assignments," he said. His voice was slightly hoarse. He looked straight at Elizabeth with a hint of anxiety in his eyes, as if he was a schoolboy hand-delivering a late assignment. They both knew this visit was inappropriate. They both knew why he had come.

"Come in," she said. These words meant she could not plead innocence. She had become a willing accomplice in what was bound to happen next. He stepped across the threshold. Like an automaton, she took a step forward. Stephen kissed her lightly on the mouth. He crushed her against his chest. "I couldn't wait to see you again," he whispered. "What about you?"

Elizabeth looked up at Stephen with a mixture of astonishment and joy. He kissed her again. Then, spontaneously, they were kissing with a mounting intensity — frantically, hungrily. The last coherent thought in Elizabeth's mind was, *How did this happen?*

As she lay in bed after he had gone, her heart told her that something momentous, something life-altering had just taken place. The 'French lessons' were to take over her life. They now met in Elizabeth's apartment rather than at the embassy. During the first month of their affair, Elizabeth experienced a happiness she had never felt before. Fellow teachers told her that she looked radiant. There was a sparkle in her eyes, her skin glowed. Life could have been perfect if only she could be with Stephen more often. He could not see her on weekends due to his 'situation'. They hardly ever mentioned his 'situation'. Elizabeth tried not to think about the fact that he was a married man. Yes, her Catholic upbringing taught that adultery was a sin, but Elizabeth did not feel guilty. She followed her heart, and her heart ignored all laws; it accepted no rational or moral objections. It ruled like a tyrant.

In July, Stephen's wife left Bangkok to join their daughter in England. Laura and Christine would return to Thailand in early August. Most evenings, when Stephen did not have official engagements, Elizabeth sneaked up to his apartment to spend the night.

Elizabeth would remember that July as 'our honeymoon'. Doing the most ordinary things with Stephen, whether watching videos or loading the dishwasher, was sheer bliss. She discovered so many new facets of his personality. He was an excellent dancer. Elizabeth would glue herself to

Stephen as they swayed to Tony Bennett's rendition of 'I Left my Heart in San Francisco'. Alone in his apartment on the top floor of a high-rise, with floor-to-ceiling windows, dancing above the flickering lights of a city dotted with shimmering golden temples and the moon reflected in the meandering curves of the Chao Praia River — what perfect, absolute happiness!

On the last Sunday of July, after they made love in the afternoon, Elizabeth was lying on the couch, wearing earphones and watching a Jennifer Aniston comedy. Stephen, in shorts and a T-shirt, was reading the *Financial Post*. Elizabeth dug her toes, nails painted bright orange, under his thigh. She could not bear not to touch him for one single moment.

"I'm hungry," said Stephen, putting down the paper and stretching.

"No take-out tonight! Let's go to a restaurant for a change," said Elizabeth.

"No, that wouldn't be a good idea — you never know who I could run into. I'll cook for you myself. What would mademoiselle like? We have shrimp and scallops. Come, I need help."

"I could make a shrimp cocktail sauce with ketchup and lemon juice."

"Ketchup! Perish the thought! Would mademoiselle like a shrimp bisque and then Coquilles Saint Jacques? Or a seafood gratin with *Nantaise* sauce?"

"Whatever you feel like — you know I can't cook."

"I'll open the Chablis, and you can shell the shrimp." He took time to make the *Nantaise* sauce. "Here, taste! What does it need?"

"I don't know. I cook with Hamburger Helper."

The seafood was delicious. After the dishes were done, Stephen poured himself a cognac. "Elizabeth, darling, I want to tell you something," he said, as he sat down on the couch and put his arm around her shoulder. "This is very difficult for me… This is our last night together — for about a month."

"What do you mean, last?" His words felt like stabs to her chest.

"You know I love you, sweetie pie, but I can't see you while my daughter is visiting. If you love me, you have to understand."

"You see me while your wife is here!"

"That's different."

"I don't understand."

"Neither do I, but I will not indulge in amateur psychoanalysis."

"How long is your daughter staying?"

"About four weeks."

"A month! Stephen, I won't survive!" *He will never survive a whole month without me. He'll call, I'm sure.*

The telephone rang. It was Rajimi, Stephen's new personal assistant. "Yes, Rajimi, leave a message with the car company, that's all. Call back to check tomorrow morning. Yes. Goodbye, Rajimi."

"Why does Rajimi phone you at home?"

"She's very young and very insecure. She's no Mrs O'Donnell."

That night, as they made love, she looked deeply into his eyes. Elizabeth felt as if she was pouring her soul into Stephen. She knew the landscape of his eyes, the little flecks of gold and green in the hazel iris. She and Stephen were one. How could anyone else exist outside this perfect union?

When Christine arrived, Elizabeth's perfect world dissolved. Like in a flash flood, her happiness was washed away and was replaced by an ache that no amount of sunshine could burn off, and no amount of wine could drown. She called his office, ostensibly to ask about the French lessons. The new secretary, Rajimi, said she would give him the message. He did not call back. *How can he live without you, Lizzie, daughter or no daughter? Doesn't he know what I am going through? Isn't he in pain, too?*

At the end of August, Christine went back to England, but Marie-France did not return to Bangkok. Her mother died that summer, and she stayed in Montreal to settle the estate. Elizabeth felt guilty because although she missed her friend and was genuinely sorry, her entire life now revolved around Stephen. Without Stephen, there was no sun — day was night. Elizabeth came to life again when the 'French lessons' resumed in September. She was surprised how quickly she forgot her torments. He was back, that was all that mattered. However, the French lessons began to dwindle. There were six lessons in September. On one occasion, he had to cancel because of a reception at the American Embassy. When Stephen walked through her door the following week, Elizabeth could not control her tear-filled voice as she told him how much she missed him.

"I had to babysit a group of Canadian businessmen," he said in a weary voice.

"I thought you had a reception at the US Embassy."

"I was working most evenings last week. Can you blame me for not keeping the days straight?"

Elizabeth, with tears welling up in her eyes, sat pouting.

"Don't you trust me?" he asked, with a smile that did not entirely hide his irritation.

She saw him only four times in October. Elizabeth did not ask why his workload had suddenly increased. She never doubted any of his reasons for cancelling. She always experienced heightened nervous anticipation before meeting Stephen, followed by tears and long bouts of lethargy if he cancelled.

At the end of October, Elizabeth received an email from her sister. Catherine would arrive in Bangkok in the middle of December and stay for the holidays. She had plans to visit Angkor Wat in Cambodia and then fly home through Singapore. Elizabeth was overwhelmed by guilt as she read the email. Instead of feeling happy at the prospect of seeing her sister, her first thoughts were about Stephen. Where would they meet?

During a French lesson in early December, Stephen told Elizabeth that he would be leaving for an extended business trip to Hong Kong and Tokyo, and then on to Ottawa for home leave. His whole family would spend Christmas in Vancouver with his parents.

"What? That's two months!" Elizabeth gasped. "Why did you not tell me this before?"

"Please, darling! Don't you understand that these decisions are made in Ottawa?"

That evening, their lovemaking was so tender and so heartbreaking. Elizabeth cried softly in his arms as he kissed her ever so gently.

Stephen's departure date for Hong Kong coincided with her sister's arrival in Bangkok. Stephen agreed to let Elizabeth ride to the airport in the embassy car. As Elizabeth stood in front of the Abdul Rahim Palace, Stephen arrived with the third secretary, Rob White. Elizabeth was disappointed — she had expected to be alone with Stephen, but had to sit in the front seat, next to the driver. Above the din of the traffic and honking horns, Rob said, "The potash delegation is arriving tomorrow, so when you and Rajimi come back from Hong Kong next week, you'll have a few days to read my report before you brief the ambassador." But last night, he had said that he would not be back, that he would be flying on to Canada for home leave. Why is Rob saying that Stephen would be back in Bangkok next week? The realisation reverberated through her body like a shock wave. *He lied to you, Lizzie! Rob mentioned that Rajimi was going to Hong Kong, too. Pretty, young Rajimi. Boy, oh boy, Lizzie, have you ever been blind! Blind like a lovesick kitten.*

As the car neared the Suvarnabhumi Airport's departure area, Elizabeth glanced in the rear-view mirror and noticed that Stephen cast furtive glances at Elizabeth and lowered his voice. Elizabeth bit her lower lip to hide the quiver. When they got out of the car, Rob busied himself with his boss's luggage, while Stephen tried to catch Elizabeth's arm. Without a word, without even a glance in his direction, Elizabeth ran as fast as she could towards the airport's arrivals section. Inside the glass tubular terminal, Elizabeth locked herself in a cubicle in a ladies' room and cried. *How are you going to hold it together, Lizzie? You're not going to dump all this broken-heart stuff on Catherine! You were an idiot, Lizzie. Now deal with it!*

Catherine had a slim, athletic body and short auburn hair. Upon arrival, she looked as if someone had spilled pools of blue ink under her eyes.

"I've been travelling for thirty hours! Get me to bed! Please!"

Holding her sister tightly in the taxi, Elizabeth burst into tears. "It's so good to see you!"

"Why are you crying, Lizzie? Do I look that bad?" Catherine, her head bobbing, slumped over and fell asleep on Elizabeth's shoulder. Elizabeth was grateful that her sister would not see the steady trickle of tears running down her face. In the apartment, she let Catherine sleep for a few hours while she kept reliving the conversation in the embassy car. *Perhaps I misunderstood? I'll call the embassy when it opens on Monday.* The thought cheered her up.

"Sleeping beauty, time to get up!" said Elizabeth as she gently roused her sister. "I have a bottle of cold white wine and some delicious Thai food."

Catherine declined the wine, but drank gallons of bottled water. They both nibbled on crab-stuffed wonton dumplings, vegetable spring rolls, and lettuce wraps. They talked about home, jumping from topic to topic.

"What about Amanda and Rob? Are they planning to start a family?" Elizabeth asked about their oldest sister.

"Not for another five years or so — first, they want to build a Jacuzzi in the backyard and take a Mediterranean cruise."

"I think that Amanda's life will be like a continuous Volvo ride along a smooth highway. I have a feeling that my road will be full of potholes, roadblocks, washed-out sections…"

"Wha-a-at?" Catherine yawned. "Why all the gloom and doom? You've had too much wine. Look, I'm going to take a shower and then go back to bed. I'm so looking forward to your guided tour tomorrow."

Elizabeth did not go to bed. She poured herself some cognac from the bottle Stephen kept in a kitchen cupboard. There was nothing left in the bottle when it rolled under the couch, and Elizabeth fell asleep.

Catherine woke her sister at nine a.m. "How could you sleep on that tiny couch? Look, I've been reading about this river/canal cruise and the floating markets. Can't wait to get started!"

Elizabeth felt groggy; her mouth was parched, and her head throbbed. Going out into the hot, exhaust-filled air of Bangkok would require superhuman strength.

"Boy, you look like shit, Lizzie. How much cognac did you have last night? I didn't know you even drank the stuff."

"I have a lot on my mind," Elizabeth said, and gulped down a tall glass of orange juice.

Catherine showed off her new tablet, then ran off to the bedroom.

Elizabeth overcame her nausea and got dressed. During the canal and river cruise, Catherine took dozens of photographs: the banks of the Chao Phraya River, the silhouettes of Buddhist temples, the golden palaces, and glittering high-rise buildings. Then the tourist boat moved into a maze of canals edged by houses on piles.

"Now I know why Bangkok is called the Venice of the East," said Catherine, aiming her tablet at people as they went about their daily routines, lifting buckets of water from the canals to do the washing or to water plants. She took photos of children throwing scraps of bread to large, fat, whiskered fish that poked their heads out of the water to swallow the crumbs.

"Look at all the floating gunk, fruit peels, marigolds, garbage! Do they flush their toilets into the canals? Do they even have toilets? Do they use the same water for drinking?" Catherine kept asking questions.

"If the fish survive, it must be relatively OK," Elizabeth said without thinking. She was still absorbed by her analysis of Stephen's behaviour. Had he lied, or was it a misunderstanding? By midday, their tourist boat left the canals and returned to the Chao Phraya River, but despite the cooling breeze, Elizabeth felt even more nauseous as their boat rocked in the wake of a larger vessel. Elizabeth bent over Catherine's knees and retched into the dark grey water. She lay across her sister's lap with her head hung over the side, her body convulsing. When she opened her eyes, she saw her own fractured reflection in the waves. If a face reflects the soul, I look like I'm in hell — only I'm not dead.

"OK, we're going home," said Catherine in a take-charge tone of voice.

It was getting dark when Elizabeth woke up. She splashed water on her ashen face and went into the living room. "I'm so embarrassed. I so hoped we would make the most of this Sunday. I'm back at work tomorrow."

"I'm a big girl. I know what I want to see. Would you care to tell me what's going on?" asked Catherine, as she poured hot water into a cup of instant chicken soup. Elizabeth sipped in silence.

"Can't you tell me?" said Catherine, and sat down beside her sister.

Suddenly, Elizabeth felt as if some inner dam had burst and the story of her affair with Stephen gushed out, punctuated by sobs and tears. Catherine leaned over to kiss her sister on the cheek. "Poor, poor Lizzie. I'm so sorry for you. But I really don't see why you're making it into such a big deal! What was your first boyfriend's name? Tom? When you broke up, you didn't go all crybaby!"

"That was puppy love!" said Elizabeth. "And we didn't break up."

Tom, a boy with kind blue eyes and red hair, went to Banff to work as a bartender for the summer and did not return to Montreal. Elizabeth accepted the separation easily. They still kept in touch by email.

"Look, in a few weeks, you'll forget this guy! So you were dumped! Find somebody else — preferably not married!"

"Catherine, you don't understand! Have you ever been really, really,

really in love?"

"Do people in love lose their ability to think? How did you think this was going to end?"

"Sure, I saw the flashing red lights. I read the big sign — 'Heartbreak Inevitable'! I didn't have the strength to let go."

"What did you think you meant to him? Men like to add notches to the old bedpost before they descend into impotence and old age."

"What if I misunderstood?" Elizabeth interrupted Catherine. "Should I call the embassy tomorrow and find out?"

"No! Go to bed!"

"I can't sleep. I keep thinking…"

"Look, Lizzie, isn't it obvious? It's over! You are far too sensitive. It's as if your heart is outside your body. Mother was like you. Me and Amanda, we're not so thin-skinned. I guess we both take after our father."

"Our father was a creep who ran out on a young wife and three little girls!"

"You were Grandpa's favourite. He spoiled you. Not all men are like Grandpa. You've got to toughen up, Lizzie!"

That first week in Bangkok, Catherine toured the city while Elizabeth struggled to teach her classes. She resolved to believe Stephen's story and repressed the urge to call the embassy to ask whether he was back. Several times, she began to dial, only to drop the phone. In the evenings, Catherine showed off her photos — the Royal Grand Palace in Bangkok, with guards in white pith helmets; ferocious-looking stone statues in monkey masks; and the tall spires of Buddhist monasteries. Catherine took far too many photos of the exotic floating gardens. On Saturday, they booked a boat ride and toured Ayutthaya, Siam's ancient capital. Catherine photographed every single temple, particularly the ruins overgrown by monster roots of banyan trees. She snapped away at the hundreds of statues — colonnades of Buddha statues, the golden Buddha in a glass cage, the colossal reclining Buddha. Elizabeth could not pretend to share Catherine's enthusiasm. She did her best to hide her inner pain.

By the second week of December, Elizabeth still had not called the embassy. She decided to believe that, by now, Stephen was on home leave in Canada. On Friday, she finished work early, and the sisters strolled over to the lake in Lumphini Park, Bangkok's vast oasis of greenery. They sat on a bench and fed the ducks as they watched families in paddle boats with prows shaped like white swans. They admired the skyline of high-rise buildings, including the Abdul Rahim Palace that housed the Canadian Embassy. Then they walked back towards Rama IV Road.

"I'm taking you out to a really nice riverside restaurant tonight," said Catherine. "We'll take the Skytrain."

They walked back along a winding path edged by banyan trees, palms, and thickets of bamboo. The stairway leading up to the elevated Skytrain train was hidden behind an island of oleander bushes. Suddenly, Elizabeth stopped in her tracks and grabbed Catherine's arm. "Wait!" she said, and pulled down an oleander branch. She was not mistaken; it was Stephen's voice. He was embracing the diminutive Rajimi, who stood on her tiptoes while Stephen bent down to kiss her lips. Rajimi, in a red silk Thai dress, ran up the stairs to catch the Skytrain. Feeling as if someone had punched her in the stomach, Elizabeth doubled over in pain. It took a full minute to catch her breath.

"What's the matter? You look like you've seen a ghost!"

"Stephen, he was kissing Rajimi," Elizabeth stammered, gasping for air. Then she bolted across the street and ran all the way back to the apartment. Catherine could have outrun her sister, but she had to wait for the light to change.

"Look, Lizzie, we have a reservation...," Catherine began as she entered the apartment. She didn't finish the sentence. Elizabeth was sobbing, curled up in a foetal position on her bed. Elizabeth lay in bed all weekend. On Monday morning, Catherine, holding a mug of coffee, approached her sister.

"Lizzie, get up, you have to go to work. You've been in bed for two days! Don't you think that's more suffering than the bastard deserves?"

"I can't," Elizabeth managed to say, and began to sob into the pillow.

The school sent a doctor, who diagnosed severe depression. The International School released Elizabeth from her contract before Christmas, and the sisters flew back to Montreal on 1st January.

Chapter 2

The flights seemed endless: fourteen hours to the west coast of Canada, two hours in the Vancouver transit area, and some five more to Montreal. Throughout much of this ordeal, Elizabeth's mind was in a fog, her body leaden. Crammed into an economy seat, she kept her head on Catherine's shoulder with a blanket over her face to hide her teary eyes. The oldest of the three Burgess sisters, Amanda, was waiting at the airport in Montreal. Wearing a fur-trimmed leather coat, she stood behind a cart full of parkas and boots. 1st January was the coldest day that winter. As they ran across the outdoor parking lot, Elizabeth felt the wind cut into her face with what seemed to be a thousand icy needles.

Elizabeth spent the next three months in Catherine's dingy apartment on Marlowe Street, where all the dusty windows faced brick walls. Catherine was mostly away at her computer courses and spent weekends waitressing at a pub. She also managed to keep the refrigerator reasonably stocked (frozen pizza) and did their washing when the overflow from the laundry basket spread across the bedroom floor. The bedroom furniture consisted of two single beds, a red plastic milk crate that served as a night table, and a blue and white Wedgwood-style lamp. There was also a scruffy old dresser with peeling green paint.

For the next three winter months, Elizabeth's nights were filled with painful dreams of Bangkok and bouts of insomnia. She spent the days in pyjamas in the living room, lying on the lumpy couch. She watched the entire *Poirot* TV series several times over. Elizabeth told her sisters that this was far better therapy than any of the psychiatrists they suggested.

Amanda, who worked at the Royal Bank head office in downtown Montreal, was married, lived in the suburbs, and did not visit often. She did call, usually to dispense advice. Elizabeth always gave her the same reply: "How do you mend a broken heart?"

As the days became longer, Elizabeth's inner fog began to dissipate. One evening, as Catherine prepared supper — removed a frozen pizza from the microwave — Elizabeth said, "I have no idea what to do with my life. I don't want to go back to teaching!"

"This is the first time you've brought up the future. Do you have any ideas about what you would like to do?" asked Catherine.

"None whatsoever!" Elizabeth said with a sigh.

"I have a friend at work whose older sister works in an employment agency. Just yesterday, she told me that they are looking for someone to work as a research assistant." Catherine rose from the rickety plastic table and brought back her purse. "This might interest you." She gave Elizabeth a business card.

"Do you think I'm ready?" asked Elizabeth without looking at the card.

"Do you want to spend the rest of your life on the couch, moping about Stephen?"

"You're right. I'm suffering while he's…" Elizabeth winced.

"The opening is for a fluently bilingual research assistant with computer skills. The only downside is that you would have to live and work in the Laurentians, somewhere in the vicinity of Mont Tremblant. On the other hand, it's just for three months, extremely well paid and…"

"I still don't go out much. I don't sleep very…"

"OK, so you were dumped by the love of your life! Get over it!"

"I do need the money… What else do you know about the job?"

"All I know is that this guy is writing some sort of history book. He retired as president of his company or corporation or whatever and has been living like a recluse on his estate. He's supposed to be a little eccentric, but nothing too crazy — just a stickler for privacy and confidentiality."

"An estate… I don't know…"

"Look, talk to the agency yourself. Ask for Francine."

After some inner turmoil, Elizabeth did call, and agreed to the first stage of the process — the online application. She filled in forms, uploaded test translations, and sent a photograph — a flattering one, taken by Catherine on her cell phone. Elizabeth convinced herself that she would not be invited for an interview. To her surprise, the invitation came two weeks later. The thought of going into the outside world was terrifying. She had to force herself to take that first step out the door.

The agency was downtown, in Place Ville Marie. After hibernating all winter, Elizabeth felt like a country bumpkin on a visit to the big city. As she walked out of the elevator on the twenty-third floor, she paused to look at her own reflection in the mirrored wall and experienced a tiny surge of confidence. Her swing skirt flattered her shapely legs, and the short, black jacket she borrowed from Amanda made her look more confident than she felt.

The office did not have the coveted view of Mount Royal — it overlooked Mansfield Street. Francine, a fortyish, slim brunette in a grey suit and horn-rimmed glasses, was all business.

"Please sit down. Let me see…" Francine opened a thick file. "First, your security check… All OK," she said without looking up.

"You did a security check on me?"

"Yes, my client insisted." Francine continued to look through the file. "I already sent him your photo. You did very well on all the translations. I see you graduated from Concordia University with a BA, majors in English and French. You also have an ESL certificate. Your transcripts show quite an eclectic mix of electives: Sociology, Psychology, French Literature… What is your first language?"

"I grew up bilingual. Grandpa John was Irish, and Grand Maman was French Canadian."

"But what language did you speak at home with your parents?"

"My father left us when I was very young, so we all lived with my mother's parents. Mother was an elementary school teacher. She was bilingual, too."

"I see. Now, let's review the contract." Francine handed Elizabeth some printed pages.

"The contract is for three months, starting on 12th May. You will be required to live at Mr Agnew-Simpson's estate, just north of Mt Tremblant. Very isolated. Cell phone reception rather iffy. You will have access to a landline with your own extension number. You will have a small suite of rooms."

Elizabeth was stunned. She could not quite process this information. "Do you mean I'm hired?"

"Yes, provided you agree to the conditions. Do you have any questions so far?"

"No."

"Mr Agnew-Simpson is very security conscious and puts a premium on confidentiality. No visitors. His former assistant, a young man, did not take the 'no visitors' requirements as seriously as he should have. One day off — Sunday." Francine pushed another document across her desk. "Please read this confidentiality agreement carefully. Mr Agnew-Simpson insists on absolute confidentiality. Would you like a few minutes to read the contract?"

With a tight knot in her stomach, Elizabeth said, "I'm ready to sign."

"Good," said Francine without a smile. "Please sign here and here and here and here."

"So I'm really hired?"

Francine's shapely eyebrows shot up over her horn-rimmed glasses. "Yes. You start on 12th May. I'll email more information. Feel free to call me if you have questions."

Chapter 3

May twelfth was a Monday. Elizabeth was still awake at dawn. She had packed the previous night and spent the morning drinking too much coffee and tidying the apartment. Her new boss, Mr Theodore Agnew-Simpson, was to send a driver who would arrive some time before noon. She was expecting his call. At eleven, she went into their bedroom. The purple sheet on Elizabeth's bed was wound into a thick python — evidence of a sleepless night. A pillow covered Catherine's head.

"Catherine, get up. The driver will call soon." Incoherent moans emanated from under the pillow as Elizabeth rolled out her battered suitcase.

The doorbell rang. Elizabeth buzzed in Amanda, who rushed in holding a large, orange Michael Kors handbag and a stack of computer printouts.

"It's always so dark in here," she said, as she pulled up a Venetian blind.

"And hello to you, too," said Elizabeth, kissing Amanda on the cheek.

"Look, I don't have much time. You do realise that I work! Look at what I found online!" said Amanda, and she thrust some printed sheets at Elizabeth. "Perhaps you should reconsider accepting the job before it's too late!"

"Too late for what?" Catherine yawned, as she came out of the bedroom wearing men's plaid boxer shorts and a white T-shirt.

"Just listen!" said Amanda. "This all happened about a year ago." She began to read out loud. "Mont Tremblant is known as Quebec's international ski resort with a trendy après ski scene. Many international jet setters have homes in the area. The mysterious death of Madame Mathilde Agnew-Simpson, wife of the reclusive Canadian multimillionaire, stunned the entire world. A maid discovered Madame Mathilde's body, clad in a pink chiffon negligée, at the foot of the grand staircase in the secluded mansion north of Mont Tremblant. The police have been very tight-lipped. Cause of death? The coroner's report is still delayed for reasons that have yet to be made clear."

"The poor woman probably slipped on a banana peel! But that's too boring — won't sell any papers," said Catherine, pouring herself a mug of coffee.

"OK, I know the source is the gutter press, but…" Amanda continued reading. "Residents of Mont Tremblant are reticent to talk about this mysterious death. According to rumours circulating in Mont Tremblant village, her death was not an accident. 'That night, I was on the other side of the lake, across from the Agnew-Simpson mansion,' said a witness, who wishes to remain anonymous. 'There was a full moon. I heard a wolf howl. I saw a naked woman standing on the edge of the pier of the Agnew-Simpson mansion. She raised her head and howled in response.'"

Catherine doubled over with laughter.

"Amanda! You have a college degree! How can you read this drivel?" said Elizabeth with a smile.

"So, we're sending our sister to be the next victim of some Bluebeard of Mont Tremblant, who lives in a gloomy mansion with bats in the attic. And there is a ghost, in a pink chiffon negligée, wandering the corridors at night!" Catherine exploded in peals of infectious, child-like laughter.

Amanda was impervious to her sister's teasing. "They even did a write-up in *Hello* magazine. Agnew-Simpson has a son, a professor or a scientist — somebody brainy — and he…"

"Now that is much more interesting!" said Catherine. "Wow, Lizzie, you'll be working for a millionaire, who has a son!" Her stage whisper was full of exaggerated deference. "What if sonny boy turns out to be your knight in shining armour?"

"Catherine, please shut up! Knights in shining armour! What a bunch of horseshit!" Elizabeth hated any references to romance.

"I just want you to be aware of where you are going," said Amanda. "It's not too late to change your mind."

"If that woman died in some slum tenement, no one would have cared!" said Catherine, and she went back into the bedroom to change.

The phone rang. Elizabeth finally found it in the kitchen alcove, hiding behind a plastic pitcher with blue daisies. "*Oui, moi-même… Oui… oui… À bientôt.* It's the driver, he'll be here in about fifteen minutes."

The three Burgess sisters sat down to wait. The only seating in the room was the blue velvet sofa inherited from Grand Maman. The sofa had not aged well. A neat pile of bricks replaced one of its carved legs. When they were little, their mother dressed them up in frilly pink dresses and sat them on the sofa while Grandpa John said, "Cheese." The sisters, aged eighteen months apart, were now in their early twenties — petite, slim, with short auburn hair, and large blue-green eyes.

Catherine broke the silence. "I bet the car looks like a hearse, and the driver is a hunchback with a black eye patch and…"

Elizabeth had no time for jokes. "Catherine, I'm nervous as it is! I am counting on you! As soon as that tax refund arrives, deposit it into my account!" she said, and jumped off the sofa.

"I don't understand why you don't have a cell phone," said Amanda.

"I'm too poor," Elizabeth replied. "In case of an emergency, like if Catherine lands in jail or something, call the number I gave you. It's a landline." And in a pleading voice, she added, "Please come and visit me! I'll be so lonely."

"You know I would if I could," said Amanda, hugging her sister. "But Rob always needs the car for golf on weekends."

"I'm a starving student. I work weekends," said Catherine. "I think we should go outside in case he's early. There's never any parking on the street."

The sisters made their way along the dusty corridor to the vestibule with rows of dull, metallic mailboxes. The old, four-storey brick apartment building was in an area of Montreal still waiting to be gentrified. They stood on the sidewalk next to two squares of scruffy grass strewn with cigarette butts.

"It's not forever," Catherine whispered, and she hugged Elizabeth.

"It's a great opportunity!" said Amanda, as she leaned over to kiss Elizabeth on the cheek.

"Thank you for everything," said a tearful Elizabeth. "I don't want to screw it up! I really, really don't!"

Chapter 4

The driver, Monsieur Gervais, a thin, wiry man of medium height, was perhaps sixty. His grey hair was neatly parted on the side. He looked tidy in his crisply pressed khaki slacks and a white long-sleeved shirt. He greeted Elizabeth politely and placed her suitcase in the trunk of the silver Cadillac. He motioned to the back seat. The front seat was filled with boxes from Birks.

"My wife, Madame Gervais, insisted I place the crystal glasses in the front seat. She's the housekeeper."

Monsieur Gervais drove north on Highway 15. Elizabeth barely noticed the green hills dappled in lime-green foliage. Exhausted by a sleepless night, she dozed, cradled by the plush softness of the velvet seats, lulled by the humming tyres. This dream was new. She was crawling through a boulder-strewn desert under a scorching sun. Then she was falling, falling endlessly into a deep gorge, and landed prone at the bottom. With bloodied fingernails, her face smeared with dirt and sweat, she finally completed the torturous climb and pulled herself over the edge, only to see the same never-ending desert, scorched by a pitiless sun. Elizabeth awoke as the sign for Mt Tremblant flashed by. *I hope this dream isn't prophetic.* The car rhythm changed as they left the highway and began to climb. The Cadillac turned into a private road that sliced a perfectly straight swath through pine trees that stood straight and tall, like an honour guard. They drove up to a massive metal gate that opened as if by magic. Elizabeth bolted forward — the towering mansion did look like a medieval castle. *It's even got a turret, for God's sake! All it needs is a moat! Only some crazy Brit would build a Gothic mansion in the wilds of Quebec. Trimmed hedges and manicured lawns! So, if this is a castle, who are you, Lizzie? Cinderella or some sacrificial maiden offered up to the Bluebeard of Mont Tremblant?*

Monsieur Gervais stopped the car next to stone stairs leading to an oak door with a gryphon adorning the brass crest. Elizabeth could not help but notice the roving eye of a video camera.

"Leave your suitcase, I will bring it up."

They were met by Madame Gervais. "*Entrez, entrez, ma belle!*" Like her husband, Madame Gervais was grey-haired and about sixty. She looked efficient in her crisply starched grey cotton uniform and white apron. "My, but you are a pretty one!"

Elizabeth was always surprised when she was complimented about her looks. She did not find anything exceptional in her short, copper-auburn hair, blue-green eyes, and bow-shaped lips. Today, instead of her usual jeans and T-shirt, she wore an A-line swing skirt that showed off her shapely legs and pretty feet in black wedge sandals. Her toenails were painted bright orange. She looked much younger than her twenty-three years.

Madame Gervais prattled on in French as they walked through the vast, vaulted entrance hall. Gothic glass doors opened to a terrace with a magnificent view of the lake. Elizabeth could not help but notice the flicking red light of the security system. They rode up to the third floor in an antique elevator with a folding brass door.

"This is your little suite. You have a bedroom and a small sitting room," said Madame Gervais as she stopped to straighten a lace doily on the dresser. "And here is Monsieur Gervais with your suitcases. You must be tired, *ma chère*. Settle in, and when you are ready, come down for a cup of tea in the kitchen."

Elizabeth thought that if she was ten, she would have loved this bedroom with blue and white floral wallpaper, mounds of flounced pillows scattered over the bed, and a myriad of velvet violets in porcelain pots.

The sitting room was small, with a white desk and white bookshelves. A royal blue velvet love seat stood in front of a television. But the bathroom! Huge! All white, with ornate fixtures and a deep, old-fashioned, freestanding tub. *Wow! I've never had such digs!* Elizabeth unpacked and began to descend the mahogany staircase that smelled of lemon polish. She wondered whether the former lady of the house had fallen down these very same stairs. Gingerly, she touched the dark wood panelling, as if expecting to find fresh bloodstains. It was quiet — solemn — like in an empty church, where the silence is heavy and significant.

How am I going to survive in this mausoleum?

Elizabeth tiptoed into the living room on the left of the vestibule. The stiff brown leather furniture looked as if it belonged in a monastery waiting room. There was a large portrait over the stone fireplace that did not fit the décor. The woman was rather too angelic, with baby-soft, short blonde hair, and large blue eyes. She had a delicate milky complexion and a rosebud of a mouth. *This must be the late Madame Agnew-Simpson. I wonder what Monsieur looks like?*

"Ah, there you are, *ma chère*," said Madame Gervais, as she walked into the living room. "Yes, that was our angel, Madame Mathilde. I still cannot believe she is gone." Madame Gervais stood looking at the portrait with something like religious adoration. As they walked up to the Gothic glass doors leading to the veranda, Madame Gervais took out a cloth from her apron pocket and stopped to polish a faint smudge on a brass doorknob.

"What did she die of? I hope you don't mind my asking." Elizabeth was curious about what the housekeeper had to say about this well-publicised death.

Madame Gervais's body stiffened. "It was an accident... a terrible accident," she said rather too curtly, as they walked into the kitchen.

"That's according to the morons on the police force," said Monsieur Gervais. He was unpacking the box of wine glasses.

"Marcel! Please!" Madame Gervais looked at her husband as if he was an errant schoolboy.

Monsieur Gervais, looking chastised, walked out of the kitchen carrying the discarded packaging.

The kitchen was modern and fully equipped. An enormous picture window framed a gorgeous lake view, reflected in the glass doors of the double refrigerators.

"I made a pot of rosehip tea. It was Madame's favourite."

Carefully, Elizabeth picked up the '*fleur-de-lys*'-patterned teacup. The matching pink and gold teapot looked out of place against the chrome counter.

"Do try the scones. Mr Ted always has scones for tea. I make the raspberry jam myself," Madame Gervais prattled on. "I don't need a large kitchen now. We hardly ever have guests any more. Mr Ted always eats alone, but today he has asked you to join him for a glass of sherry at six and then dinner."

It was soothing to be fussed over by a woman who reminded Elizabeth of her French-Canadian grandmother. They sat at the polished oak table by the picture window, drank tea, and chatted.

"Both Marcel and I were born in the village of St Jovite. I don't see why they had to rename it Mont Tremblant. Marcel's father used to work for Mr Ted's grandfather, so we consider ourselves to be almost part of the family. We adored Mathilde." Madame Gervais let out a deep sigh. "And little Alexander — he was such a joy! Unfortunately, I couldn't have children myself."

"I presume Alexander is Mr Agnew-Simpson's son. Where is he now?"

"He's a professor at a university in London," she said proudly. "Now, tell me about your family, Elizabeth."

"I have two older sisters. I don't remember my father. My grandparents told me he walked out of the house when I was four years old and never returned. We found out later that he went back to the Maritimes. We always lived with my grandparents in NDG. My mother died of breast cancer when I was sixteen. Grand Maman died of breast cancer, too, just before I graduated from university. Grandpa John had a heart attack six months later. My grandparents were inseparable, so I guess he couldn't live without her."

"Oh, you poor dear," said Madame Gervais, patting Elizabeth's hand.

"We weren't rich, but I never felt deprived," said Elizabeth. "My sisters and I were loved."

"You don't know how lucky you are! Money does not always bring happiness," said Madame Gervais rather too forcefully. In the next moment, she seemed to retreat into her private thoughts. Then she looked at the clock and jumped up.

"Time to start supper. Remember — sherry at six. I'll come to show you the way."

Elizabeth had relaxed while talking to Madame Gervais, but a knot formed in her stomach at the thought of meeting her employer. She took a luxurious bath. *So what is the worst thing he can do? You'll be fired, Lizzie! That's all.* She changed into a white silk blouse bought in

Thailand. She had but that one black skirt. Appearing in jeans did not seem appropriate. *"What did you get yourself into, Lizzie? What kind of a queer duck is this Mr Theodore Agnew-Simpson?"*

At precisely six, Madame Gervais escorted her to the study door in the middle of the second floor. Elizabeth took a deep breath and knocked.

"Come in, come in." Agnew-Simpson took Elizabeth's elbow and guided her towards two maroon leather love seats that formed a conversation corner.

A massive mahogany desk, stacked high with books and papers, stood in the middle of a vast room lined with wooden panels and bookshelves. A small, round dining table, set for two, stood in front of the tall glass doors overlooking the balcony and the lake.

"So young! So pretty! I almost feel guilty for luring you to this monastic retreat. At your age, there should be music, dancing, charming young men... Oh, my... Oh, my... Although, I must admit that my guilt for tearing you away from the big city lights is tempered by my anticipation of the pleasure of admiring so beautiful a creature. Sit here where I can look at you in the afternoon sun. Yes, yes... Pretty... very pretty... May I offer you a glass of sherry?"

Elizabeth had to draw on every last ounce of self-control to simulate composure. She could not allow her face to reflect her shock at Mr Agnew-Simpson's appearance. What did the lovely Mathilde find attractive in this man?

"My grandfather was a business associate of Joseph Bondurant Ryan, the American who built Mont Tremblant lodge. In the old days, they came up to ski from Montreal on the *P'tit Train du Nord*. Grandfather built this grand house. He always said that he had but one talent: he could make money. Whatever he tried — railways, timber, mining — he made money. Quite a bit, actually."

Elizabeth sat demurely with her legs crossed and listened politely, but at the same time she was analysing Agnew-Simpson from head to toe. *He's probably just five feet five in his socks. His chest looks caved in. That left shoulder has a bit of a bulge. Does that make him a hunchback?*

"Did I offer you a glass of sherry, my dear?"

While sipping her sherry and making sure to return Agnew-Simpson's smiles, Elizabeth thought, *Sir, can't you afford a fashion consultant? Your clothes look two sizes too big. That shapeless tweed jacket belongs at the Salvation Army! Why wear rimless glasses that only magnify your pale, watery eyes? Your eyes seem to be zigzagging back and forth all the time! Do you have some sort of involuntary nervous tic or what? That ginger beard is nicely trimmed, but you probably grew it to hide a weak chin. Villains have weak chins! How old is he? Fifty? Sixty? Who cares, he's decrepit! What could have attracted that angelic Mathilde to this unfortunate-looking gentleman? Oh yes, he is filthy rich.*

"By way of entertainment," Agnew-Simpson continued, "I hope you enjoy water sports. We have a canoe and boats at your disposal. The library is full of books and videos. If you start coming down with cabin fever," he chuckled, "you can accompany the Gervaises to the village on Sundays."

After a second glass of sherry, Elizabeth began to relax. She did not find him threatening or repulsive. Perhaps it was his manners: the exaggerated *politesse* of an age gone by. Should she send her sisters Agnew-Simpson's photograph with a note attached? *No, I'm not in the Bluebeard fairy tale. This is more like 'Beauty and the Beast'.* Elizabeth had to bite her lip to suppress a smile.

"I was hoping you would give me the pleasure of getting to know you a little better. I am, as you see, a recluse. Although, as they say, I am wired. Is that the right expression? All these gadgets." He pointed his thin finger in the direction of the computer section, nestled in an enormous wall of books that rose up to the ten-foot ceiling in motley, dishevelled rows.

"I live mostly in this room, like in a cocoon. I can bring the entire world into my study without leaving the house. At my age," he said, smiling coquettishly at Elizabeth, "it's not such a bad thing."

Elizabeth noticed, or thought she noticed, that he tried to look into her eyes and that his washed-out, watery blue eyes acquired an elfish sparkle. *Is he flirting? Do old people flirt? Was it the sherry? The man is definitely weird!*

"Being a recluse, I enjoy hearing about other people's adventures. Now, tell me all about your teaching in... was it in China...? Ah, yes, Thailand! You taught English? And French, too. Sounds fascinating!"

Tell me all about it! Of course, he wants the tourist/tour guide description. Almost no one knew about her emotional roller-coaster affair with Stephen. Elizabeth told him the sanitised version.

At precisely seven, Madame Gervais came in, pushing a trolley. Supper was a bowl of consommé, fillet of sole in a light lemon-butter sauce, yellow rice, and steamed baby vegetables. He poured only one glass of absolutely delicious French Chablis. Then herbal tea and a wafer-thin cookie. After a loud, and it seemed to Elizabeth, a staged slurp of the last drops of tea in his cup, Agnew-Simpson looked straight into Elizabeth's eyes and said, "Thank you so very much. It has been a pleasure." His tone turned cold. "Good night, Elizabeth."

"Good night, sir," said Elizabeth. *I gather I have just been dismissed. After all, I am just the hired help.*

Elizabeth could not fall asleep in her new bed. She replayed the conversation with Agnew-Simpson. The questions about Thailand triggered those relentlessly recurring memories. Images began to seep into her mind: the cleft in Stephen's chin, the speckles of green in his left eye, the fleeting expression of guilt on his face that last day when... She pushed the images away, over and over again. That night she dreamed of Bangkok.

Chapter 5

Elizabeth remembered the dream. She and Stephen were standing in a dark room, locked in a tight embrace. Her head was on his chest. She could hear the beating of his heart. They were one being, merged by love. A ray of sunlight burst the blissful dream. Elizabeth was overwhelmed by an all-enveloping sadness and felt too tired to get out of bed. *Get yourself out of this funk! You have a job! Get up!* Laboriously, she sat up and stared at her bare feet on the floor. Then she forced herself to take a shower.

"*Ah, voice la belle Elizabeth,*" said Madame Gervais, smiling broadly. "I hope you slept well."

"Yes," Elizabeth lied, as she accepted a steaming mug of coffee. "Do I smell freshly baked croissant?"

"I always make them from scratch — with real butter!" said Madame Gervais. "Please sit down. Too bad about the weather."

Elizabeth sat down at the polished oak kitchen table and looked through the windowpane, blistered in trembling raindrops. A pale, tear-stained sky. A veil of mist over the dull, metallic surface of the lake.

After breakfast, Elizabeth took a black umbrella from the rack and walked down the stone steps to the water. She stood on the pier by the boathouse, breathed in the misty air and listened to the silence, punctuated by the intermittent cries of nameless birds. *Breathe, Lizzie, breathe. Breathe in. Count to ten. Hold your breath. Count to ten. Breathe out.*

At precisely nine o'clock, she knocked on the study door. Agnew-Simpson greeted her with a sly smile.

"Nothing like a good brisk walk in the morning, even in this weather. Yes, yes, I watched you from the window. Have to keep tabs on you young people. Before I give you the assignments for the day, I will introduce you to my father and grandfather." Agnew-Simpson took Elizabeth by the elbow and gently guided her to two portraits that hung over the stone fireplace. "As you know, I am working on my family history."

"You don't look like them," Elizabeth blurted out without thinking. She noticed the corners of Agnew-Simpson's mouth turn down. *Why can't you keep your opinions to yourself, Lizzie? From now on, zip-zip.*

His tone became cold and businesslike. "This is Leonard Agnew-Simpson, my illustrious grandfather, the self-made tycoon."

Elizabeth studied the stout man with thick grey hair neatly parted in the middle. He was standing next to a model train.

"Pappy had nerves of steel," continued Agnew-Simpson. "A tough old bird. No one could outsmart him in business."

Elizabeth kept her mouth shut. Agnew-Simpson then pointed to the portrait of a tall, handsome man with a thin brown moustache.

"He has a medal," Elizabeth said, and looked furtively at Agnew-Simpson, hoping that this was an appropriate comment. *How could such a handsome man have such an ugly son?*

"Victoria Cross and all that. A real man's man," said Agnew-Simpson without enthusiasm.

They walked across the room to the love seat corner. Last night, she had not paid attention to the dozens of framed photographs that covered the wall. There were groups of men sitting in boardrooms, men speaking into microphones, men with shovels planting trees, men boarding trains or airplanes. With Big Ben in the background, there was a photograph of a skinny little boy in short trousers and with knobbly knees standing between two men in bowler hats. There were many other photographs of the three Agnew-Simpsons in various exotic locations. Elizabeth was afraid to ask why there were no women. There were no photographs of Mathilde or Alexander either.

"You will work at the computer in the library on the first floor. I will send assignments by email." He handed her a red file and a typed sheet of instructions. "For today, here is a list of references to check, and some articles from French newspapers to translate. In the afternoons, and only if you have free time, I would like you to work on my late wife's journals. They are on the desk in her boudoir. I could not touch them. I still cannot," he said with a sigh. "I would like you to transcribe and translate them into English. My angel's handwriting was so atrocious."

Elizabeth carried the file and instructions to the wood-panelled library on the first floor, across from the main salon. Her desk and computer were set up on a long desk under the Gothic windows facing the front lawn. These first assignments were simple. Once completed, she emailed them to Agnew-Simpson.

At noon, she went to the kitchen to inquire about lunch. The Gervais couple were out, but Madame Gervais had left a plate of sandwiches and fruit with Elizabeth's name attached by a little green cocktail umbrella.

After lunch, Elizabeth walked up to Mathilde's suite in the left corner of the second floor. The sitting room suite was pink and white. Neat rows of leather-bound books filled the lacquered shelves. A pink chaise longue with floral pillows stood in a corner. There was also a bedroom with a large, white cross over a bed covered in a simple, white crocheted bedspread. Silver-framed photographs stood on the dresser and side tables — pictures of parents, grandparents, and large family gatherings presided over by a serious-looking cleric. Elizabeth looked for wedding photos. She was curious to see images of Agnew-Simpson as a young man. She did not find any.

During the next two weeks, Elizabeth settled into a routine. She spent most mornings working on Mr Ted's family history project. After lunch, if the weather permitted, Elizabeth looked forward to a swim or a canoe ride. She began to appreciate the healing power of nature as the painful memories of Bangkok faded. In the afternoon, she returned to the library or Mathilde's boudoir. Agnew-Simpson wanted the 1976 journals transcribed first. The first journal described the year before Mathilde and Agnew-Simpson were married. It turned out to be all about family gossip, descriptions of parties, and visits with friends from convent school days. Dullsville! Mathilde studied Art History at the University of Montreal, but she barely mentioned anything to do with that part of her life. Elizabeth had never seen such handwriting — it was neat but minuscule. She asked for a magnifying glass.

Like the Gervais couple, she began to call her boss Mr Ted. In the evenings, Elizabeth was sometimes invited for sherry with Mr Ted at six. She looked forward to it. The sherry dissipated some of the strain she still felt when alone with her boss. Mr Ted was amusing in a quaint, old-codger kind of way. He did most of the talking. Mostly about himself. Elizabeth learned that Agnew-Simpson's father, Theodore Sr, was paralysed by a stroke right after Mathilde gave birth to Alexander. He never regained consciousness and died a few months later. Agnew-Simpson was forced to assume the responsibility of running the vast family empire.

"Luckily, my father hired competent people to do the heavy lifting!" Agnew-Simpson also told her that some ten years ago, he delegated the day-to-day running of his business interests and retired to his mansion in the Laurentians. On another occasion, he confided that when he was a young man, he was more interested in literature and poetry than in business.

"You look surprised, my dear. Is it because you cannot imagine that I was interested in literature or that I was once a young man?" He chuckled. "Yes, I was young once and very romantic. I even wrote reams and reams of terrible poetry. There was a young woman I admired — secretly. She was the girl next door, our neighbour in Outremont. More than admired, actually. I was obsessed. She was so very lovely and delicate, and I was so very shy. Underneath my rather — how shall I put it? — less than handsome exterior I was a highly sensitive young man. I suffered. How I suffered!" Mr Ted poured himself more sherry.

Elizabeth did find it difficult to imagine Mr Ted as a young man. The topic of love made her uncomfortable. Rather clumsily, she changed the subject. "I applied to work as a substitute teacher this fall, but I'm not looking forward to it."

"Then why on earth don't you change professions?" He looked at her point-blank, eyebrows raised over his watery eyes.

"It's difficult to change things, and…"

"You are young, you are free. You can do anything!"

"I don't know what I want to do. I'm stuck, I guess."

"Change is not easy. It can be frightening. But if you don't try, if you don't dare, you may always regret it." Agnew-Simpson's words seemed to hold some inner meaning for him. He put down the sherry glass, picked up the crystal decanter, poured himself two fingers of scotch and drank deeply. "My father and grandfather believed in accepting responsibility for one's decisions. They were of a different age! They believed in duty! They believed in honour! Elizabeth, do you know that men used to fight duels? They risked their lives to defend their family's good name. Today, so many celebrities are scrambling to confess to all sorts of depravities! Their ghost-written memoirs are nothing but a litany of sordid deeds." Agnew-Simpson poured himself more scotch. "What can you expect, if the only thing that sells is filth and scandal? The notion of shame no longer exists!"

What's got into him tonight? Elizabeth sat in silence, not daring to interrupt his impassioned speech. She noticed red blotches on his face.

"But don't let me start," he said, and shook his head as if shaking off a cobweb. Then, returning to his usual bantering tone, he said, "Let me ask you a question, Elizabeth. Do you consider yourself to be free?"

"Well... Yes, I guess... It's not something I think about."

"Do you want to remain in the teaching profession?"

"No, I suppose not. I only started teaching because it would allow me the opportunity to travel and see the world. My friend, Marie-France, and I..."

"Then why don't you do something else?" Agnew-Simpson interrupted.

"I don't know what else I could do. It's difficult..."

"Yes, I agree, making choices is difficult. It can be excruciating. And the choices one makes may not come with a built-in warranty of success. Sometimes, it's easier not to choose and remain locked in, even if one is unhappy," he said, slipping back into a mournful tone. "Later, we agonise about why we were so cowardly. Why we chose to live in bad faith."

"Bad faith. That's a term from Jean-Paul Sartre, isn't it?"

"Have you read Sartre?"

"In my Twentieth Century French Literature course. But I've forgotten the name of the play."

"*No Exit*. The characters are in Hell, but not because of conventional sins; they are guilty of not taking responsibility for their decisions. That's what Sartre calls 'bad faith'. Have you noticed how many people often blame something or someone for their problems? Parents who were very, very bad or much, much too good. On being very, very poor or too, too rich? My father always said that we are the masters of our fate, and we are responsible for the life we create for ourselves." Agnew-Simpson looked across the room to the portraits over the fireplace. "Yes, my father taught me to accept responsibility for every decision I made!" The red blotches on his face flared up. "He taught me that promises are sacred! He certainly did that," said Agnew-Simpson, and he drank the last drop of scotch from his glass.

Elizabeth did not know how to respond, and said the first thing that came into her mind. "My friend, Marie-France, is going to law school at the University of Ottawa in September. She says I should apply for the January semester. They hardly ever accept anyone in January…"

Elizabeth was interrupted by Madame Gervais pushing the trolley. It was precisely seven o'clock.

Agnew-Simpson turned to Madame Gervais and said with a smile, "Louise, did I tell you that Alexander is coming soon? Not quite sure of the exact date yet."

Madame Gervais almost dropped a dish cover. *"Dieu Merci!* We have not seen him since the funeral." Her wide smile, the sparkle in her eyes, made her face look younger.

"I had to summon him," Agnew-Simpson said with a scowl. "He did not decide to grace us with his presence himself. Papers to sign."

Elizabeth was not invited to dinner that night. She got up and began to walk towards the door.

"Elizabeth, you mentioned Ottawa. Alexander said something about a position at the University of Ottawa. Or was it at Carleton? He's a professor, you know. He is working on a book or an article. Economics? Politics? Something in that vein."

"Have a good evening, sir," said Elizabeth. *Wouldn't a proud father know what book or article his son was working on? I guess the rich are different.*

Chapter 6

Awkwardly, holding a pile of books and files under her chin, Elizabeth walked into Agnew-Simpson's study and went directly to the far end of the room, to the freestanding bookcase on wheels that was dedicated to his family history project. As she put the books back on the shelves, she could hear Agnew-Simpson yelling into the telephone. "No, I will not change my mind! I have scientific proof! DNA! Mortimer, have you become a Luddite?"

Elizabeth placed some files on his desk. Agnew-Simpson looked up and pointed to a pile of colour-coded folders. Elizabeth picked them up and waited for further instructions.

Agnew-Simpson's face became red. "Scandal! What do I care about a scandal?" He waved his hand at Elizabeth in a motion of dismissal.

As she made her way to the door, Agnew-Simpson continued to yell. "Mortimer, have you ever considered that I might marry again and sire an entire brood of offspring? Now wipe that crooked smirk off your face! Yes, Mortimer, I expect you here next week — Friday! You will stay the night, of course."

All morning, while working on translations in the library, Elizabeth replayed Agnew-Simpson's conversation. DNA? Who's DNA? And the idea that Agnew-Simpson could sire progeny seemed somehow absurd.

By noon, Elizabeth was happy to leave the library and step into the patio sunshine. She loved eating outside, next to the sparkling lake. Madame Gervais served plain food for the staff — Campbell's chicken noodle soup and ham and cheese sandwiches.

"You'll have to do so much cooking for company!" Monsieur Gervais said, blowing on his soup. "Dr Jordan tonight, the lawyer next week. And Alexander, he should be here any day."

"Alexander didn't say when exactly." Madame Gervais looked up from her notepad. "Dr Jordan does not eat meat, so Marcel, right after lunch, bring me some trout from the fisherman on the lake. Next week, drive over to Labelle to that sheep farm and pick up my order. I'll marinate the lamb for the lawyer."

"You see, Elizabeth? I am just an errand boy!"

"Who's Dr Jordan?"

"Oh, yes! You haven't met him. Dr Jordan is Mr Ted's friend from university. He's been away in the States for a month or so," said Madame Gervais. "He owns The Wellness Centre — it's a spa with a cosmetic surgery wing and a psychiatric clinic."

"One-stop shopping," said Monsieur Gervais with a chuckle. "First, you go to the cosmetic clinic because you have an ugly nose. They fix your nose, and then they tell you that you are also suffering from an ugly nose neurosis. So they send you to their psychiatric clinic. If you start screaming when you see the bill, they recommend the spa to calm your nerves!" Monsieur Gervais winked at Elizabeth. "Dr Jordan is always looking for victims to disfigure in his clinic. In the village, they say the wife of an American millionaire is suing him. Her plastic surgery went wrong, and her face slid to one side! They say he's on the verge of bankruptcy!"

"Marcel, since when do you repeat village gossip?"

"It's not gossip! My niece, Collette, has a friend who works as a cleaner at the clinic. They all say that the doctor is very strange — he sleeps in a coffin!"

"*Voyons!* Marcel!"

Elizabeth put her hand over her mouth to hide a smile.

"Well, I don't believe it's a coffin — probably just black sheets. You know how people exaggerate! But I don't trust that Dr Jordan." Monsieur Gervais sighed deeply. "Madame's accident happened on the same night Dr Jordan brought her back from his clinic."

"Marcel! Enough!"

This was the opening Elizabeth followed up. "The internet is full of fantastic stories about Madame Mathilde's death. I've read all sorts of nonsense. One blogger even speculated that her death was a satanic ritual sacrifice."

"Elizabeth, please! I don't want to hear any malicious gossip!" Madame Gervais put her palms over her ears, and her cheeks turned bright pink.

Elizabeth bit her lip. The topic of Mathilde's death was off-limits for Madame Gervais. Monsieur Gervais, on the other hand, seemed bursting to talk.

"I'm sorry, Madame Gervais, I didn't mean to upset you, but I would like to know the truth. There is so much nonsense on the internet! Can you tell me what happened?

Madame Gervais sat silently with her head bowed. Elizabeth, however, did not want to miss this opportunity. "I read that Madame Mathilde had a sleep disorder."

"She had problems with sleep all her life, but it got worse during the last few years," said Madame Gervais.

"She was a *somnambule*. That's why Dr Jordan was treating her. Everyone at the clinic knew that," said Monsieur Gervais.

Madame Gervais glowered at her husband.

"I'm not giving away any secrets," Monsieur Gervais said defiantly.

"A sleepwalker?" Elizabeth put down her sandwich.

"Marcel! We do not talk about the family!" said Madame Gervais, as she brusquely removed her husband's soup bowl.

Elizabeth picked her words carefully. "Please, Madame Gervais, you know I signed a confidentiality clause. You can count on my discretion. The only information I can get is from the tabloids. I would like to know the truth. As I understand it, Madame was walking down the stairs at night, slipped and fell and broke…"

Monsieur Gervais interjected. "You probably also read that the coroner, the one from the *Sureté* in Ste Agathe, ruled it a suspicious death. Then, for some reason, they brought in another forensic specialist from Montreal, who decided it was an accident after all. The first forensic guy suddenly got a big promotion and moved away! Now that's fishy…"

Madame Gervais interrupted. "It was not a big promotion! I know that for a fact! He retired early and moved to New Brunswick to be with his daughter." Madame Gervais took a deep breath. "All right. I'll tell you what I know so you won't believe all that salacious gossip. It was six in the morning when I found Madame Mathilde. She was at the bottom of the stairs. She was wearing her beautiful pink negligée." Madame Gervais dabbed her eyes with a white handkerchief. "Her eyes, she had such beautiful blue eyes… They were wide open. That's how I knew she was dead," said Madame Gervais, her voice choking.

"Louise picked up the knife…"

"It was not a knife! It was a silver letter opener in the shape of a cross. It was a present from her uncle, the cardinal," said Madame Gervais. "His Eminence spent many years at the Vatican."

"I did not read anything about a knife. Did Madame stab herself during the fall?" asked Elizabeth.

"No, thank goodness," said Madame Gervais with a deep sigh. "She dropped it on the stairs. I took it up to her boudoir and put it back in its place."

Elizabeth did not utter her thoughts out loud. *So does that mean you tampered with evidence?*

Monsieur Gervais continued with the story. "I was in the kitchen having coffee when Louise walked in. Her face was white, white like chalk! Even when I saw the body, I couldn't believe she was dead. I ran up to Mr Ted's bedroom, and he was…"

"Marcel!" Madame Gervais glared at her husband.

Monsieur Gervais continued, "I went to the guest bedroom. Dr Jordan was spending the night. He often does that when he and Mr Ted have too much to drink. Dr Jordan told me to call an ambulance…"

Madame Gervais interrupted. "Then, the ambulance and the police arrived. You cannot imagine how horrible it was! The police and all those people in white plastic suits with tape measures, cameras and things. They were coming and going. I put coffee, muffins, and sandwiches on a trolley in the vestibule. I don't know how I survived!" There were tears in Madame Gervais's eyes. Monsieur Gervais took his wife's hand.

"Oh, I'm so sorry, I did not mean to bring back painful memories."

"It is all right, *ma petite*." Madame Gervais wiped her eyes and blew her nose. "Now you know the truth." They ate the rest of their lunch in silence.

Coming back from a short canoe ride, Elizabeth stopped in the kitchen to make herself some herbal tea. The Gervais couple were at the oak table.

"Marcel, what do you think of my menu for Alexander's visit? *Cipaille, tourtière, ragoût de boulettes*. I'm making his favourite dessert — *tarte au sucre*."

Elizabeth was happy to see Madame Gervais was smiling again.

"Alexander prefers *tarte aux citrons*," said Monsieur Gervais.

The couple were still arguing about dessert when Elizabeth went back to the library to return to a tedious translation. Her mind kept springing back to the lunchtime conversation. *Why did Madame Gervais remove the knife? Why was Mathilde walking with a knife? Was Mathilde sleepwalking?*

Elizabeth could not help herself; that same afternoon, she searched the internet for more information about Mathilde's death. One online tabloid, *Gossip Queen*, claimed that during her stay at a clinic, Mathilde was tied down in her bed at night because she walked around and got into bed with male patients. Was it true? Was someone at the clinic spreading malicious lies? No wonder Agnew-Simpson was paranoid about confidentiality. She decided to research somnambulism in her free time.

Chapter 7

Every Sunday, the Gervais couple drove to church in their personal car, a twenty-year-old Mercury Impala. It looked brand new — a gleaming, golden body, sparkling chrome and not one speck of dust on the plush seats. Madame Gervais wore a white pillbox hat and a grey linen suit with a crisply ironed, box-pleated skirt. Monsieur Gervais wore a navy-blue blazer and a white shirt. He always smelled of Aqua Velva.

On her first day off, the couple invited Elizabeth to the church in the village and then to their family lunch at the home of Bernadette, Madame Gervais's widowed sister. She did not want to intrude on their private time and spent the morning by the lake, swimming, sunbathing and reading *Ten Little Indians* by Agatha Christie. In the afternoon, she took a canoe ride around the lake. The water was crystal clear and calm. It was quiet, except for the gentle rustle of leaves and the occasional bird call. As if by osmosis, she absorbed the peaceful serenity of nature.

That afternoon, she called Catherine. After six rings, the answering machine responded. "You have reached Catherine the Great. Please leave your name and number. I will call you back if you deserve my attention."

"It's time you changed that message! Don't tell me you are still sleeping? All OK here." Then, after a pause, "I miss you."

She dialled Amanda's number.

"Lizzie, finally! How are you?"

"Country living has been good for me. All this sunshine — great therapy! I think I'm almost back to my old self again. But I'm so lonely."

"Ah, poor baby! Why such cryptic emails? Why didn't you phone earlier? I was beginning to worry."

"All the computers are connected here, and I don't feel comfortable talking on the phone. I'm probably paranoid, but whenever I pick up the house phone, I hear a click. My boss is obsessed with security, confidentiality and all that stuff, so I don't want to discuss anything on the telephone."

"Aren't you getting paranoid yourself? How does your boss treat you?"

"He is not an ogre. He is usually nice, but at times he can be weird."

"Weird? How? Weird funny or weird dangerous?"

"Don't know — just a feeling. I phoned Catherine, and she didn't pick up."

"Catherine has two jobs. Works nights at a bar and sleeps the rest of the time. I keep telling her she's killing herself. She wants to save money now, so she won't have to work so much during the semester. Tell me something about your life up there." Then, in an aside to Rob, Amanda yelled, "In a minute, I'm talking to Lizzie. Sorry. He's upset because I forced him to paint the living room this weekend. Go on, tell me about your work."

"I didn't think that translation would be so difficult! Checking footnotes is tedious. What I enjoy are the research assignments and…"

"Sorry, Lizzie, my lord and master is calling me again."

When Amanda returned to the phone, she said, "Lizzie, can you call me back this evening? Rob is having golf withdrawal symptoms. Wants me to hold the ladder."

"Tell Rob, I said he's a big baby. Can you come up to Tremblant on a Sunday?"

"Next weekend we are off to Rob's company golf tournament in Montebello, and then the weekend after that we're at Rob's parents' cottage. I'm so sorry, Lizzie! I will come later, I promise."

By her second week on the estate, Elizabeth began to experience cabin fever. She gladly accepted the next invitation to visit Mont Tremblant village. Monsieur Gervais parked the Impala in the church parking lot, a typical nineteenth-century grey flagstone building with a silvery metal roof. A stone statue of Jesus, arms spread wide, welcomed all. The couple joined the trickle of churchgoers, a steady procession of neatly dressed people. Monsieur and Madame Gervais, walking arm in arm, nodded to some parishioners and stopped to chat with others. The sun's rays reflected off the tall, silver steeple. The church bells rang. It was Sunday.

Elizabeth felt like a tourist as she strolled Rue Principale, lined with white, French-Canadian clapboard cottages with silvery sheet-metal roofs.

The narrow porches abutted the sidewalk and in times past, on Sunday evenings, the inhabitants used to sit on rocking chairs, drink Cokes or beer, and watch the procession of cars drive back to Montreal. Since the Provincial government poured millions into making Mont Tremblant a world-class ski resort, many family homes became boutiques or souvenir shops featuring local *artisanat* selling paintings of Laurentian landscapes, postcards, and photographs of the Mont Tremblant ski resort — white in winter, green in summer, red and gold in the fall. There were many French bistro-type restaurants — *Le Petit Chateau, Le Vieux Four* and several *cases-croute*. The square, modern buildings housing the pharmacy and supermarket looked out of place on a street where hanging pots of pink petunias and bluebells decorated the lamp posts.

Elizabeth walked into a coffee shop, ordered a cappuccino, and sat at a table with a red-and-white chequered tablecloth to read a local tourist flyer. She discovered that Mont Tremblant hosted music festivals: a blues festival in July, followed by a succession of free outdoor concerts by Quebecois artists. She made a mental note to invite Marie-France. It would be such fun to sit in an outdoor café together or ride the gondola to the top of Mont Tremblant and marvel at the magnificent view. Sightseeing alone was not quite the same.

She looked up from the paper and watched a young couple walk up to the counter. Both wore khaki shorts and dark blue hoodies. As they waited for the coffee, the girl nuzzled her nose against the young man's shoulder; he bent over to kiss her on the cheek. The scene triggered memories. Elizabeth left her unfinished cappuccino on the table and walked out of the café.

She found a bicycle rental. A young man with a long, greasy black ponytail and tattoos on his hands showed her a map. Bicycle paths ran next to the railway track of the former *Petit Train du Nord*, but Elizabeth decided to cycle along Chemin des Voyageurs instead, past the Congress Centre and the pedestrian ski village at the foot of the mountain, with its narrow cobblestone streets, high-end hotels, boutiques and restaurants. It looked like a Swiss village, with white or cream buildings and red, green, or grey roofs. Cycling up the slope, Elizabeth stopped to look at a water-ski competition on Lac Tremblant. Then she followed Chemin de la Chapelle up the hill under the shadow of the Tremblant Fairmount Hotel.

After two hours of cycling, exhausted, Elizabeth returned the bicycle and stopped at a *casse-croute* — a trailer painted with red and white stripes. She ordered poutine, the *crème de la crème* of sinfully fattening foods. After the first bite of the thick, greasy French fries smothered in brown sauce and stringy cheese curds, Elizabeth let out a loud grunt of guilty pleasure. Embarrassed, she stole a furtive glance at the two teenage girls sitting at the next table. They smiled at her.

Returning to the bicycle rental shop, Elizabeth looked up at a map posted on the wall. Those familiar names — Ste Agathe, Ste Adele, Ste Marguerite du Lac Masson. These place names triggered a rush of memories — a dark brown cottage with red shutters... Grandpa John smoking a pipe, sitting on the green rocking chair on the porch... Grand Maman in her chequered apron... a kitchen that always smelled of freshly baked cookies. Ste Marguerite du Lac Masson! How many childhood memories! *I want to see it again.*

That Sunday felt like the longest day in her life. At five o'clock, she arrived at the church parking lot just as Monsieur Gervais drove up in his golden Impala. Later, she telephoned Marie-France. She no longer cared whether Agnew-Simpson or anyone else was listening; she needed to talk to a friend. Elizabeth was ecstatic. Marie-France agreed to visit the following Sunday and meet Elizabeth in front of the church at ten a.m.

Chapter 8

Elizabeth was waiting outside the church as Marie-France arrived in a tiny orange car. Pink-cheeked and smiling from ear to ear, she ran to hug Elizabeth. The two young women jumped up and down and squealed like six-year-olds.

"What's with this oversized sardine can?" Elizabeth asked, as she got into the car.

"It's a Mini Cooper. Her name is Daisy. She's perfect for me!"

"Hello, Daisy," said Elizabeth, and patted the dashboard.

Elizabeth had planned the itinerary. First, they would drive to Ste Marguerite and visit the old cottage. As a child, Marie-France had been a guest there, too. It was about fifteen minutes away, south on Highway 15.

On the way, Elizabeth talked about her life and work on the estate. Her description of Agnew-Simpson made Marie-France laugh out loud. "He is supposed to be a multi-millionaire, but he dresses like a hobo. Always the same tweed jacket with elbow patches and baggy grey trousers with frayed cuffs! And his eyes — they always seem to be shivering behind those tinted glasses."

"I'm so glad you can laugh again," said Marie-France, as the car turned onto a narrow road that wound up the hill overlooking Lac Masson. To the left were snatches of blue water, white picket fences, and neat hedges.

Elizabeth read the names on the mailboxes: Miller, Lefebvre, Hutchison, Lamoureux. They found the log cabin with the red shutters. The name on the mailbox was different.

"When was I here last?" asked Marie-France.

"I think we never came back after Mother died," said Elizabeth, as they got out of the car. "It looks empty. Let's take a quick peek."

The old rocking chair still stood on the porch facing the lake. Much of the green paint was gone. Elizabeth experienced a memory flashback. "I remember, I scraped my knee. I must have been five or six. I sat on

Grandpa's lap and cried. I pressed my cheek against Grandpa's chest and listened to the thump, thump, thump of his heart. I felt so safe, so secure — nothing bad could happen to me while the chair rocked gently and Grandpa's heavy hand patted my leg."

"You were the youngest, Lizzie, and you were pampered." Marie-France sighed. "Your grandfather was a rock!"

Elizabeth stood looking at the rocking chair and felt her eyes well up. They walked down to the lake, to where, once, a wooden rowboat was tied to a peg. "Remember how Grandpa used to dig for worms! Then he would row us all — you, me, Catherine and Amanda — to that little island, and we would all squeal when he baited the hook or gutted the fish."

"And your grandmother fried the fish outside, on that old electric frying pan. No fish has ever tasted so good."

The sound of a car in the driveway disrupted their reminiscences. Elizabeth and Marie-France hurried back and almost ran into a young woman carrying a baby in a shoulder strap. Behind her came a tall young man in shorts and flip-flops. Wide-eyed, they stared at Elizabeth and Marie-France.

"Are you looking for someone?" the young man asked.

"Sorry for trespassing. My grandparents used to rent this cottage when I was a kid," said Elizabeth. "We just wanted to see it again."

They drove back to the Mont Tremblant ski village, left the car in the parking lot, and walked along the cobblestones to *La Crêperie*, a restaurant with a red roof and dormer windows. Inside, it had cosy booths, wood panelling, and a collection of kitschy pig figurines. Elizabeth ordered the house white and crêpes stuffed with ham, cheese and asparagus. Marie-France took a long time to decide, and finally opted for crêpes filled with strawberries, bananas and whipped cream.

"I missed you so much! I don't have anyone to talk to! I mean, talk! If my boss hadn't made me sign a confidentiality agreement, I'd share something that's been on my mind."

"Sounds so mysterious! Mmm! Good wine," said Marie-France, as she took a long sip from the blue-tinted goblet. "Why can't you tell me? You know I won't tell anyone."

"If I tell you, I will have to kill you!"

"So what? You would only get life imprisonment! Is that any reason to keep secrets from your best friend?" Both Elizabeth and Marie-France exploded in peals of raucous laughter.

"Do you know anything about sleepwalking?"

"Sleepwalking?" Marie-France's eyes opened wide. "Now that's a bizarre question!"

"I have been researching sleepwalking. Here, look at this..." Elizabeth was about to take some printed pages from her purse, but the young, freckled waitress brought their crêpes, and for the next few minutes conversation gave way to moans of delight.

"Now that you mentioned sleepwalking, I do remember my brother used to sleepwalk as a kid. The only weird thing he did was to pee in his closet."

They finished the crêpes, and Elizabeth took a few printed sheets from her purse. "Listen to this: 'Some sleepwalkers have been known to engage in sexual activities while asleep and completely unaware. These behaviours can occur whether they share a bed with a partner or not. Engaging in sexual behaviours while asleep and unaware is called sexsomnia. Stress, anxiety, fatigue, sleep deprivation and drug use can all contribute to this condition. Like sleepwalking and other sleep disorders, people tend not to remember behaving this way.'"

Marie-France looked at Elizabeth with her eyes opened wide. "Lizzie, what's it all about? OK, I won't ask. Tell me what you can."

After her conversation with the Gervais couple, Elizabeth had researched sleepwalking. She assumed that on the night she died, Mathilde went to her husband's bedroom for sex. *But why did she bring the knife/letter opener? Did Mathilde plan to kill her husband? Why? What was the motive? Do sleepwalkers need a motive?*

"One of the articles I read claims that most sleepwalkers are not dangerous to anyone but themselves."

"I heard it's dangerous to wake up a sleepwalker. Do they become violent or what?" asked Marie-France.

"I'm not sure. Most people just babble or wander around the house for a bit. A few even go outside and then wake up wandering down a highway in their pyjamas. I also read about a murder committed while sleepwalking."

"Come on, that's just an excuse!" said Marie-France.

"Not according to the jury!" Elizabeth read from a page: "'Evidence of abnormal brain waves during REM and deep sleep has convinced past juries that crimes committed in this state weren't intentional and shouldn't be punished.'" Elizabeth stopped reading and looked up at Marie-France for effect.

"You mean like the Twinkie defence? Your honour, I'm innocent! I was high on chocolate when I killed my husband with an axe!"

"Listen to this." Elizabeth picked up another text. "In 1987 — that's not so long ago — a man called Parks was acquitted of murdering his in-laws. While asleep, he drove twenty miles to Pickering, Ontario. He used a tyre iron to bludgeon his mother-in-law to death, then he choked his father-in-law within an inch of his life. He then drove to a police station and confessed. At the trial, his lawyer argued that his client was not criminally liable. From the doctor's evidence, it was confirmed that the accused was sleepwalking. Five neurological experts also confirmed that he was sleepwalking during the time of the incident. The jury acquitted Parks."

"They must have picked a jury of village idiots!"

"The Supreme Court of Canada upheld the acquittal!"

"You are kidding me! Now that's scary!"

Elizabeth looked up at the big cuckoo clock. "We should be getting back to the church," said Elizabeth, and she picked up the check.

There were hugs and kisses in the parking lot. There were tears in Elizabeth's eyes as the Mini Cooper drove away.

Chapter 9

One evening in June, as Elizabeth walked into the study for sherry hour, she heard voices drifting in from the balcony. A guest, his back to Elizabeth, leaned over the stone balustrade above the shimmering lake. He was wearing crisply pressed black slacks and a long-sleeved, black silk shirt.

Agnew-Simpson's voice was shrill. "Tig, the piggy bank is closed!"

"Yes, Ted, you were right, and I was wrong! Bit off more than I could chew! *Mea culpa*! I would not ask again, but my life's work is at risk! Can't you see that? Can't you try to sort it out with your accountant? After all, whose money is it — yours or his?" The guest turned to look directly at Agnew-Simpson and raised his voice. "After everything I have done for you, particularly that night..."

Agnew-Simpson sounded irritated. "How often will you keep bringing up that night? It's beginning to sound like a threat."

"How can you even suggest such a thing? Do you want me to leave?"

Agnew-Simpson changed his tone and placed his arm around the man's shoulder. "You know I will always take care of you. You know that I have written you into my new will. You will inherit..."

"And a lot of good that will do me! With my luck, you will live forever! I don't know how long I can delay the creditors."

"Sell your fancy cars! Do you need that bunker of a house?"

"That was cruel, Ted."

"You are such an ingrate! Not even a thank you?" Agnew-Simpson laughed. "You have been there before. In the end, you always survive — nine lives, like a cat! Get some of your rich old hags to subsidise you."

Elizabeth slowed her step. "Ahem!" She coughed into her fist.

"Ah, my lovely assistant, Elizabeth! What did I tell you, Tig?"

"Congratulations! You always had the knack of surrounding yourself with beautiful women!"

"Elizabeth, meet Dr Jordan, owner of our world-renowned Wellness

Centre! And I will tell you in confidence, he is Mont Tremblant's international man of mystery!"

"Man of mystery, indeed! He is trying to scare you, Elizabeth!"

Elizabeth noticed that the doctor's fingers, wrapped around a crystal whisky glass, were manicured and lacquered. To her surprise, he kissed her hand. His lips were cold, and she sensed a certain chill emanating from his body as if he had just stepped out of a crypt. She almost took a step back as the cloying, musky smell of his cologne wafted past her nostrils.

"Let's go in," said Agnew-Simpson. "Getting cold out here."

Elizabeth made an effort to smile as she analysed Dr Jordan. *Why dye your thinning hair such an unflattering tar-black? Tinted glasses — part of your man of mystery get-up? And Doctor, no matter how expensive the cologne — less is more.*

"My dear, let me pour you a sherry — unless you want something stronger?" said Agnew-Simpson. Elizabeth noticed that both men were drinking scotch and that both had consumed substantially more than one drink.

"Sherry is fine."

"Elizabeth, you must visit my sanatorium! A massage, a steam bath — absolutely *de rigueur* after a day with Ted!" He gave Elizabeth his card. "My treat. Please, do come next week. I insist!" Dr Jordan took Elizabeth by the elbow to guide her to the love seat corner.

Elizabeth noted that Dr Jordan smiled with his mouth only. His face remained immobile like a granite bust.

"What is a sanatorium? Is it like a spa? I'm not sure."

"Sanatoriums used to be very fashionable in Europe at one time. You may have heard of Carlsbad, now Karlovy Vary, in the Czech Republic. People go there for the mineral waters, to cure everything from gout to baldness. Unfortunately, here in Tremblant, we don't have natural springs, although we use hydrotherapy."

"Waterboarding?" asked Agnew-Simpson.

Elizabeth smiled at the joke and asked, "Dr Jordan, are you a plastic surgeon?"

"No, heaven forbid! Although we do have a wing dedicated to cosmetic surgery. I'm CEO of the entire complex and chief psychiatrist. I work with patients who suffer from addictions or sleep disorders. My specialty is in neuropsychiatric disorders: insomnia, narcolepsy, night terrors, sleepwalking..."

"Sleepwalking? I thought it was an old wives' tale, like people turning into werewolves when the moon is full."

"In the past, people associated sleepwalking with a full moon. In fact, in some languages, 'lunatic' is the word for a sleepwalker. Sleepwalking only became the focus of neurological study at the end of the nineteenth century. Now it is a treatable condition."

"How do you treat it?" asked Elizabeth.

"We use a combination of drugs and hypnosis," Dr Jordan continued. "I published several papers on the subject, and I am just back from a speaking tour in..."

Agnew-Simpson interrupted, slurring slightly. "Hypnosis! Really! It sounds like a parlour trick! You wouldn't be able to hypnotise me! And that is a fact!"

"I wouldn't be too sure about that!"

"Try it! Try to hypnotise me now! I bet you couldn't," said Agnew-Simpson, sounding belligerent.

Elizabeth, seeing that her boss had had too much to drink, began to fidget and stole a surreptitious look at her wristwatch.

"Ted, you are making Elizabeth uncomfortable."

"Oh, we can't have that, can we? Tig, why not entertain Elizabeth with your famous family history story?"

"*My* famous family history story? It's *your* story! You tell it, Ted; you do it so much better than I do."

"Tig is a descendant of Vlad the Impaler. He was born in Transylvania..."

"Pay no attention to Ted. I was born in Algeria."

"You're Algerian?"

"No! My father was Bulgarian, my mother was Armenian. 'Jordan' is an anglicised version of 'Iordanov'. I was named after my Armenian grandfather — Tigran. Everyone calls me Tig."

"Tig is too modest to tell you that he is a descendant of Bulgaria's King Boris, who defeated somebody or other in the eleventh... or was it the twelfth century? Despite this illustrious past, the family fortune was lost during the war. The Iordanov clan accommodated themselves quite nicely to Nazi occupation, but were forced to flee when the Russian tanks moved in." Agnew-Simpson looked at Dr Jordan with a wicked smirk.

"Regrettably, that part is true. Papa escaped to Spain; then, he moved to Algeria, where eventually I was born. When Algeria was liberated from colonial oppression, we were kicked out and landed in Canada. I graduated from McGill, met Ted, and lived happily ever after."

"Don't you think it's a fascinating story, Elizabeth?"

"No, Ted! I did not live happily ever after! As you know, my whole life's work is at risk! I will admit to bad management, but it's not only about me! What will happen to my drug rehabilitation clinic? Apart from my paying clients, every year I take in a number of young Inuit from northern Quebec. *Pro bono.* If the clinic folds, they'll be out on the street!"

Agnew-Simpson looked unmoved. He had a wicked and sly smile on his face. "On the street! We do have socialised medicine in Canada! So, Elizabeth, don't believe Tig's Mother Teresa routine!"

Before Elizabeth could react, they were startled by the sound of female voices in the hallway. The door to the study was flung open, and a statuesque blonde rushed into the room. She was followed by a breathless Monsieur Gervais. Standing behind them in the hallway, looking uncomfortable, was a tiny, thin woman wearing a loose white pants suit and red high-heeled sandals.

"I told Madame Holt that I would need your permission before she could go upstairs, but she…"

"Thank you, Marcel," said Agnew-Simpson in a severe tone. "How did you get past the gate, Zsuzsanna?"

Zsuzsanna was dressed in beige linen slacks, a cream silk blouse, and sandals with two-inch crystal heels. A pair of flat shoes was sticking out of her oversized straw handbag. There were masses of pearl chains around her neck. Her buttercup-yellow hair was swept up in a chignon.

Elizabeth noted the contrast between the woman's smooth, heavily made-up face and the age spots on her hands.

"Honestly, Ted!" said Zsuzsanna, as she approached Agnew-Simpson with her arms open wide. Agnew-Simpson took a step back. Zsuzsanna ignored his reluctance. "Are you under prison guard? I drove up last week and yelled into the intercom at the gate! You do not answer my emails or calls! What is a woman to do to get your attention?"

Agnew-Simpson, his face red, was about to open his mouth, but Dr Jordan took him by the arm and said, "Zsuzsanna, darling, you must forgive Ted's little eccentricities."

"How did you get in here?" asked Agnew-Simpson without any effort at civility.

"And it is so nice to see you, too, Ted. Even though you decided to live like a hermit, I can't believe you've forgotten your manners." Then, turning towards the open door and seeing her companion standing in the hallway, Zsuzsanna said, "Forgive me, Dina. Please come in. Ted, this is Dina Levinson from New York City. She inherited the property across the lake and hired me to make the place presentable before it goes on sale. Would you be interested in buying the property by any chance?"

"No," said Agnew-Simpson.

"You may be sorry when some rock band buys it and has practice sessions all night long. I already have a potential client."

"You did not answer my question," said Agnew-Simpson without a smile. "How did you get onto my estate?"

"Ted, won't you offer the ladies a drink?" asked Dr Jordan.

No one introduced Elizabeth. She sat on the maroon couch and watched, wide-eyed.

"First, tell me how you got in," reiterated Agnew-Simpson, raising his voice another notch.

Zsuzsanna stretched her red lips into a smile, and ignoring his tone, said, "While Dina and I were inspecting her house, she asked who lived in the gorgeous house across the lake. We came across in a rowboat."

"Sherry or scotch?" asked Dr Jordan.

"Scotch," said Zsuzsanna.

"Sherry," said Dina.

With a scowl on his face, Agnew-Simpson walked the ladies to the love seats. He introduced Elizabeth as his assistant. Dr Jordan poured the drinks at the built-in bar.

"How do you do," said Zsuzsanna, stretching her full, red lips into a smile. She turned to Dina and said, "So young, so pretty. Men, no matter how old, are always attracted by youth. Women our age don't have a chance!"

Elizabeth found the courage to reply to this tactless comment. "Mr Agnew-Simpson hired me as a research assistant for his history book," she said without a smile.

The conversation turned to the upcoming golf club fundraiser. Zsuzsanna made transparent hints that she would like to invite Agnew-Simpson to sit at her table. "Why have you ostracised yourself, Ted? So many people, most of them women, may I add, would love to see you. Although I gather that you are not bored," she said, and looked at Elizabeth.

"I gave up golf years ago," said Agnew-Simpson.

Elizabeth tried not to study Dina too openly. Here was a woman of undetermined age, who wore oversized, orange-tinted glasses. Her facial skin was pulled as taut as a drum. Her fashionably full lips (probably botoxed) looked too big for her thin birdlike face. *She should wear a wig to hide that wispy red hair with grey roots. And the jewellery — enough gold for a Mayan breastplate!*

"I forgot all about the house on the peninsula," said Agnew-Simpson.

"Out of sight, out of mind," said Dr Jordan.

"Many years ago, there was some unpleasantness that almost turned into a blood feud. Father went to court. I don't remember how it all ended. Was the owner named Levinson, too?"

"No, Frascatti. He is my uncle on my mother's side of the family. He moved to California years ago," said Dina with a coquettish smile. "I married Aaron Levinson. You may have heard of my late husband. Wall Street?"

"Do you have any children or grandchildren interested in the property?" asked Agnew-Simpson.

"Grandchildren! Heavens, no!" said Dina with a girlish giggle.

Elizabeth noticed that Dina's teeth were very white. Why is it, Elizabeth thought, that thin women, especially those who have never had children, think of themselves as perpetually young? They hide the sagging skin and cover up the age spots with make-up, but don't they realise that these subterfuges don't fool anyone?

"Has anyone expressed interest in the property?" asked Agnew-Simpson.

"Not yet. We plan to spruce it up before the open house," said Zsuzsanna. The house phone rang. Agnew-Simpson picked it up, listened for a few seconds and said, "Another fifteen minutes."

Elizabeth understood that it was Madame Gervais asking when to serve supper and whether to include the additional guests.

When Agnew-Simpson returned to the guests, he said rather unceremoniously, "Ladies, may I suggest that you take the boat back across the lake before it gets dark."

Dina's orange-tinted eyebrows rose above her glasses, while Zsuzsanna's red lips drooped.

"Of course," said Zsuzsanna, as she stole an inquisitive glance at Dr Jordan. She rose, took Agnew-Simpson by the arm and said, "The golf club is celebrating our fiftieth anniversary. I am selling tickets and—"

"My dancing days are over," said Agnew-Simpson.

"Can I ask you for a donation? It is a fundraiser!"

"I will write you a cheque," said Agnew-Simpson. He went to his desk and quickly wrote the cheque. "I will detain you no longer." Then, turning towards Dina, he added rather stiffly, "It has been a pleasure."

As the two women got up to leave, Dr Jordan said, "Ladies, I would like to invite you both to a party. It's next week, Thursday, at six. I'm not sending invitations; just a few friends. It's my birthday, my thirty-ninth." Doctor Jordan paused to allow everyone to laugh at his little joke. "I promise that Ted will be there, even if I have to tie him up or drag him by the hair."

Agnew-Simpson gave his friend a withering look, then took Zsuzsanna by the elbow and walked her to the door. "Goodbye. I am sure you will find your way out."

Neither Zsuzsanna nor Dina were smiling as they left the room.

As soon as the door was closed, Agnew-Simpson turned to Dr Jordan.

"The first thing I will do tomorrow is to call my lawyer and tell him to buy that house across the lake. I forgot that the entire lake was not part of my property."

"Ted, you were a wee bit harsh with poor old Zsuzsanna. She is quite harmless."

"I know she is your girlfriend, but..."

"She is not my girlfriend," said Dr Jordan. "She is a useful contact —

I give her free facial treatments, and she brings clients. The woman knows absolutely everyone, even the people who fly in on their private airplanes."

Agnew-Simpson walked out onto the balcony. "I want to be sure they leave," he said.

Elizabeth remained seated on the love seat. Before leaving, she wanted to ask Agnew-Simpson for the next assignment, but taking one look at his crimson face, she decided to wait until the morning.

Seemingly oblivious to Elizabeth's presence, Agnew-Simpson confronted Dr Jordan.

"Since when do you throw birthday parties? You do not have a birthday! What is this all about? Don't think you can fool me!"

"Calm down, Ted! I am asking you for a favour! A potential investor will be there, and your presence will give me a certain gravitas."

"What sort of scheme have you cooked up?"

"I just need you to show up…"

Elizabeth heard the rumble of Madame Gervais's dinner cart in the hallway. It sounded like the cavalry rushing to her rescue. Thankfully, Mr Ted did not invite her to stay for dinner. Dr Jordan followed Elizabeth to the door, kissed her hand, and reminded her of the invitation to visit his spa.

Elizabeth went down to the kitchen, where Monsieur Gervais was drinking a Molson Light and watching the news on a small portable television.

"There will be hell to pay tomorrow," he said, turning off the TV. "I don't know how we missed them. They must have walked in through the back door. I will tell him to his face: if you want complete security, hire somebody to sit and watch the cameras all day long!"

"Was Zsuzsanna a friend of Madame Agnew-Simpson?" asked Elizabeth.

"No, she was never invited here as a guest. Mr Ted must have met her at the golf club. He used to play golf. She lives in a chalet she got in a divorce settlement. They say her last husband, some rich guy from New York, ran off with his secretary. He made her sign a prenuptial agreement, so she certainly didn't get much," said Monsieur Gervais.

"The poor woman has to work as a real estate agent. That's what happens to so many women," said Madame Gervais with a sigh. "She has no children, no family, so she will be completely alone in her old age. Who was that woman with Zsuzsanna?"

"She inherited the peninsula across the lake. Zsuzsanna is helping her sell it," said Monsieur Gervais. "There is also a house, but we can't see it from the lake. I forgot, there was a court case long ago."

"My nephew, the plumber, expects to get work from Zsuzsanna soon. He said that she hired Mako to paint some house."

"Who is Mako?" asked Elizabeth.

"He's a former patient of Dr Jordan. He arrived as a teenager, and Dr Jordan kept him on to work at the clinic. The boy is strange!"

"Boy!" said Monsieur Gervais. "He must be close to thirty by now! One day, believe me, that young man will land in jail."

"And Dr Jordan, what a strange character!" said Elizabeth. "He gave me his card and invited me to his spa."

"I can drive you. It's about ten minutes from here. Lots of people from Montreal come up for the weekend Nordic spa experience. First, you sit in a steam room until you shrivel up into a hot, wet prune, then you jump under an ice-cold waterfall. Still want to go?"

The ice-cold waterfall did not frighten Elizabeth, but she could not shake the uneasiness she felt about Dr Jordan.

Chapter 10

One morning in late June, everyone was waiting for Alexander to arrive. Elizabeth was at the computer in the library when the screen went blank, and the lights went out. She made her way to the picture window in the kitchen and watched as a black tide spread across the sky and swallowed a flock of little grey clouds. Gale-force winds whipped the lake into a frenzy of bulging waves.

There was Monsieur Gervais by the boathouse, struggling to close the door. His hair was standing on end as he turned his shoulder into the wind to push through the downpour. Madame Gervais was rolling up the umbrella over the patio table, her hair soaked and flat against her scalp. She lost the struggle, and the umbrella tumbled down the grassy incline. A cracking sound came from the direction of the garage. Elizabeth ran to the dining room and looked out the window. An old pine tree had collapsed across the driveway and pulled out an enormous soil ball, with roots dangling like torn intestines.

Monsieur Gervais walked into the kitchen, creating puddles under his feet. The house phone rang.

"Yes," he said, "I will try to start the emergency generator right away. I will tell Louise to bring up the candles."

That evening, as the wind howled, Elizabeth, holding a flashlight, made her way to Agnew-Simpson's study for sherry at six.

"Did you hear the news, my dear? Alexander arrived about an hour ago. I wonder how his car did not blow off the road. He's changing now. Got drenched to the bone, had to leave the car outside because of the fallen tree."

The rain beat a staccato rhythm against the window panes as they waited for Alexander by the light of two tall silver candelabra. Agnew-Simpson paced the room. He stopped in front of Elizabeth and whispered dramatically, "Isn't this fun? We can pretend we are in an Agatha Christie murder mystery — a clap of thunder, the lights go out, and somebody is found dead."

"What about a gothic novel, with a castle full of skeletons and ghosts rattling chains?" Elizabeth asked with a smile. "It's the perfect time for ghosts to come out."

"Yes," said Agnew-Simpson, "I would like them all to come out soon."

Elizabeth noticed that the bottle of Glenlivet was half empty. Agnew-Simpson poured Elizabeth a glass of sherry and more scotch for himself. *He looks different, somehow. Red blotches on his cheeks. How much scotch did he drink?* Elizabeth did not hear Alexander enter the room. She turned around because Agnew-Simpson looked towards the door. She had assumed that the son would resemble his father and not the angelic Mathilde. But here was a handsome man — not yet thirty — dressed casually in jeans and a black T-shirt, stretched taut over muscular shoulders. He was about five foot ten inches tall and slim. His hair, cut very short, was thick — coal-black, like his eyes. Alexander's dark olive complexion was a startling contrast to his father's pasty skin. Was the candlelight distorting Alexander's features? *He must be adopted! That is the only logical conclusion.*

As if reading Elizabeth's thoughts, Agnew-Simpson said, "No, no, my dear, he was not adopted. The Beaudry family claim to have Iroquois blood. Genes do funny things sometimes. I was at the hospital when Alexander was born. It was a difficult birth, and Mathilde could not have more children after. Pity... I always wanted another son."

Talk about tactlessness! What a horrible thing to say about your son — in front of a stranger. Is it because he doesn't look like you?

She looked furtively at Alexander to see how he reacted to his father's words. Alexander's face was inscrutable. It was not tense, not angry. Calmly, he looked straight at his father with his lips pressed together tightly.

"Alexander, did I forget to tell you that I hired an assistant for the summer? Alexander, Elizabeth. Elizabeth, Alexander."

"How do you do?" said Alexander. Rather than choosing one of the love seats, he sat in a straight-backed chair.

When he presses his lips together like that — they practically disappear. And Al, can't you manage a smile — even a fake smile? You know, like those mechanical smiles for greeting door attendants, waiters, female assistants.

"Don't you think I have a pretty assistant, Alexander?" asked Agnew-Simpson, as he sat down on the love seat opposite Elizabeth. "Don't you think that she has beautiful eyes? Such a rare colour. They remind me of a lake in the Rockies. Lake Moraine? No, no. Lake Maligne. Turquoise, like Elizabeth's eyes. Elizabeth, you are blushing! Such modesty! You must have received many compliments. Many times! Many, many times! Am I not right, Elizabeth?"

Is there some innuendo that I'm not quite getting? I feel as if I am being inspected, like a horse. Will he want to look at my teeth next? Should I tell him that I feel uncomfortable? On the other hand, perhaps Catherine was right. I am too sensitive.

"Yes, she is beautiful, Ted. She must also be competent because I know you would not employ just a pretty face."

Thank you, Al! You have redeemed yourself. But why does Alexander call his father Ted?

"It's so much more delectable when brains and beauty come in the same package," Agnew-Simpson giggled. "Alexander, please forgive me. Your drink." He poured Alexander two fingers of Glenlivet and sloppily splashed more scotch into his glass.

"Did you drive through the storm?" Elizabeth asked Alexander.

"The rain started around St Jerome, and by the time I reached Ste Adele, I thought the wind would blow the car off the road. The radio called it the storm of the century. Transmission lines, trees, even roofs blew away in some areas."

"We are talking about the weather! How mundane! People with nothing meaningful to say will be talking about this storm for years!" said Agnew-Simpson, and he rolled his eyes. "Tell me, Alexander, what is the topic of whatever you are writing about?"

"I've been asked to write a chapter for an anthology about the Quiet Revolution in Quebec. The editor is Professor Abelard Legault of Carleton."

"And what is your thesis, may I ask? I am very interested in the subject myself."

"At one time, it was fashionable to treat the FLQ crisis in the context of de-colonialisation. I'm sure you've read *Negre Blanc de L'Amerique*, by Vallière. However, I think..."

"Yes, yes, I remember — bombs in mailboxes, the attack on the Armoury. The FLQ issued a manifesto, something completely asinine. 'Students, peasants, and workers of Quebec unite — you have nothing to lose but your chains', or was it 'your brains'? But I still chuckle when I think how it scared the pants off the Yanks. What year was that? 1960?"

"They bombed the armouries in March 1963," said Alexander. "In my opinion, the Marxist analysis is outdated. My thesis focuses on the secularisation process..."

The blotches on Agnew-Simpson's cheeks flared red. "Why do professors waste time on useless theorising? For whom are you writing? For other professors, locked in their ivory towers?"

"Ted, I am quite familiar with your propensity to argue with me when you have had a few; however, as a historian yourself, how can you...?"

"There is a difference," Agnew-Simpson interrupted. "I am writing about real people. My grandfather and my father were men who built the wealth of this country! They were men of action! They certainly did not waste their time cooped up in musty libraries, scribbling about esoteric theories or counting how many devils danced on Marx's head." Agnew-Simpson got up, glass in hand, and stood in front of the two portraits over the fireplace. "My book will be an homage to their ingenuity, their energy, and their will. My book will inspire the younger generation."

The expression on Alexander's face remained inscrutable. His eyes seemed locked onto his glass of scotch. Elizabeth wondered whether Alexander's eyes seemed so dark because of the candlelight. If eyes are the mirror to the soul, how can you see inside such black eyes?

"I do have a theory," said Agnew-Simpson, and he began a rambling tirade about Jesuit colleges and the French-Canadian élite. Elizabeth did not understand most of what he said. *Mr Ted is on a roll. No way to shut him up short of stuffing a rag into his mouth.*

"Alexander, have you noticed that intellectuals never want to get their hands dirty? They are incapable of creating anything practical, and yet they claim the right to control the economy in the name of the oppressed masses. They nationalise the wealth and anoint themselves in charge of distribution and allocation. And they certainly do not short-change themselves! Compassion for the oppressed masses! What a crock! It's a power trip!"

Alexander's voice was calm when he said, "Ted, you are boring Elizabeth."

"Perhaps, but I am enjoying this conversation," replied Agnew-Simpson. "I don't have many opportunities to discuss serious topics."

Sure, Elizabeth and I talk about celebrity gossip and fashion. We exchange cake recipes.

There was a soft knock on the door, and a downcast Madame Gervais rolled in the trolley laden with cold cuts and cheeses. "Monsieur Gervais could not get the generator working," she lamented. "The electricians, well, you can imagine how busy they are tonight."

Elizabeth took this opportunity to excuse herself. She went down to the kitchen and told Monsieur Gervais that she was tired and would take a cold plate up to her room. She wanted to avoid any discussion of her boss and his son. Later, as she lay in bed, she could not concentrate on her novel or stop thinking about the contrast between the pasty-skinned, watery-eyed Agnew-Simpson and his dark-eyed son.

Chapter 11

The electricity was back when Elizabeth woke up the next morning. The day turned out to be hot and sunny, as if the weather gods were making amends for yesterday's rampage.

Except for the sound of Monsieur Gervais's electric saw, cutting up the fallen pine tree, it was as if the storm had never happened. She did not see Agnew-Simpson or Alexander that morning, and continued to work on assignments in the library. At lunch with Madame Gervais, they listened to the local radio station describe the litany of the storm's destruction. Elizabeth finished her tuna sandwich and took a carton of apple juice to the dock. She sat, debating whether to go up to her room and change into her bathing suit. She did not hear Alexander's approach.

"Care to join me on a canoe ride? We can check out any damage to the trees around the lake." Alexander was in shorts and flip-flops.

"Sure, but I have a lot of work to finish."

"So do I, but perhaps we both need a short break."

There was almost no wind. Like a mirror, the lake reflected a clear, azure sky. For some ten minutes, they paddled in silence. *So, Lizzie, is Alexander what they call the strong and silent type, or does he not talk to the hired help?* Halfway across the lake, they passed the peninsula Elizabeth now knew belonged to Dina Levinson.

"Look, a boat," said Alexander. "I've never seen a boat there before."

"Neither have I. Last week I met the lady who inherited that house. She and her friend rowed over to visit your father."

"A house? I thought the entire lake belonged to the estate. But then again, I don't know much about Ted's property."

Ted's property? Why doesn't he call him Father? "Do you spend much time at the lake?"

"Not since I was a child. After I went away to university, I only came back for a few days to see my mother."

Only your mother? What about your father?

In silence, they paddled to a tiny islet at the far end of the lake. It was little more than a rock with one scraggly bush. Alexander pulled up the canoe and stood looking into the crystal-clear water. Elizabeth did not want to intrude on his private thoughts. She waited before she asked, "Did you come to this rock as a child?"

"This was my favourite place," he said.

"Did you fish?"

"No, Monsieur Gervais and I used to fish over there." He pointed to a narrow inlet on the other side. "I came here to read."

"How old were you?"

"Probably about twelve. Mother made Monsieur Gervais sit in a rowboat nearby and watch me," he said with a sad smile.

As they paddled back, Alexander asked, "What do you do for Ted?"

"Translations, some research, checking footnotes, that sort of thing. When I have free time, I transcribe your mother's diaries. Her handwriting is practically illegible; I need a magnifying glass."

Sitting at the helm, Elizabeth could not see Alexander's face. Yet, inexplicably, she sensed that his body stiffened. There was a long silence before he asked, "How many diaries are there?"

"I'm not sure."

"And Ted wants you to transcribe them all?"

"No, just the diaries from 1976 to 1977."

"I was born in 1977."

"I haven't reached 1977."

"I would like to read them."

They are your mother's diaries, for heaven's sake! You don't have to ask for my permission!

"They are on the shelf next to her desk. I'm still working on the 1976 diaries. That was the year she started at the Université de Montréal. But there are large gaps. Your mother stopped writing about ten years ago."

"That would coincide with the progression of her illness," he said in a matter-of-fact tone of voice. "Have the Gervaises filled you in?"

"They are very protective of her. They did mention sleep problems."

"As long as I can remember, she always had bouts of depression and insomnia. As a child, I was aware that she had to go away from time to time. Ted told me that he sent me to a boarding school at seven because of her illness. She didn't want me to go. I remember how she cried on the day I left."

"Were you always away at boarding schools?"

"Yes, then in prep school in the United States, and there were always ski trips and summer camp. Then Harvard, then Oxford. I should have…" He didn't finish the sentence.

"My mother died when I was sixteen. It was a shock — probably, because I expected her to always be there for me. I was selfish. I still feel so guilty."

The silence seemed long and heavy. *Alexander didn't ask about my mother! He is not interested in my life! I can't figure him out. First, he barely talks, then it's suddenly True Confessions. I guess the lake brought back all kinds of memories.*

Alexander helped Elizabeth disembark. She could not explain why she was so conscious of the touch of his hand. She was not sure how it made her feel. Since her heartbreak over Stephen, Elizabeth joked with Marie-France that her heart was in a sling — wrapped in bubble-wrap to prevent re-injury. She smiled up at Alexander. *His dark eyes seem warmer, softer. It's probably the sunshine!*

"When are you leaving?" she asked.

"I have to be in Ottawa for a meeting on Thursday. But Ted wants me back on Friday for dinner with his lawyer."

"My friend Marie-France is studying law at the University of Ottawa, and she is trying to convince me to join her and get another degree."

"I will be in Ottawa, too — teaching at Carleton."

Elizabeth returned to the library and found instructions from Mr Ted to bring up some papers. When she walked into the study, Agnew-Simpson looked up at her with undisguised irritation. His watery eyes were cold and metallic. "What with all your boating, my dear, do you have time to keep up with your work?"

Elizabeth was struck dumb by his openly aggressive tone. Didn't he see her in the canoe most days?

"Has Alexander been flirting with you? You should be careful, my dear, he is a serial womaniser. Likes to reel them in, then lets them go. Some silly women imagine that he is a rich heir. Hope you don't carry such illusions."

Elizabeth gasped. She felt the insult physically, as if her oxygen had been suddenly cut off. She ran out of the room. *Did he just call me a gold digger? How dare he!*

All afternoon she continued to agonise over the insult. Should she demand an apology? Should she miss sherry hour? Should she quit? She had no savings left from Thailand. Practical considerations put a damper on her anger. Mr Ted will probably forget all about it by the evening, she rationalised, and decided to act as if nothing had happened. *You can handle this, Lizzie. If he mentions it again, tell him, very politely, very, very politely — tell him to fuck off.*

That evening, Agnew-Simpson acted as if nothing had happened. He morphed back into his charming self.

"At least no trees were blown down into the lake," said Alexander. "But whose boat is that on the peninsula?"

"I just found out that some old biddy from New York inherited the peninsula. I've instructed Mortimer to buy the property. Discreetly. If I show any interest, the real estate vultures will jack up the price."

"I know how you value your privacy," said Alexander. "The new owner may rent it out to…"

"A rock band," Agnew-Simpson finished the sentence.

The phone rang, and Agnew-Simpson went to the desk. "Tig! We were talking about your harem. What harem? The two ladies who crashed last week! No! I have no desire to leave the confines of my study. You do not have birthdays! Do you think I'm dying to play pin-the-tail with all your other little guests? Insist as much as you want! My answer is still no! Goodbye, Tig!"

Agnew-Simpson returned to the conversation corner with a puzzled expression on his face. "A birthday party? He's going gaga! Wants me to meet some bigwig investor from Miami! Poor Tig — always scrounging for money!"

"You should socialise more, Ted!" said Alexander with a sly smile.

"I am not interested in those people! Particularly the women! That Zsuzsanna practically swam across the lake just to see me. Some women will stop at nothing! Soon they'll be jumping from parachutes!" Agnew-Simpson laughed at his joke.

Elizabeth smiled. *What are we to conclude — that you are God's gift to women or that all women are gold diggers?*

Madame Gervais knocked on the door and rolled in the dinner trolley. That night, Mr Ted dined alone. Alexander took a tray to his room to wait for a conference call, and Elizabeth had supper with the Gervaises. She was in no mood to talk and was happy to listen to Madame Gervais's reminiscences about Alexander's favourite dishes. Elizabeth skipped dessert and retired to her room. *How much longer? Four more weeks! Four more weeks till 14th August. Then freedom!*

Chapter 12

On Thursday morning, Elizabeth finished the tedious translation and went down to the kitchen, where Madame Gervais was frying *Croque Monsieur* sandwiches. Monsieur Gervais was washing his hands in the kitchen sink.

"Alexander has already gone to Ottawa, but the poor boy will have to drive right back tomorrow night. Mr Ted insisted that Alexander should be here for supper with Maître McDougall. Marcel, don't forget to vacuum the guest room. The lawyer will stay the night. I've already marinated the lamb. It's his favourite and…"

The house phone rang. Monsieur Gervais answered. "I'll do it right away," he said, and put down the receiver. "Mr Ted wants me to chill a bottle of champagne for tonight."

"But he only drinks champagne on New Year's Eve!"

The house phone rang again. "Yes, Elizabeth is here."

"Hello," said Elizabeth. "Yes… Of course. I'll be there." Then, turning to the Gervais couple, she said, "He wants me to go to Dr Jordan's birthday party with him tonight."

"What?" Madame Gervais stopped cutting a tomato. "He never leaves the house except for his annual check-up."

"I heard Mr Ted refuse Dr Jordan's invitation. Why did he change his mind?" Elizabeth asked.

"That man has too much influence on Mr Ted if you ask me!" said Madame Gervais. "But at least you'll get a chance to see the house. In the village, they call it the bunker. It's all cement with no windows in the front."

"I've only seen the garage," said Monsieur Gervais. "It has a heater that thaws the snow from under the cars. Can you believe that the driveway and the steps are heated, too? Very fancy! Dr Jordan has two cars — a white SUV for clinic business and a black Aston Martin."

"Since Dr Jordan says he's descended from royalty, he should drive a Rolls-Royce," said Madame Gervais.

"I don't know how he can afford any of it — the house, the cars. The whole village knows he's bankrupt," said Monsieur Gervais, as they sat down to their *Croque Monsieur* sandwiches and tomato salad. "And you'll meet Mako! Another freak."

"Marcel, please!" said Madame Gervais. "I feel so sorry for the boy! He's an orphan! He had a horrible childhood! At least Dr Jordan gave him a home."

"I will not repeat what they say about that relationship in the village," said Monsieur Gervais.

"Marcel! Enough!"

That evening, Elizabeth put on eye shadow and added a little mousse to her hair. She wore her only 'good' clothes — the black swing skirt, white silk blouse, and black wedge sandals. Elizabeth painted her toes a bright orange for the occasion. When Agnew-Simpson came down to the car, she was surprised to see that he was wearing the same misshapen tweed jacket. He motioned to Elizabeth to get in the back seat of the Cadillac.

"Marcel, did you bring the champagne?"

"Yes." Monsieur Gervais raised the gift-wrapped bottle from the front seat.

"Is the party informal?" asked Elizabeth.

"I don't know. These *nouveau riche* women probably wear diamonds to the supermarket!"

Elizabeth smelled scotch on his breath. Not a good sign!

"I expect you to work at this party. I didn't invite you to flirt! Your job is to stand next to me to ward off those widows and divorcees. If they think you are my girlfriend, they'll stay away."

"I don't feel comfortable playing that role. I will tell everyone that I am your research assistant," she said in a firm voice.

"Tell them whatever you want. They won't believe you."

In about ten minutes, the Cadillac turned into a private road with a large billboard at the turn-off. It read 'Health and Wellness Centre — Spa — Clinic — Sanatorium'. The car climbed the slope and arrived at a low concrete building that looked like a Second World War bunker. Expensive cars stood parked on the road and on the wide driveway.

"Marcel, park up the hill and wait. I don't think I can last for more than one hour. Into the lion's den," said Agnew-Simpson, as he and Elizabeth stepped onto the green slate floor of the vestibule.

A young man dressed in a black silk pyjama-style outfit met them. Like Dr Jordan, he wore tinted glasses, although his were round. He sported a braided pigtail under a round black cap and wore red embroidered slippers on his feet.

"Ah, Mako," said Agnew-Simpson. "Is it Hallowe'en? Should I have worn a costume, too? Here, this is for Tig." Agnew-Simpson tried to hand him the champagne.

"I am sure that Dr Jordan would much prefer to receive this gift from your own hands," said Mako with a low bow. "The clothes are an *homage* to my heritage," replied Mako, leading them across the vast living room. He took mincing steps, and his body seemed folded into a perpetual bow.

He's doing a lousy imitation of a stereotypical Chinese servant from an old Hollywood movie. Overdoing it a bit with the bowing and scraping routine. Elizabeth followed her boss. They walked past an enormous golden crest depicting a crowned lion holding a shield that hung over the white marble fireplace. A wall of glass at the end of the room framed a flagstone patio and an infinity pool. About twenty middle-aged people stood in clusters — men with men, women with women. The women were expensively attired and perfectly groomed. The men, some silver-haired, some balding, some slim, some pot-bellied, all had the aura of self-confidence that comes with wealth and status. With his wispy red-grey hair and baggy tweed jacket, Agnew-Simpson looked like a homeless person who had accidentally wandered in from the street.

"Darling!" Zsuzsanna's shrill contralto rang out like a bell. Everyone turned to look at the latecomers. "How wonderful to see you again!" Zsuzsanna, wearing a red and gold floral print caftan, flew up, sleeves flapping, and if Agnew-Simpson had not stepped back and placed the bottle of champagne between them, she would have smothered him in an embrace. Zsuzsanna led them to Dr Jordan.

"So good of you to come, Ted." Dr Jordan tore off the wrapping from the bottle of champagne. "*Mumms*, my favourite! Much appreciated! Thank you, Ted! Ah, the beautiful Elizabeth!"

Elizabeth felt the overpowering musk of his cologne as his thin, cold lips touched her hand. Dr Jordan wore a silk pyjama-style outfit and patent leather loafers with tassels. Turning to the cluster of men in his group, Dr Jordan said, "I promise I will bring him back very soon." Then, taking Agnew-Simpson by the elbow, he said, "Come, Ted, there is someone who is dying to meet you." He dragged his friend towards a tall man with slick black hair — the only man in the room wearing a pin-striped suit. The man was standing alone at the bar. Elizabeth was about to follow her boss, but Zsuzsanna caught her elbow and manoeuvred her to a group of women standing by the picture window.

"Ladies, let me introduce the lovely Elizabeth — she's Ted's research assistant." From Zsuzsanna's lips, 'research assistant' sounded like a dirty word. Elizabeth noticed the repressed smiles as the women looked her up and down, before returning to their conversation. Dina Levinson, in a white palazzo jumpsuit and masses of gold chains, barely acknowledged Elizabeth. She continued talking about a New York acquaintance who came to Montreal for a routine cosmetic procedure — an eye lift. "She died in the recovery room! Can you imagine?"

"In a posh private clinic!" Zsuzsanna interjected. "Dr Jordan's cosmetic clinic has a one hundred percent safety record."

Elizabeth did not follow the rest of the conversation about the upcoming golf club fundraiser. She positioned herself to watch Mr Ted, ready to come to his rescue should any woman approach him. *Boy, is Mr Ted ever delusional! Where are the hordes of attacking widows and divorcees?* After about five minutes, Dr Jordan guided Mr Ted towards the open door of his office. Elizabeth followed.

As if by magic, Mako appeared and blocked her path. "You do not have a drink, Miss Elizabeth." Mako clicked his fingers, and one of the waiters, a young man with a black bow tie, appeared with a tray of glasses and flutes. "May I recommend the pink champagne?" said Mako, as he took her ever so gently by the elbow and guided her away from the study door. Before Dr Jordan shut the door, Elizabeth did manage a peek inside. She saw a gleaming, black, lacquered desk with a sword in an ornate scabbard hanging on the wall behind it.

In a sweet, cloying voice, Mako said, "Miss Elizabeth, have you seen the view from the patio? Please allow me to show it to you."

Outside, the soft evening sunlight lit up the green hills. Elizabeth walked up to the edge of the infinity pool and looked over the steep edge to where the water formed a solid sheet before it crashed into rocks and boulders of a mountain stream. Suddenly, Mako was gone, and Zsuzsanna was standing next to her. This changing of the guard, performed so seamlessly, looked rehearsed. Elizabeth tried to go back inside.

"They will be discussing business, so he may not be out for a while," said Zsuzsanna.

"Who is Mako?" asked Elizabeth. "Why is he dressed like that?"

"Mako?" Zsuzsanna's lips stretched across her face like a red, elastic band. "He's Dr Jordan's assistant. He likes to dress up and role-play sometimes. One of his little eccentricities. I always tell him he should become an actor!"

"Where is he from?"

"I'm not sure. I think Mako is of mixed race, but I could be wrong. Mako tells so many stories about his origin." She ushered Elizabeth back into the living room, where servers carrying trays loaded with glasses or appetisers weaved among the guests. "Try the deep-fried crab claws — absolutely delicious," said Zsuzsanna, and she left Elizabeth in the middle of the room.

Elizabeth made her way to the study door and stood next to it, like a sentinel. No one approached her. She watched as Mako, with a take-charge air, gave instructions to the servers. Then he transformed himself into a subservient servant again and began flitting among his guests. *Zsuzsanna is right; he really should be an actor.* The study door flew open, and Agnew-Simpson burst back into the living room. There were red blotches on his pale cheeks. A grim Dr Jordan, his olive skin a shade darker, followed and attempted to pull Agnew-Simpson back, while Mako tried to block Agnew-Simpson's path.

"Out of my way!" Agnew-Simpson growled, and he pushed Mako aside. "Elizabeth, we are leaving!"

The guests stopped talking. Everyone was wide-eyed. Before they were out the door, Elizabeth heard Agnew-Simpson hiss, "How dare he foist that gangster on me?"

As they walked up the hill towards the car, Agnew-Simpson continued to rant. "So I'm the bait! If he owes them money, let him sell his bloody house! Sell his fancy cars! It's his mess! How much of this blackmail does he think I'll take?"

On the ride home, no one said a word. Agnew-Simpson rode up the elevator as an emotionally exhausted Elizabeth went into the kitchen. "I'm hungry," she said.

"Didn't they feed you?" asked Madame Gervais, looking up from the local grocery store flyer.

"Mr Ted and Dr Jordan had a big fight," said Monsieur Gervais.

"They will probably make up in a few days, as usual," replied Madame Gervais, and she put a pasta casserole into the microwave.

They all sat down at the oak table. "I have never seen so many rich people in one room," said Elizabeth. "And this Mako, what a strange young man!"

"Bernadette's grand-daughter's boyfriend works as a bartender at the Crazy Caribou bar," said Monsieur Gervais. "Mako is a regular — he drinks a lot and tells everyone that he is Dr Jordan's illegitimate son. He claims that Dr Jordan had an affair with a Japanese woman, a samurai general's daughter. Then she died, and Dr Jordan brought Mako to Canada."

"Do they still have samurai in Japan?" asked Elizabeth.

"The boy certainly has a vivid imagination!" continued Monsieur Gervais. "Another time he told the barber that his mother was a famous Mexican actress who had an affair with Dr Jordan. She had to abandon him to pursue her career."

"Poor boy," said Madame Gervais. "All I know is that he had a horrible childhood. No wonder he tries to escape into a fantasy world!"

"Did you know that last year, when Dr Jordan was away, Mako took the Aston Martin to the golf club, got drunk, and smashed it into a pole? So now Mako is not allowed to drive that car."

"Bernadette's grand-daughter says Dr Jordan bought him a second-hand Honda Civic," said Madame Gervais.

"What does that tell you about their relationship?" asked Monsieur Gervais. But after one look at his wife's face, he changed the subject. "They say that Mako sells stories to the tabloids. I wouldn't be surprised if he's the mysterious anonymous source for all the filth they wrote about Madame Mathilde."

That night, Elizabeth slept fitfully. She dreamed that she was still at the party and that everyone was dancing a wild, frenzied waltz. Agnew-

Simpson was dancing with Zsuzsanna, Mako was dancing with Dina, and Elizabeth was dancing with Dr Jordan, who kept trying to kiss her hand. She woke up in a cold sweat — terrified.

Chapter 13

Madame Gervais was grumbling to herself when Elizabeth came down for lunch on Friday. "And what am I supposed to do with all this lamb? Marcel could have asked Mr Ted if the lawyer cancelled or postponed his visit. Should I freeze the lamb? Of course, it won't be as good..."

Monsieur Gervais walked into the kitchen. "Louise, I just talked to Mr Ted again. Whoever called this morning did not have all the information. Mr McDougall is in hospital. He had a heart attack. The entire office is in a panic."

"A heart attack!" Madame Gervais sat down. "Poor man. I hope he gets better soon. Let me know the minute you find out anything more! And what about Alexander? Will he be back for supper if the lawyer will not come?"

"I don't know."

"Should I still serve the lamb?"

Elizabeth took a juice box and a sandwich to the canoe and paddled across the lake. There were no new assignments from Agnew-Simpson when she returned, so Elizabeth went to Mathilde's boudoir to continue work on the diaries.

Mathilde's 1983 diary lay on the desk. She concluded that Alexander must have left the volume open. There was no way he could have read it without a magnifying glass. Elizabeth's magnifying glass was still in a side drawer. She took it out and began to read.

12th March. Today was my little Alexander's sixth birthday, and it should have been the happiest day of his life, but the day started so terribly. What Ted did at breakfast is unforgivable! I have never seen such a cold hatred on his face! Ted accused Alexander of breaking the Chinese vase in the vestibule and shouted that boys have to tell the truth even at the age of six. He said he would send Alexander to a strict boarding school because I am spoiling him. He even threatened to cancel the birthday party unless

Alexander confessed. Alexander kept his head high, looked straight at Ted and pressed his lips together so tightly. He did not cry. He is not like me; he never cries. Such a distant child. If it wasn't for Monsieur Gervais, I don't know how it would have ended. Marcel must have heard Ted's tantrum, because he walked in and told us that he accidentally broke the Chinese vase last night as he was bringing in the logs. He offered to pay for it from his salary! Ted did not apologise to Alexander. Ted left the house and did not come home for the birthday party. I will pray that God softens Ted's heart. I will say Hail Mary one hundred times tonight and ask the Holy Mother to intercede. Let God punish me, not my little Alexander.

Was Mathilde an over-indulgent mother? Mr Ted was certainly unfair! And cruel! And Alexander was distant, even as a child. She went back to the transcription of the 1976 diaries. Mathilde wrote about visits with her convent school friends — parties — who danced with whom, who wore what. Elizabeth found the journals vacuous. She got up to stretch her legs and looked through the bookshelf for something to read; she found *Madame Bovary*, *Jane Eyre*, *La Dame aux Camellias*, and half a dozen Danielle Steele romance novels. She picked up a slim volume, *La Princesse de Clèves*. It turned out to be an empty box holding a stack of letters tied in a pink ribbon. They were mailed to a Montreal post office box from a *poste restante* in Casablanca. They were addressed to 'my beautiful gazelle' and signed Hassan. They were written in French, in a flowery style that Elizabeth characterised as mushy. *"When we are together, nothing else matters, nothing else exists; I am no longer in this world, I am in paradise."* This guy's been reading too many Harlequin Romances, was Elizabeth's first reaction. *"When I awake each morning, it is your radiant image that I see before me, and my heart begins to ache. You are far away! Without you, I only pretend to be alive. The sun does not shine... The day has no joy. I long for the night. I pray for dreams of you. Every day, no matter where I am, I will suddenly feel the touch of your hand caressing my cheek or brushing the hair from my forehead. I tremble at the very thought of your touch."*

In another letter, written on Ritz Carleton Hotel stationery, Hassan wrote: *"The memory of our night together will haunt me forever. I remember our every caress, our every kiss. Making love to you, my beautiful gazelle, is sheer bliss. When we are together, nothing else exists; I am no longer in this world, I am in paradise."* Another letter posted in Casablanca was full of longing. *"You are with me from dawn to sunset. When I awaken each morning, it is your radiant image that I see before me — and my heart begins to ache. You are far away! Without you, I only pretend to be alive. The sun does not shine... The day has no joy. I will be truly alive only when I look into those violet eyes once more. I long for the night. I pray for dreams of you."*

As Elizabeth continued to read, her initial disdain for the florid style gave way to empathy. Did she not understand the longing, the pain? Elizabeth continued to sit at Mathilde's desk with tears in her eyes. Was she crying for Mathilde or for her own broken heart? Then another realisation: Mathilde, the saint with the angelic face, was having an affair — an affair with a Moroccan! *And Alexander, his complexion, his eyes, hair...* Elizabeth sat down again, her knees weak. It was six o'clock, sherry time. *How can I show these to Mr Ted?* Her mind was racing. She tied the pink ribbon around the packet with trembling hands and put the letters back into the hiding place.

As Elizabeth walked down the hall to the study, she heard Agnew-Simpson shouting. She raised her arm to knock, but afraid to intrude, stood motionless with her fist in the air. The door swung open, and Alexander rushed out. His mouth was set in a firm, thin line. "Excuse me," he snapped, and walked briskly down the dark hallway.

"Come right in, my dear, don't just stand there, eavesdropping." Agnew-Simpson's tone was venomous. He approached Elizabeth and gripped her arm.

She could feel the urgency in his fingers as he pulled her to the maroon love seat. He stood over her, cheeks blazing. "How much have you heard? No matter! I will repeat it again, in case you missed something. Yes, after Mattie's funeral, I did get a DNA sample from Alexander without his consent," he said, riveting Elizabeth with his pale, watery eyes. "I couldn't do it while she was alive. I received the tests some months ago, but my lawyer insisted on yet another verification. I summoned Alexander only after the final confirmation. We were all meant to have it out in the open at dinner, but McDougall decided to have a heart attack!"

Elizabeth, frightened by his rage, kept her eyes down and stared at what must have been Alexander's glass. A thin shard of ice was floating in the amber liquid. *I can stand up and walk out of this room. I don't have to listen to this.* Her body did not respond.

"Alexander is not my son! Of course, in my heart, I always knew, even without the DNA," he said, and he began to pace the room. "I still loved her, my angel. Of course, I hated her, too." Agnew-Simpson downed the rest of the scotch. "The Beaudry family, they were all in on it. Everyone knew that they made their fortune in the fur industry, so they invented the charade about some ancestral *coureur de bois* who married an Iroquois woman. What nonsense! I tried to keep Alexander away at boarding schools as much as possible. Didn't like to look at him much. Now my angel is gone, and I am free."

Elizabeth looked up at him, her mouth open. She felt as if a fog had clouded her brain, and she could barely process the information. *He must have invited the lawyer to write Alexander out of his will. No wonder Alexander stormed out!*

Agnew-Simpson continued to pace the room. "I couldn't do it before, you see. I promised them," he said, pointing his glass of scotch to the portraits over the mantelpiece. "I promised them to keep my marriage vows!" He stood looking at the photographs, then sat down across from Elizabeth. His tone became intimate, as if he was opening his heart to a trusted confidante. "You see," he said, as he leaned towards Elizabeth, "I was so much in love with her. We all lived in Outremont. She was the girl next door. I wrote her long, lovesick poems and finally a marriage proposal in verse. I received a polite refusal from her mother, Madame Beaudry. I was mortified. Then, unexpectedly, her mother invited me to tea with Mathilde. Of course, I melted on the spot. I turned into a lovesick poodle. When I was leaving, Madame Beaudry walked me to the door. She took me by the arm and asked me whether I still wanted to marry Mathilde. The family would agree, she said, provided I converted to Catholicism. I was ready to convert to anything they wanted — Catholicism, Maoism, Paganism! And what about Mathilde, I asked? Does she…? Would she marry me?"

"'Mathilde confessed to me that she would,'" her mother replied.

"'You must understand she is very shy,'" she said. Agnew-Simpson leaned over the table and poured himself another two fingers of scotch.

Elizabeth, in her new, imposed role of confidante, sat frozen, her back stiff.

"I believed every word Madame Beaudry said. She promised to confer with the family. I was on tenterhooks until she called me two days later. The family wished to have the wedding as soon as possible. Madame Beaudry's brother, the cardinal, was a very sick man, she said. His dying wish was to officiate at his niece's marriage ceremony. Because of the cardinal's illness, the marriage would be private and within two weeks. I could not believe my ears. All I could think of was that I would walk down the aisle next to this ethereal creature in a diaphanous, white gown, a creature so beautiful, so delicate, and so pure that it was almost a sacrilege to touch her."

Elizabeth realised that he was barely aware of her presence. It was as if an inner dam had burst and Agnew-Simpson could not hold back the torrent of innermost secrets. After reading Hassan's letters, it all made sense: the devoutly Catholic Beaudry family forced their daughter into a loveless but respectable marriage to avoid scandal. Perhaps they justified this decision by rationalising that Agnew-Simpson, who so adored Mathilde, would accept the child as his own and that Mathilde would grow to love her husband.

"How I hated that conniving mother-in-law." His tone became aggressive again. "Would not let her into the house after Alexander was born. Now they are all dead. Only Alexander…"

"And your father?" Elizabeth asked, her curiosity overcoming her discomfort.

Agnew-Simpson jumped up, and weaving slightly, walked up to the portraits. "Father and Grandfather, they said the usual — you are too young, etc. etc. They threatened, they cajoled, they tried to bribe me. Finally, Father said, 'I raised you as a rational man. Surely you can see beyond instant gratification.' I told him that nothing he said would change my mind. I will never forget Father's final words: 'I will give you my blessing, provided you make me a solemn promise — promise me that you will never break your vows. You promised to convert. Catholics do not believe in divorce.'

"I jumped for joy! Fool that I was! I never kissed my father, even as a child, but at that moment I wanted to kiss him. 'Thank you, thank you,' I babbled." Then, raising his glass to the portrait, Agnew-Simpson said, "You should be proud of me, I kept my word!"

Elizabeth sat mesmerised. She poured herself a glass of sherry. Unsteadily, Agnew-Simpson walked back to the love seats. "Yes, I kept my word. I did my duty." He began to laugh, a tittering laugh that resembled short sobs. "From the very beginning, there was a cuckoo in my nest!" he said bitterly, fell back into the couch, and closed his eyes.

Elizabeth, thinking that he was asleep, got up to leave.

"Sit down, Elizabeth." His tone was now businesslike. Elizabeth did as she was told. "I was hoping that you would find something in the journals."

"What do you mean?" asked Elizabeth. She felt her heart rate quicken.

"Don't pretend to be such a dolt! Who is Alexander's father?"

Elizabeth had to make a decision. She knew she was obligated to tell her employer about the letters, yet she could not! Slowly, as if speaking was a great effort, articulating every word, Elizabeth asked, "Is that why you hired me?"

"Partially. Now I have DNA proof, but I want the man's name. There must be some clues in the journals," he said, and he looked sternly at Elizabeth.

Elizabeth visualised the hidden letters tied in the pink ribbon. For an instant, she wavered. But looking up at Agnew-Simpson's face, so distorted by hatred, she decided that she would not give him any more ammunition to exact revenge on Alexander. Elizabeth, her body rigid, spoke slowly. "Everyone has been wearing a mask," she said, as if she had just made an important discovery.

"And you, my Elizabeth — have you not been wearing a mask?" he asked, and looked at her with a venomous smirk on his face. "Or perhaps two masks — one for me, and one for Alexander? Yes, I know you were trying to seduce Alexander. You thought that Alexander would inherit my wealth. You were wrong. You should have stuck with your original plan..."

Elizabeth felt as if Agnew-Simpson had poured a bucket of filth over her head. *How could he come to this preposterous conclusion?*

There was no stopping Agnew-Simpson now. He had spittle on his lips. His pale blue eyes were glowing with a cold metallic sheen. "I want to clear the air, my dear. I now realise that despite my appearance, I can still be a magnet for certain women. Wealth is a powerful aphrodisiac. And no, my dear, I am not susceptible to women like you. Not any more. Once was quite enough."

Elizabeth was dumbfounded. According to Agnew-Simpson, he was the victim, trapped by the wiles of the angelic Mathilde. Now he saw Elizabeth as a predator. To Elizabeth, Mr Ted seemed like a harmless old codger. She had merely laughed at his jokes and returned his coquettish smiles. Where was the harm? How could he interpret her attempt to be congenial as…? *How can he think I'm so conniving?*

Agnew-Simpson's tone became shrill. "I saw through your intrigues, my dear. Yes, yes, I admit I was tempted at first. You are of child-bearing age. And for your information, I am just over sixty. Not totally decrepit."

Elizabeth felt the room spinning. *Are you going to sit there and take it?* Then the reality of her situation dawned on her. She was innocent, and she was helpless. *There ain't nuttin' you can do, Lizzie! You can't argue with a drunken, crazy person.* It took every ounce of self-control to hide the trembling inside. Without a word, she got up and walked out towards the door of the study.

"Good! Go! Get out!"

Elizabeth collapsed into bed. Despite her conclusion that Agnew-Simpson could not be held fully accountable because he was drunk, she felt crushed and humiliated. The house telephone rang — it was Madame Gervais.

"Elizabeth, Marcel and I are having supper. You…"

"I won't be coming down, Madame Gervais, I have a horrible headache."

"Can I bring up your supper and some tea? Do you need aspirin?"

"I have everything, thank you. Good night, Madame Gervais."

Tossing and turning in bed, her mind was a kaleidoscope of flashing images — Mr Ted, Alexander, Mathilde's portrait, and the fireplace portraits. Then the images changed into masks. Mathilde wore a beautiful angelic mask to hide the face of a Jezebel. Agnew-Simpson had the face of a lunatic behind the mask of a gentleman. *Did Hassan wear a mask for Mathilde? Were his letters a pack of lies? And what about you, Lizzie? Was Agnew-Simpson right? Did you have an unconscious desire to fulfil some parody of a little girl's Cinderella dream? Wasn't Stephen wearing a mask — one for you and one for his wife?* Elizabeth decided that she had to go back to Montreal in the morning. But how to do it without seeing Agnew-Simpson again? Problem solved. She would ask Monsieur Gervais to drive her to the bus station in Mont Tremblant.

And so, Lizzie, how does the story end? The prince turns out to be an imposter. The king throws Cinderella out of the castle. Who would even believe such a fairy tale? Welcome to the real world, boys and girls.

Chapter 14

Elizabeth's few intervals of sleep were filled with dreadful dreams. She remembered only one, about the tsunami that swept her out into the ocean. She awoke, gasping for air. There was a knock on her door. Madame Gervais's eyes were red. Monsieur Gervais spoke in a faltering voice. "Last night, Mr Ted called me to his study and told me to drive you back to Montreal this morning. He asked me to give you this envelope. It's a cheque for the full amount of the contract sum." Monsieur Gervais lowered his eyes to the floor. "I am to remind you about the confidentiality agreement. Please forgive me, Elizabeth, but I have to say this — you will be sued if you divulge any information about the Agnew-Simpson family."

Elizabeth interpreted this as yet another one of Agnew-Simpson's deliberate humiliations. She could not control the tears welling up in her eyes.

Madame Gervais put her arm around Elizabeth. "*Excuse-moi, ma petite*, but he wants me to help you pack."

"Is he afraid I'll run off with the silverware?" Elizabeth bit her lower lip to prevent it from quivering. "I'm going to take a shower," she said, and disappeared into the bathroom. Elizabeth stood in the shower for a long time, hoping that the hot water would wash away Agnew-Simpson's insults that seemed to cling to her body like a slimy film.

She finished dressing and went down to the kitchen, where Monsieur Gervais sat at the oak table, looking out the picture window. "The house will seem so empty now," he said. "Louise and I have become so attached to you."

"I will call you from Montreal," Elizabeth replied. "Please say goodbye to Alexander for me."

"He's gone," said Monsieur Gervais with a sigh.

"What? When?" Elizabeth was stunned. She did not say 'why?', having witnessed the tail end of the father-son argument.

"Last night. It's not like him to leave without saying goodbye. I hope he calls later."

Elizabeth remembered Alexander's face as he left the study: his eyes flashing blackness, the firm line of his lips. Suddenly, they heard loud shrieks from the second floor. Elizabeth ran up the staircase, followed by Monsieur Gervais, slowed by his stiff knee. The breakfast trolley stood in the hallway. Madame Gervais was backing away from the desk, sobbing.

Elizabeth approached the desk. Agnew-Simpson sat in the swivel chair. His upper body lay prone across the desk. From the back, he looked as if he had fallen asleep. A faint beeping sound came from the telephone receiver. Agnew-Simpson's head lay to one side. One cheek was puffed out, his mouth and one eye were open. The glasses had slipped off his nose; the frames pointed up to the ceiling.

"Elizabeth, call 911! It may be a stroke or a heart attack," Monsieur Gervais said in a hoarse voice.

Elizabeth picked up the receiver and dialled 911 for an ambulance. Still holding the receiver, she turned towards Monsieur Gervais and said, "The operator asks whether he has a pulse?"

"I've never done this before," replied Monsieur Gervais. "I can't find a pulse, but that does not mean…"

"Now he's telling me to place him on the floor and pump his heart."

"I think he's dead," said Monsieur Gervais. "He seems cold."

"No! No!" Madame Gervais wailed. She was standing near the door, afraid to come closer.

"The ambulance can only be here in about half an hour," said Elizabeth. "Perhaps Dr Jordan can come more quickly."

"His telephone number is in the kitchen," said Monsieur Gervais, as he took his sobbing wife by the shoulder and led her out of the room.

Elizabeth felt as if her feet were welded to the floor. She continued to stare at the body. Agnew-Simpson was wearing the same tweed jacket he wore last night. For some reason, she noticed that the scotch, or was it brandy, matched the colour of his wing-tipped shoes. The man who had wilfully caused her so much pain was dead, and yet she felt only sadness, as if the finality of death wiped the slate clean. Elizabeth was dazed, not sure whether to believe or disbelieve her own eyes. She went down to the kitchen and called Dr Jordan.

"Can you come over right away? It's Mr Ted, he's face-down on his desk... Yes, we already called 911."

"Oh! You are in Montreal? Yes, the ambulance is on its way." Turning to the Gervais couple, she said, "Dr Jordan spent the night at the Queen Elizabeth Hotel. He has an appointment to see his bank manager this morning at ten. Then he will drive back."

"Is he really dead?" asked Madame Gervais. "Maybe he had a stroke? We should go up and make him more comfortable. We should put a pillow under his head!"

"Louise, he was not breathing."

Monsieur Gervais dialled Alexander's number. "The customer is not available, please call again later." He left a message.

Elizabeth served tea while they waited for the ambulance. Madame Gervais, with a shawl over her shoulders, could not stop trembling. "Elizabeth, tell us what happened last night?"

"I came up for sherry at about six. I left before you served dinner. So it must have been just before seven."

"Supper was to be at seven fifteen last night," said Madame Gervais. "Marinated lamb." She blew her nose. "Mr Ted called and cancelled just before I went upstairs with the trolley. Both you and Alexander said you didn't want supper either. What happened?"

"Mr Ted drank more than usual and told me things that I would rather not repeat." Elizabeth's mouth began to quiver. "He said some very mean things, and I decided to quit, but I guess Mr Ted beat me to it. When did you talk to him, Monsieur Gervais?"

"Before Louise and I sat down for supper; it must have been after seven. He called and asked me to come up to his study. He looked agitated. He said that he wanted me to drive Elizabeth back to Montreal in the morning. What did you say to get him so upset?"

"What did I say?" Elizabeth's face turned red. "I did not say anything! He and Alexander had a big row. Alexander left in a huff, and Mr Ted took his anger out on me!" She decided not to tell them anything more.

At the sound of the ambulance, the Gervais couple rushed to the front door. Elizabeth, feeling completely drained, took the elevator up to her bedroom and collapsed into bed. She could hear the heavy stomping of feet up the staircase and the sound of male voices.

Then it became quiet, and fatigue finally overwhelmed Elizabeth. She fell into a deep, dreamless sleep.

Chapter 15

The telephone woke Elizabeth. "It's almost three in the afternoon! Were you sleeping all this time?" asked Monsieur Gervais. "Inspector Jolicoeur is here."

"Who?"

"The police!"

The image of Agnew-Simpson's body lying on the desk flashed into her mind. Shuddering, she dragged herself to the bathroom. The face in the mirror was creased, with matted hair and inky pools under her eyes. *You look like shit, Lizzie.* She splashed cold water on her cheeks, brushed her teeth, and fluffed her hair. Walking into the kitchen, Elizabeth was surprised to see Dr Jordan and Monsieur Gervais sitting at the oak table. Dr Jordan was dressed all in black, as usual. He rose to meet her.

"My dear," he said, and he brought Elizabeth's hands up to his cold lips. The smell of his musky cologne seemed more repulsive than usual. "You must be in shock. Would you like some cognac?"

"I'll make some tea," Elizabeth replied, and walked away.

Monsieur Gervais was eager to continue his account of the day's events. "The investigating team arrived first; a couple of the guys are still here. Inspector Jolicoeur dragged me all around the estate. He wanted to see the location of the surveillance cameras. I did not realise that the camera over the kitchen door is broken. Perhaps a bird…"

"Or an intruder smashed it," Dr Jordan finished the sentence.

"If we had an intruder, they would have heard the alarm all the way in the village. The inspector wanted to know how to open the front gate and where we keep the tapes from the surveillance cameras. The police took some tapes away. I even had to give them a list of the people who come to the house regularly. Not too many — spring or fall yard work, repairmen. All are from the village — mostly relatives."

Dr Jordan interrupted, saying, "Marcel, why do you think the police are interested in all of this? It would only make sense if they suspected foul play! Were there any signs of an intruder?"

"I don't think so," said Monsieur Gervais, looking puzzled.

"Where is Madame Gervais?" asked Elizabeth, as she poured hot water into her mug.

"Louise has been on her feet since six this morning. She set up a table with coffee and cookies for the police. Then Inspector Jolicoeur wore her out with all his questions! Poor Louise collapsed from exhaustion."

"Did you reach Alexander? Does he know what happened?" Elizabeth asked.

"He called back this morning," said Monsieur Gervais. "Apparently, he drove to Ottawa last night and checked into a hotel. He left his cell phone in the car and only got my message late this morning. He is driving back as we speak. Should be here soon."

"The police are most anxious to talk to him," said Dr Jordan, getting up from the oak table. "The inspector even interviewed me! God only knows why. I wasn't Ted's physician, and I was in Montreal all day yesterday."

Elizabeth noticed that Dr Jordan had finished all the cognac in the snifter. "Dr Jordan, do you think Mr Ted died of a heart attack?" she asked.

"Unfortunately, I did not have the opportunity to examine Ted's body. Ted's body — it sounds so impersonal," said Dr Jordan, and he lowered his head. "Why do you think it was a heart attack, Elizabeth?"

"I don't know. It was so sudden. Could it have been a massive stroke? The telephone was off the hook. Perhaps he was trying to call for help?"

Monsieur Gervais, having graduated from caretaker to police expert, said, "The Medical Examiner... I couldn't tell whether the white plastic suit was a man or a woman. It was a woman. I heard what she said to the inspector. She said it could be suicide!"

"Suicide?" Dr Jordan's dyed, black eyebrows, shot up over his tinted glasses.

"Suicide?" Elizabeth shivered as if she had caught a sudden chill. "Yes, he had too much to drink, but... I can't believe it."

"I am reluctant to believe it, too," said Dr Jordan. "But let's look at the facts. With the information we have, how could he have killed himself? No gun! No noose! Were drugs found?"

"They took away the glass. There was still some cognac in it," said Monsieur Gervais.

"Autopsies are done relatively quickly. Toxicology tests could take a long time," said Dr Jordan.

"I can't believe it was suicide. He had plans... His book..."

"Who knows what mysteries lurk in someone else's heart?" sighed Dr Jordan. "Please excuse me, I really must get back to the clinic. I think I am still too stunned to grasp that my best friend is dead. Courage, my friends," he said, and he squeezed Monsieur Gervais's shoulder. He came up to Elizabeth. "Whatever you need. Call me." He took her hand and raised it to his cold, thin lips. Elizabeth had no choice but to endure his unwelcome touch and the cloying smell of his cologne.

Elizabeth and Monsieur Gervais continued to sit in silence at the oak table.

"How can the sun shine so brightly? And the birds are chirping — as if nothing has happened," said Elizabeth. "Mr Ted will never hear the birds sing again."

Monsieur Gervais sighed. "If someone told me that we would live through two deaths in almost two years..."

Elizabeth noticed that the lines on his face seemed more profound, and his complexion was ashen.

A young, uniformed police officer walked into the kitchen. "Mademoiselle Burgess?" he said with a disarming smile. "Inspector Jolicoeur would like to speak to you in the library."

She followed the young officer. *I haven't done anything wrong, but I feel that they suspect me of killing Mr Ted. I know it's irrational, but...* Only yesterday, the first-floor library was Elizabeth's office, with her desk and computer under the window. Now, sitting behind the long table at the opposite end of the room filled with leather-bound books was a large man with a droopy, black moustache. His double chin hid the top of his shirt collar. Both his shirt and hand-knitted tie were the same colour — a drab olive green. Inspector Jolicoeur raised his bulky figure to greet Elizabeth, and as he extended his hand, she noticed his firm, egg-shaped belly and sweat stains under his armpits. He grimaced in pain as he lowered himself into the chair. Elizabeth noticed the bottle of Advil painkiller on the table and concluded that the inspector suffered from backaches.

"Inspector Alphonse Jolicoeur, Sûreté de Québec," he introduced himself. "Please sit down, Mademoiselle Burgess."

Elizabeth sat on the edge of the chair, her back rigid. *What a peculiar-looking man. With that moustache, he looks like a walrus.*

"And so, Mademoiselle Burgess, first, some routine questions."

A smiling Constable Fortin got up from behind his computer at the end of the table and handed Elizabeth a clipboard with forms. She read the first sheet and looked up at Inspector Jolicoeur. "You see, since I came back from Bangkok, I have been staying in my sister Catherine's apartment in NDG, so I am not listed in the phone book, and I still don't have a cell phone, so I can only give you her landline, which I do not know by heart because I always email her."

"Here is my card — send me your contact information. Do you have any objections to our taping this interview? It's common practice."

"I guess. If it's normal." The library's ventilation was always poor, and Elizabeth felt perspiration beads form above her upper lip.

"When did you start working for Mr Agnew-Simpson, and what were your duties?"

Elizabeth gave a detailed account of her work, omitting for some reason the translation and transcription of Mathilde's journals. Was it a simple oversight, or was it a conscious omission?

"I understand you met your employer in his study last night. What time did you go in, and at what time did you leave?"

Elizabeth gave him the information.

"What was Mr Agnew-Simpson's mood?" Inspector Jolicoeur asked.

"He was agitated. He was drinking scotch."

"Was drinking scotch unusual?"

"He usually drank sherry at cocktail time, but sometimes he drank scotch. Last night, he drank more scotch than usual."

"Was Alexander Agnew-Simpson with him when you came in?"

"Alexander was leaving as I came in."

"And what can you tell me about Mr Alexander's demeanour?"

"He looked upset, although I could be mistaken…"

"Miss Burgess, tell me exactly what happened. Please give as many details as possible."

"Nothing happened. Mr Ted had too much to drink. He was agitated.

I left as soon as I could."

"What was he agitated about?"

"He was talking about the past. I really didn't understand much of what he was saying."

"Was he so drunk that he was incoherent? Could you please be more specific?"

"He talked about his father and grandfather. He talked about private things, things that I should not repeat. It would be like an invasion of his privacy," said Elizabeth, squirming in her seat.

"Mademoiselle Burgess, I have a daughter, perhaps a little younger than you are. I understand how young people are sensitive about privacy issues. However, I am investigating your employer's death. When the cause of death is not clear, we refer to it as a suspicious death. Please tell me everything you can remember." His voice was gentle.

"Mr Agnew-Simpson told me about how he proposed to his wife. How he used to send her poetry."

"Did he mention his wife's death?"

"No. He talked about how much he was in love with her before they were married. That did not come out right. I'm sure he loved her after they were married, too."

Inspector Jolicoeur wiped the perspiration from his forehead with a chequered handkerchief. "Did he say anything about his son?"

"He was so drunk that I am not sure he meant what he said."

"Please tell me what he did say, Miss Burgess."

"He said some mean things about Alexander... But he probably didn't..."

"Miss Burgess, I see that you are not forthcoming with your answers. I could terminate this interview and invite you to come to the police headquarters," said Inspector Jolicoeur with a deep sigh.

This threat achieved the desired results. "Mr Ted said something about a DNA test. He was expecting his lawyer for dinner that night."

"Did he say what he planned to discuss with the lawyer?"

"No, not really."

"What are your impressions of the relationship between Alexander and his father?"

"They were not close. Alexander only came back to the estate to visit his mother. Alexander called his father 'Ted'. Look, Inspector Jolicoeur, I don't want to get Alexander in trouble."

"Miss Burgess, I understand that Monsieur Gervais was to drive you back to Montreal this morning? Why? Your contract was to end..." He looked through some files. "On August fifteenth?"

Elizabeth blushed. *Of course he knows — he's already interviewed Monsieur Gervais.* "Mr Ted fired me. He accused me of absolutely incredible things," she blurted out, and instantly regretted her frankness.

"Incredible? Go on, please."

"I can't." Elizabeth's face reflected a great deal of discomfort as she tried to smother her tears.

"Constable Fortin, please bring Miss Burgess a glass of water."

"He said crazy things! He accused me of trying to seduce both him and Alexander! False accusations don't wash off. People always believe the worst about others."

"What did you do after Mr Agnew-Simpson's accusations?"

"I got up and left — no use arguing with a drunken man. I decided to quit the next morning, but Mr Agnew-Simpson beat me to it." She took another Kleenex to wipe her nose.

Constable Fortin came back with a glass of water. Elizabeth drank half the glass.

Inspector Jolicoeur changed his line of questioning.

"Miss Burgess, please describe what you saw on the desk in Mr Agnew-Simpson's study this morning. Try to remember every detail, no matter how trivial."

Elizabeth gave a detailed account: mounds of books and files, the beeping telephone receiver.

"Did you notice any pieces of paper? Handwritten notes?"

"No, not that I can remember."

"Is there anything else you remember about what was on the desk?"

"No."

"Sometimes, if you close your eyes and try to picture the desk, you may remember something you overlooked."

"I will try." Elizabeth closed her eyes. "No, nothing else. When can I go home?"

"I may have follow-up questions tomorrow. You can leave after you have signed your statement."

"Statement?"

"Interviews with witnesses are part of the documentation I have to include in my report."

Another police officer poked his head into the library and said, "He's here."

"Thank you, Miss Burgess," said Inspector Jolicoeur, as he rose laboriously from his chair. "Someone will call you tomorrow."

In her room, Elizabeth kept mulling over the interview. She should not have mentioned Alexander's DNA tests. Did she tell the inspector about what Mr Ted said about the DNA results? She couldn't remember. Was Mr Ted planning on disinheriting Alexander? Is that why Alexander left in a rage? Surely, Alexander did not have anything to do with Mr Ted's death. And the lawyer? What was the purpose of his visit? She vaguely remembered something that Agnew-Simpson said to Dr Jordan on the balcony. Something about writing him into his will. It was all a jumble. She lay in bed with a throbbing headache. *I want to go home. I want to hug my sisters.* No longer concerned that Agnew-Simpson may be listening, Elizabeth dialled nine for the outside line and called Catherine. No answer. Amanda and Rob were away for the weekend. When Marie-France picked up the telephone, Elizabeth burst into tears. Choking back sobs, she began her disjointed account of Agnew-Simpson's death and the police interview. Marie-France did not interrupt.

"Why do millions of people all around the world live normal lives? What have I done to offend the gods?" asked Elizabeth.

"Don't be so melodramatic!" said Marie-France.

"I thought I could expect some support from my best friend," said Elizabeth between sobs.

"Look, get some rest. If you're not home by Saturday, I'll drive to Mont Tremblant and bring you back myself! No more depressions! Be strong!"

Elizabeth felt herself relax a little. "I'll call you as soon as I know when I can get out of here."

Chapter 16

At eight the following morning, the Gervais couple sat slumped over the kitchen table. Monsieur Gervais smiled weakly and told Elizabeth that the people in white plastic suits were back in Agnew-Simpson's study.

"*Bonjour ma petite*," said Madame Gervais. "I made muffins for everybody this morning."

Elizabeth noticed that Madame Gervais looked smaller and thinner. She poured herself a mug of coffee as Alexander came into the kitchen. His shoulders, usually so straight, seemed to sag a little. Taking Elizabeth by both shoulders, he asked, "How are you bearing up?"

"I want to go home. I want to see my sisters," said Elizabeth, her voice choking.

"Inspector Jolicoeur will have your statement ready today. I will drive you to Montreal myself."

No one was in a talkative mood. Elizabeth went outside and sat in an Adirondack chair. She listened to the birds calling to each other across the lake. A cloudless, warm day, azure water sparkling in the sun. *How strange*, she thought. *Nature is basking in the glow of summer, while inside, the lingering pall of death.*

At noon, Alexander phoned Elizabeth's room to tell her that the police forensic team was finished with Agnew-Simpson's study. "Inspector Jolicoeur is with Monsieur Gervais now and would like to see you again later. Can you please join me in the study?"

The study looked the same. Elizabeth half expected to see Agnew-Simpson sitting at his desk in his tweed jacket. She had never seen this room without Mr Ted in it. Alexander, wearing his signature black T-shirt, stood over the desk.

"I know Ted had his heart set on finishing his family history book," he said, pointing to the mountain of books and files on Agnew-Simpson's desk. "I gather that Ted was in the process of polishing his first draft. The estate office will probably hire someone to finish the project. How did

Ted organise your assignments?"

"Mr Ted placed books and files with instructions on this book trolley. I worked on assignments following a colour-coded priority system. The urgent assignments were in the red file. That bookshelf was dedicated to family history." She pointed to the tall freestanding shelf on wheels at the far end of the room.

"We will have to figure out what we should send to the publisher." The phone rang. "Monsieur Gervais just opened the gate for Dr Jordan. I suppose I can't refuse…"

"I don't want to see him," Elizabeth interrupted, and she pushed the book trolley behind the freestanding bookcase. As she was replacing the books, Dr Jordan walked in. He was accompanied by Zsuzsanna.

"Alexander, dear Alexander," said Dr Jordan. "My condolences, my sincerest condolences." He took Alexander's hand and held it. Elizabeth, with no desire to reveal herself, peeked through the volumes. She could see that Alexander looked at Zsuzsanna with surprise.

"Zsuzsanna Holt," she introduced herself. "Your father was a dear friend. We became quite close this summer," she said, and she tried to embrace Alexander. Alexander stepped back and held out his hand. Zsuzsanna, like Dr Jordan, was dressed all in black. She wore a wide-brimmed straw hat and dark glasses. Her wide mouth was painted a bright red.

"My sincerest condolences! And to think I saw your father just a few days ago! He invited me to the golf club dinner dance next week," said Zsuzsanna, dabbing her nose with a tissue.

Elizabeth put her hand over her mouth to suppress a gasp. *How can that woman lie so brazenly? Hadn't Agnew-Simpson told her, rather unceremoniously, to row back across the lake?*

"I still cannot believe it. What do the police say? Was it suicide?" asked Dr Jordan.

"Let's wait for the autopsy," said Alexander.

"Yes, of course," said Dr Jordan. "Is there anything I can do to help?"

"I think I can manage."

"And the funeral?"

"We will have to wait for the autopsy. The estate office tells me that Ted left precise instructions for the funeral in his will."

"Ah, yes, the estate office. I feel rather uncomfortable, but circumstances force me to bring up Ted's will," said Dr Jordan.

Alexander looked surprised. "Ted and I never discussed his will."

"Alexander, believe me, I take no pleasure in this. I realise this is not the right time. The only reason I raise Ted's will now is because the big bad bank is threatening to bankrupt me. I am hanging on to my clinic, to my life's work, by my bloody fingernails. This is not just about me. I am very concerned about my psychiatric patients. I treat young addicts from the north — *pro bono*. What will happen to them? Ted, bless his heart, promised to help. Please do not hold this against me, but the last time I spoke to Ted, he said that since I was his oldest and truest friend, he promised to bail me out. You may be surprised, but when he came to my birthday party... last week..." Dr Jordan seemed to lose his self-confidence. "On Thursday... He actually signed a new will. Zsuzsanna was a witness."

Elizabeth, still hiding behind the tall bookshelf, felt her jaw drop. She distinctly remembered that Zsuzsanna was not in Dr Jordan's study with Mr Ted. She was circulating among the guests. And Agnew-Simpson came out of the study livid, shouting that he never wanted to see Dr Jordan again! Definitely not the behaviour of someone who had just made Dr Jordan his beneficiary!

Alexander stood with his lips pressed tight — eyes glued to the floor.

"In fact," Dr Jordan continued, "Ted told me that he would send this new will to his lawyers. Did he send it? Did you find a copy of the new will in his files?"

"I have no idea. The police just removed the yellow tape about five minutes ago. You should deal directly with the estate office lawyers. I can provide you with their number." Alexander took out his cell phone.

"As God is my witness," said Zsuzsanna, "I was standing right here, on this very spot, two weeks ago — I think it was a Tuesday — when Ted said that he would leave Tig well provided for in his will. Ted was so grateful for Dr Jordan's loyalty and for his help with poor Mathilde."

"I thank you for your help with 'poor Mathilde'." Alexander's tone was dry, verging on sarcasm.

Elizabeth was disgusted by Zsuzsanna's outright lies. Although after Ted's tirade about Alexander's DNA, she could not be sure whether Mr

Ted had changed his will or not.

The telephone rang. "Yes, I will be right down," said Alexander. "You will have to excuse me." Alexander addressed his guests. "Let me walk you out."

"Of course, of course," said Dr Jordan. "A thousand apologies for the intrusion."

Before the study door shut, Elizabeth heard Zsuzsanna's voice say, "There will always be a special place for Ted in my heart! We were so close!"

Elizabeth came out from behind the bookcase. She sat down on the love seat, feeling shaken. After five minutes, she made her way downstairs. The door to the library was open, and Alexander motioned for her to come in. Inspector Jolicoeur and Constable Fortin were ensconced at the same table at the back of the room.

"I told Inspector Jolicoeur that you are anxious to go home," Alexander said. "Your statement is ready."

Inspector Jolicoeur, wearing a sky-blue shirt and matching knitted tie, looked fresher. The painkillers were doing their job.

Elizabeth read and signed the page-long statement, which turned out to be a summary of the information she had provided the night before. There was no reference to her conversation with Mr Ted. Inspector Jolicoeur had a few more questions.

"Did you have keys to Agnew-Simpson's study?"

"No," said Elizabeth. She did not have any keys at all. The rooms that she used — Madame Mathilde's boudoir, the library and Mr Agnew-Simpson's study — were always open. Inspector Jolicoeur reminded her that he would call her should other questions arise. He shook her hand and wished her a safe trip back to Montreal.

It was almost two in the afternoon when Elizabeth, luggage in hand, took the elevator down to the kitchen. Madame Gervais had prepared a quiche and a salad for lunch.

Alexander appeared with a briefcase and a suitcase. They sat down to lunch together.

"The house will be so empty now," said Monsieur Gervais.

"I will call you," Elizabeth promised.

After a tearful goodbye, Elizabeth got into Alexander's Audi, and they drove out the gate. Elizabeth did not look back for a last glimpse of the mansion. As the car headed south along Highway 15, both Elizabeth and Alexander were absorbed in their own thoughts. Elizabeth recalled her arrival at the estate in May. It was now the first week of July, and it seemed that she had lived an entire lifetime. Bangkok and Stephen were light-years away. The pain of her heartbreak resurfaced only occasionally now, as a dull ache rather than a piercing stab. Despite the shock of Mr Ted's death, Elizabeth realised that she had survived another ordeal. Exhausted by two sleepless nights, Elizabeth dozed off.

Chapter 17

Elizabeth awoke as Alexander's Audi crossed Rivière des Prairies onto the island of Montreal and Highway 15 became Boulevard de l'Acadie.

"Can't believe I slept all the way," said Elizabeth, stifling a yawn.

"I was about to wake you up. Where do you live?"

"In NDG. Take Boulevard Metropolitan to Décarie Boulevard and then turn east on Sherbrooke. Oooh! I forgot to tell you!" Elizabeth was suddenly wide awake. With a trembling voice full of indignation, she began to speak at a breakneck speed. "That woman you met today — Zsuzsanna — she was lying! Last week, when Dr Jordan came for supper, Zsuzsanna was not even invited. Did you know that she actually rowed across the lake and sneaked into the house through the kitchen? She practically begged to stay for dinner, but Mr Ted told her to row right back. She offered to sell Mr Ted that house across the lake!"

"If she's a real estate agent, that kind of behaviour is considered normal," Alexander interjected in a calm, neutral tone.

Elizabeth had not yet exhausted the depths of her outrage. "And Dr Jordan! Last week, I heard them talking on the balcony. Mr Ted was obviously joking when he said he would adopt Dr Jordan. But today, Dr Jordan told you that Mr Ted changed his will and that now he will inherit the Agnew-Simpson fortune! And Zsuzsanna claimed she witnessed the signing of the new will. I was with Mr Ted at the party, and Zsuzsanna did not go into the study! Why are they both lying?" Elizabeth's face was red, her voice raised in indignation.

"Perhaps Ted really did write Dr Jordan into the will," said Alexander. "I have no idea. I never discussed wills or money matters with Ted."

Elizabeth noted the contrast between Alexander's coolness and her own agitation. *He's right, Lizzie! Calm down!* She decided not to tell Alexander what Mr Ted told her about Alexander's DNA tests. *Perhaps Alexander already knows. Why else would he storm out of the study that night? Should I tell him about the letters from Hassan? No, Lizzie! Mind your own business! Get your own life in order.* The car turned east on Sherbrooke. "Now turn south on the next street."

As usual, there were no parking spaces on Marlowe Street, and Alexander parked in the lane next to Catherine's apartment building. To the sound of screeching feral cats and toppling garbage bins, Alexander gave Elizabeth his card. She promised to call once she bought a cell phone.

"Let me walk you to the door," said Alexander, as he took her suitcase out of the trunk.

"You don't have to," said Elizabeth. "You're parked illegally."

"I'll risk it."

After being away for almost two months, she was embarrassed by the shabbiness of the old building. Elizabeth led Alexander along the dirty beige corridor that smelled of cigarettes and somebody's curry dinner. At the door to Catherine's apartment, Alexander put down the suitcase. "You have been through so much. Don't let it get to you," he said, and he gave Elizabeth a friendly hug. Elizabeth looked up at him in surprise. His dark eyes seemed a softer, warmer brown. Impulsively, she put her head on his chest and began to cry.

"There, there," he soothed, and rocked her gently. A warm, salty tear ran into her mouth before she pulled away.

"I wet your shirt," she said, and wiped her nose with the back of her hand.

"Get some rest," he said, then squeezed her shoulder and walked away.

It was eight in the evening. Elizabeth opened the door and saw Catherine sitting on the blue velvet couch, watching TV and eating vanilla ice cream from a carton. The room looked as if it had been ravaged by a mini-hurricane, with overflowing laundry hampers, discarded pizza containers, clothes, and shopping bags.

"Hey, why are you even home?" asked Elizabeth.

"And it's good to see you, too," said Catherine, jumping up to hug Elizabeth. "I got off work early to wait for you. You sent me an email — remember? Marie-France phoned and filled me in about the murder or suicide or whatever it was. It must have been a real shock!"

"I'm so glad to be home!" Elizabeth's voice was quavering as she sank into the couch.

"Marie-France says that you were hysterical on the phone." Catherine put her arm around Elizabeth's shoulder. "I will not let you have another depression!"

"What do you mean, hysterical? Who wouldn't be upset? I saw him. He was dead, lying across his desk! Have you ever been in such a situation?"

"No, I have never been in many of your situations!"

"Why are you always so flippant?"

"Sorry! Look, your boss was obviously very weird or a total nut case. It's all over the news. Everyone at my restaurant is talking about it. Everyone thinks he killed his wife last summer and then offed himself. He probably couldn't live with the guilt."

"Just because you took Psych 101 does not give you the right to pontificate," said Elizabeth.

"I don't even know what pontificate means! What do you think, Sherlock?"

"I still can't think straight. I'll wait for the autopsy results. I think I'm upset because Mr Ted said such nasty things to me the night he died. He was very drunk, but still… I felt so humiliated!" Catherine saw tears well up in Elizabeth's eyes. "I was going to quit, but he fired me first!"

"Did he have issues with your work?"

"No, none at all."

"I don't understand. Did you get paid?"

"In full and for the entire contract period — fifteen thousand dollars."

"So, what's your problem? Who cares what he said! He was drunk! There are lots of bastards out there, Lizzie." Then, patting her sister's arm, she said, "You've got to toughen up, baby sister! You are so supersensitive!"

"Supersensitive! Who wouldn't be after what I've been through? I expected a little more support."

"Sorry!" Catherine whispered, and kissed her sister's damp cheek. "Everything will be all right. You'll see."

Despite another night of tossing and turning, Elizabeth was up early. Catherine was still asleep, so she made coffee, washed the dishes, straightened the apartment and began a to-do list: deposit cheque, buy a cell phone, clothes…

Yawning, clad in what looked like men's boxer shorts and a tank top, Catherine came out of the bedroom and poured herself some coffee.

"Did you check your emails? Did Amanda write?"

Elizabeth sat down on the couch, opened her laptop and found emails from Amanda and Marie-France. "Marie-France wants me to visit her in Ottawa next weekend. She sent something from a newspaper." Elizabeth read, "'Mont Tremblant. On Saturday morning, police were summoned to the estate of Theodore Agnew-Simpson, the reclusive millionaire. This scion of one of Canada's most renowned families was found dead in his study. Pending the release of the autopsy report, the police are treating the demise as a suspicious death. Neither Mr Agnew-Simpson's legal representatives nor his son, Alexander, could be reached for comment.'"

"So what do you think?" asked Catherine.

"I think it was either a heart attack or a stroke."

"Somebody mentioned suicide by poisoning."

"I think that's far-fetched, although the toxicology test results won't be available for a while." Elizabeth turned back to her computer. "There's an email from Amanda. She and Rob will be back this Sunday night. She also attached something. It's from some blog called *Gossip Queen*. Amanda warns me not to take it seriously. 'Be prepared for malicious nonsense! Love, Amanda.' So why did she even send it, if it's all malicious nonsense?"

Elizabeth began to read out loud. "'During the night of 3rd July, Mr Agnew-Simpson, heir to one of Canada's most illustrious families, died at his estate near Mt Tremblant. Almost ten years ago, he delegated the administration of his vast corporate assets and isolated himself to write books on Canadian history. According to close personal friends, who wish to remain anonymous, his single-minded, perhaps even obsessive, dedication to these projects contributed to his growing social isolation. Since the tragic death of his wife, Mathilde Beaudry, who died as a result of a strange accident last summer, Agnew-Simpson became fixated on security. Mt Tremblant is abuzz with rumours about his death. Was his death the result of natural causes? Was it foul play? The son, Alexander Agnew-Simpson, has issued no statement.

"'A source close to the family, who wishes to remain anonymous, asked whether the police have questioned Mr Alexander Agnew-Simpson. Why did he leave the estate so suddenly on the night of 3rd July? According to the same source, his departure was precipitated by a violent argument with his father. Alexander Agnew-Simpson's car was seen driving through the village at breakneck speed, wheels screeching. One can reasonably ask whether Mr Agnew-Simpson was already dead when the surveillance cameras captured Alexander's car leaving the estate.'"

Elizabeth stopped reading. "I know we have a free press and all that, but are they allowed to make such blatant insinuations?"

"Gossip sells. It doesn't even matter whether it's true, people lap it up! Some celebrities take them to court, others don't bother. That's the price of being rich and famous!"

Elizabeth returned to the article. "'This is the second death at the Agnew-Simpson mansion in less than two years. Many village residents believe that the police treat the Agnew-Simpson family with kid gloves. "The rich can always get away with murder," said one long-time resident.'"

"So, are they accusing Alexander of murdering his father?" asked Catherine.

"Probably." Elizabeth continued to read: "'A close personal friend of the late Agnew-Simpson mentioned the pretty young research assistant, who...'" Elizabeth gasped, stopped reading, and jumped up from the sofa.

"What's the matter?" asked Catherine.

Elizabeth, breathing like a fish out of water, gasped, "It's about me!"

Catherine gently took the laptop away from her sister and sat down on the couch. She continued reading: "'The same source suggests that this young lady gained near-total control over her employer and isolated him from old friends. 'The old man was besotted,' the source concluded. 'Despite the age difference, wealth can be a powerful aphrodisiac.'"

Elizabeth sat breathing heavily. Her face was red. She jumped up and stood over Catherine, her cheeks flaming. "It's that hideous Zsuzsanna! She's the anonymous source! That woman is a snake! I should sue her for defamation; I should..."

"Ignore this garbage! They did not give your name!" Seeing the distress on Elizabeth's face, Catherine said, "I will not let you stew over this! I will call in sick at the restaurant."

"No, go to work!" Elizabeth wailed. "You are making me feel so guilty!"

"It's done! Go take a shower! We're out of here! First, we'll do some practical errands, and then we'll have some fun. And by the way, you are going to buy me an expensive lunch," said Catherine with a determined look on her face.

The sisters deposited Elizabeth's cheque at the nearby TD Trust and applied for a credit card. They walked down Vendome Avenue to the metro and rode the orange line to the Lionel Groulx Station, where they crossed to the green line, and in a few minutes, emerged at the Eaton's Centre in the heart of Montreal's downtown shopping district. They found a Bell Telephone Boutique and purchased a cell phone. Over coffee in the underground concourse, Elizabeth input phone numbers — her sisters', Marie-France's, the Gervaises', and Alexander's.

"You need some decent clothes! Let's go! The summer sales have just begun," said Catherine.

They walked through the underground passage that links Eaton's Centre to The Bay department store. Reluctantly, Elizabeth tried on a black Calvin Klein pants suit. It looked terrific. "And where would I wear this?"

"It's a classic. You never know when you will have to look chic," said Catherine. She also persuaded Elizabeth to purchase matching low-heeled patent leather pumps and a large black and gold leather purse.

"What about you?" asked Elizabeth. She showed Catherine a size six, dark green sleeveless dress.

"I haven't worn a dress since my first communion," said Catherine.

"I'm buying you this dress," said Elizabeth. "It suits you."

"Hey, we've got to buy some oversized dark glasses and go to the Ritz Carleton dining room and pretend we're rich and famous," said Elizabeth.

"You don't have a credit card yet," said Catherine. "Let's eat some place close by."

"I haven't had Montreal smoked meat in years," said Elizabeth. "Just the thought of it makes me drool!"

The sisters went to Dunne's on Metcalfe Street. The restaurant window was filled with jars of pickled red peppers and hanging rows of smoked brisket. A bored, middle-aged waitress brought them smoked meat sandwiches — two inches of slivered red brisket on rye bread, slathered in buttercup-yellow mustard. Elizabeth added dollops of ketchup over the fat, greasy French fries. After the first bite, she let out moans of appreciation.

"I am amazed — I can laugh again! This morning I felt pretty shitty. Thank you, Catherine!"

"As of today, you have officially turned the page. You have begun a wonderful new life! No more bad luck! What else could possibly happen?"

Chapter 18

Elizabeth awoke the next day with resolve to focus on the future — a future that, like a new dawn, was still a faint, hazy glow, but which promised to turn into a glorious day. She remembered her promise to call the Gervais couple, but reluctant to revive painful memories, decided to wait until her own plans became clearly defined. Elizabeth did call Alexander to give him her new cell phone number. Alexander was in Ottawa. He was juggling meetings at the university and finalising a condo purchase. Alexander apologised, said he had to run, and promised to call her later.

He called back the next day. He sounded more at ease and asked Elizabeth about her plans. She told him that she was seriously thinking of going back to university in the fall.

"Good! Does that mean you are free in August? I have a project for you. About a week's work — at Mont Tremblant."

"I'm not sure..." She did not want to go back.

"I'd like to tell you more about the project. Look, I have to be back in Montreal on Thursday for McDougall's funeral — he was Ted's lawyer and friend. Are you free for supper on Friday?"

"Yes, I'm free on Friday."

"Good, I'll reserve something in Old Montreal. Pick you up at five. We can stroll around the old town first."

Why are you excited, Lizzie? It's not a date, date. But who cares? When was the last time anyone invited you out for dinner? In Old Montreal? On Friday morning, Elizabeth went to a beauty salon for a haircut. Her auburn hair now had a definite bounce. She splurged on a manicure and a pedicure. Before Alexander arrived, she took time with her make-up and highlighted her turquoise eyes. She wore her new black pants suit. It did look terrific.

Alexander drove up precisely at five. "The city suits you," he said, as he opened the car door. Alexander was wearing black slacks and a white open-neck shirt under a beige linen jacket. "I've had such a busy week," he said. "I'm looking forward to a relaxing dinner."

He drove the Audi to Old Montreal and left the car in a parking lot across from the Centaur Theatre. "My apartment hotel is right here." He pointed down St Francois Xavier Street. "It's walking distance from the lawyers' offices."

Elizabeth had not been in Old Montreal in years. Like a tourist, she was charmed by the old-world architecture, the cobblestone streets, and horse-drawn *calèches*. They walked along Rue Notre Dame to Notre Dame Basilica, where swarms of tourists aimed their cameras and cell phones at the Gothic structure.

"Let's go inside," he suggested. "When my grandmother was still alive, we sometimes attended Sunday mass here."

It occurred to Elizabeth that Agnew-Simpson did not quite succeed in keeping Alexander's grandmother away from her grandson. "My grandparents also brought us here a few times," she said. "My sisters and I loved that stained-glass window with that Iroquois woman. I always imagined that she had just seen a vision of the Virgin Mary and was instantly turned into a saint."

They walked around the cathedral admiring the carvings and the stained-glass windows. They sat in a pew and listened to an organist practice Bach's Toccata and Fugue in D Minor on the Casavant organ. Elizabeth felt transported by the music and mesmerised by the ornate beauty of the surroundings. Alexander pointed to the vivid, royal-blue vaulted ceiling studded with gold stars.

"As a child, I used to count those stars," he said.

Perhaps because of this shared childhood experience, Alexander no longer seemed so distant. They continued to amble along Rue Notre Dame and passed by the stately Hotel de Ville with its green copper roof. Jacques Cartier Square was full of tourists, milling on the square and packed into sidewalk cafés. The hanging baskets of flowers made the entire scene look festive.

They turned south on Rue St Claude to Marché Bonsecours, Montreal's old market, now full of tourist shops selling artefacts and souvenirs. They strolled west on Rue de la Commune to the St Lawrence River, where the old port was transformed into a leisure and recreation area. One could take a gourmet supper cruise, watch a film at the round IMAX theatre, shop at the flea market or ride a Ferris wheel. Returning to Place Jacques Cartier, they were lucky to find a free table in one of the terrace bars. They ordered sangria.

"You are very quiet," he said.

"I am enjoying this — just being here, looking at all these people. It's wonderful! I guess I've been isolated for a long time."

For a split second, it seemed to Elizabeth that a faint smile appeared on Alexander's face. "Here's to you, Elizabeth." They clinked glasses.

"When are you moving to Ottawa?" she asked.

"I'll be in Ottawa full-time once the semester begins. I'll use the apartment hotel in Montreal as a base."

"I suppose you have a lot of estate issues to keep you in Montreal?"

"The law firm is in a bit of turmoil after Mortimer's death. He was the senior partner and something of a one-man band. I am not really involved."

Elizabeth was surprised at his lack of involvement with his father's estate, but then she thought, *What do I know? Probably all he has to do is sign on the dotted line.* "When is Mr Ted's funeral?"

"Ted wanted to be cremated, and his ashes buried in the family vault. He also left instructions for a public memorial service, which will have to take place later. Everything is still up in the air. I did get an email from Inspector Jolicoeur. The body has yet to be released. Apparently, that is to be expected when toxicology tests are required."

"Toxicology? Is that a test for poison?"

"Yes, I suppose. The police are probably trying to 'dot every i'."

They finished the sangria and crossed the square to Restaurant St Amable.

"I've never been here," said Elizabeth. "I wonder whether this is an old historic building."

"Apparently, it is not that old, an early nineteenth-century residence. I used to come here for lunch with my mother and grandmother after church on Sundays."

A waiter in a white shirt seated them at a tiny table for two. Alexander looked around the room with interest. "This used to be a fine restaurant. But I don't remember this exposed brick wall and the waiters used to wear suits." Alexander picked up the menu. "It's standard French bistro fare now. I hope it's good."

Elizabeth made up her mind quickly. She ordered a mushroom salad followed by *moules/frites*. Alexander opted for snails *au gratin* and steak *tartare*. He chose a bottle of *Pouilly-Fuissé* and asked the waiter to bring him a glass of *Cabernet Sauvignon* for his meat course.

"I do enjoy steak tartare once in a while. I ordered it because of the French fries. I loved the French fries here as a child. And Mother always let me order the biggest dessert on the menu, even if I could never finish it." His tone was impersonal and dispassionate, as if he was speaking of the most mundane things.

There's never any emotion in anything he says. Does that make him an unfeeling person? Is that such a bad thing? Perhaps I should learn how to control my feelings better. Elizabeth did notice that his dark eyes seemed to become softer when he spoke about his mother.

"How old were you then?"

"I must have been about ten. I still remember my grandmother — she always wore a hat. For some reason, I also remember her in a brown sweater with a mink collar."

During the meal, the conversation was about food. Elizabeth was very enthusiastic about Thai cuisine. She laughed as Alexander described the dishes served in university cafeterias in England: mushy peas, pigs in blankets, bangers and mash, spotted dick.

He ordered a cheese plate for two. "It gives us an excuse to have a glass of port. What are your plans for the rest of the summer, Elizabeth?"

OK. I almost forgot why Alexander invited me out. It's a business dinner. "I am thinking of moving in with a friend in Ottawa. I plan to go back to university in the fall."

"What sort of degree?"

"My friend, Marie-France, the one in Ottawa, is enrolled in law school and wants me to apply. I don't think I am cut out for law. I'm too emotional, too highly strung. Marie-France — she's as cool as a cucumber."

"I see you as smart and level-headed," he said. "But then again, what do we really know about anyone? What would you like to do?"

"I'm not sure. I did not enjoy teaching. I know that for a fact. I enjoyed the research I did for Mr Ted. I was thinking of becoming a librarian or something research-related. There's a programme called Information Systems Studies."

"I'm sure you will do very well, and this project will be right up your alley. The estate office asked me to advise them about Ted's manuscript. The publisher will line up a historian to work on the final draft, but they need someone to organise his files and research materials. Would you be interested? The estate office is rather generous."

"I am not sure about my own plans yet. I think I have to be in Ottawa by the middle of August. I'm also applying for a part-time job at the Civil Service Language School. I won't be able to tell you before I check on the dates." *I really, really do not want to go back there.* "I'll know by the end of next week."

"I do hope you can do it. I'll call you next week. I'll have to go back to the estate to bring back some of my personal belongings, and I plan to raid Ted's library. The estate office gave permission."

"What about your mother's things? Her diaries…"

"Yes, of course. I took most of the family photographs after her death. Yes, I will definitely take the diaries."

"You should also take *La Princesse des Clèves*. It's actually not a book, it's a box with letters in it. The letters are rather personal. Don't forget to take them."

"Yes, of course." Alexander was obviously enjoying the cheese plate.

It's not my place to bring up the content of the letters. God knows how he would take the news about Hassan. I do not want to spoil the evening. I don't think he wants to talk about Mr Ted's death either. He was looking forward to a peaceful dinner. Disregarding her own advice to herself, Elizabeth said, "I think I should tell you. Someone is feeding slanderous information to an online tabloid."

"My family has been the subject of gossip for years. I generally pay no attention," said Alexander, and he sipped his glass of port.

"*Gossip Queen* quotes someone who claims you had a violent argument with Mr Ted the night he died. I just want you to know I am not the source. Although I must confess that Inspector Jolicoeur asked me about your demeanour that night. I said you looked angry. I'm sorry. I should not have said anything."

"No need to be sorry. You told the truth."

"I wonder whether the police leak information to the tabloids. *Gossip Queen* also wrote that you were seen driving through the village at breakneck speed, with your tyres screeching."

"If the tabloid suggests that I am responsible for Ted's death," he said, and cut a piece of Gruyère cheese, "I suppose they want to increase their circulation."

"They wrote some pretty awful things about me, too. They insinuated that I was more than an assistant. That I had an intimate relationship... Even though they did not print my name, I'm still upset."

"I am very sorry you were dragged into this."

"I think I know who is slandering me. Remember Zsuzsanna, the woman who told you about Agnew-Simpson's supposed promise to leave Dr Jordan loads of money? She insinuated that I was more than an assistant." Elizabeth could not control the trembling in her voice. "At Dr Jordan's party, she practically introduced me as Mr Ted's girlfriend. She must be the secret source — I'm sure of it! That woman is a witch."

"There could have been other women who saw you as a rival. After all, Ted was a widower and a multi-millionaire. Some people do strange things when money is involved."

Alexander finished his port. "You know, when I look back at the way I was raised, I must admit that up to the time I went to university, I was very naïve about money. Money was never an issue; it was always available. In prep school, I had a bank account that was always miraculously replenished. I had a credit card, and the bills were paid by the accountant.

"For some reason that I don't quite understand, I was not profligate. I was so focused on studies that my idea of a good time was to travel to conferences or buy more books. This may sound strange, but it never occurred to me to think of where the money came from or how much I had at my disposal. At university, I finally realised how privileged I was, when I saw that some of my friends had to work menial jobs to survive. It was a rude awakening. I wonder how I would have coped if I had not been born into a family sitting on a mountain of gold."

I hope you learned your lesson, Lizzie! Here you were choking to tell him about all the evil gossip, but does Alexander look concerned? Not a bit. He has people who handle that sort of thing. From now on, zip-zip — no more talk about the estate or Mr Ted. May he rest in peace! And Lizzie, learn from Al — ignore the tabloids.

It was not yet nine in the evening as they left the restaurant. Place Jacques Cartier was even more crowded. A fiddler played French-Canadian tunes, and an ice cream vendor was doing brisk business. Alexander bought ice cream cones. As they crossed a busy street, they were suddenly surrounded by a rowdy throng of revellers. Alexander took Elizabeth's hand and did not let go until he had manoeuvred them to safety. They continued to walk along St Paul Street, eating ice cream. Elizabeth was sorry that he let go of her hand.

He drove her back to Marlowe Street, and before he could get out of the car, Elizabeth said, "Please don't get out. You'll be double-parked, and the man behind you is already honking." Alexander opened his car door to more impatient honking.

"Thank you for a lovely dinner," she said.

"I'll call you next week," said Alexander, as he got out of the car. Impatient honking forced him to get back in again.

Catherine was at work. Elizabeth was sorry she had no one with whom to share her impressions of the evening. She had to admit that she did enjoy herself. Very much. She felt more at ease with Alexander now. *Mr Ted's death somehow brought us closer. He is reluctant to talk about his father. Why? Is it because Mr Ted told him about the DNA tests that night he stormed out?*

He says that money is not important, but would he be so calm if he knew that he's been written out of the will? Elizabeth pushed away these thoughts and fell asleep.

Chapter 19

Saturday was one of those sweltering July days when the air in Montreal becomes hot, heavy, and clammy. Elizabeth felt her clothes begin to stick to her body as she rolled her suitcase to the Vendome commuter train station. She was on her way to visit Marie-France in Ottawa and would stop off in Pointe-Claire to see her oldest sister. Amanda, who had just deposited Rob at his golf club, was waiting on the platform when Elizabeth arrived.

"It's a fixer-upper," Amanda said, as they drove up to a tiny white clapboard cottage.

She explained that they had bought it because of rising land values. Elizabeth listened patiently to a discourse on mortgages and then to an enumeration of expansion plans that included a state-of-the-art kitchen and an outdoor Jacuzzi.

"As you can see, the living room is still empty. I got rid of our old hand-me-down furniture. I'd rather wait and buy something decent."

Elizabeth was happy for Amanda; however, she herself did not aspire to suburban life. After a quick sandwich lunch, Amanda drove Elizabeth to the Voyageur bus stop, talking all the way. "You are absolutely right to go on with your studies, but I would definitely suggest law, like Marie-France. Whatever you choose, make sure it will give you status and a good salary. And find yourself a suitable man! Your track record has not been great."

"Mm, yes," said Elizabeth. "First, I will have to take a few qualifying courses to get into Information Studies in the winter semester."

"Is that what they call Library Science now? Are you sure you want to be a librarian? Sounds kind of boring to me."

"Thanks for the ride," said Elizabeth, as she took her suitcase out of Amanda's Toyota. The Voyageur bus rolled into the parking lot, and Elizabeth hugged her sister.

"Good luck, Lizzie. Call me."

Waiting at the Ottawa bus terminal was Marie-France with a big smile on her rosy cheeks. She drove the orange Mini Cooper to her flat, steps from the University of Ottawa. The car stopped in front of a narrow, two-storey house with a gabled roof. It looked incongruous between two stately homes — as if someone had bribed the building inspector to ignore municipal codes. The owner converted the top floor into a flat and added a separate narrow, wooden staircase from the driveway.

Marie-France parked the car on the street and took out several bags of groceries. Elizabeth rolled her suitcase towards the stairs. Before Marie-France could get back into the car to manoeuvre the vehicle through the narrow driveway to her tight parking spot at the back of the building, the landlord, in a sleeveless undershirt, ran out of the house. He was short, corpulent and middle-aged, with thick black hair and a day's growth of beard on his sweaty face. With his short legs wide apart, he planted himself in front of the car.

"How many times do I have to tell you? No parking on the street! How many times? If I get a fine, you will have to pay. I will not..."

"Mr Villanueva, please. We were just unloading the groceries. I will park right away."

"Do you know that the police have cameras everywhere? Even satellites!" Mr Villanueva pointed a short, hairy finger into the sky. "They are watching right now!" His face became red, and spittle sprayed from his mouth. Then, seeing Elizabeth and the luggage, he said, "If you think you can sneak another person into the flat without paying, you are wrong! Do you know the cost of water and electricity?"

"Please, Mr Villanueva. My friend is just visiting. If she likes the flat and decides to stay, we will make an adjustment to the rent."

"Why wouldn't she like it? A beautiful, furnished apartment, two minutes to the Rideau Centre, walking distance to..." A woman knocked on the front window of the house, and Mr Villanueva rushed back inside.

"You'll get used to him if you stay. His name is Angel Villanueva, but I call him the Angel of Doom. The guy never smiles. I suppose I wouldn't either if I was in his position. His wife has some sort of heart condition — needs a walker and a wheelchair. He drives her to the doctor's about three times a week. And he also takes care of his aged parents. I feel for him, but God forbid, if I leave the car in front of the house for even a second, he comes charging out like a bull."

They climbed the rickety stairs to an enclosed landing that also served as a mudroom. "The flat is small, hot in the summer, and expensive. But at least I walk to all my classes. You can crash on the couch this week, but you'll have to buy a bed if you move in. I hope we'll be able to cram it into the bedroom."

The apartment had a bedroom under a slanted roof and one tiny bathroom with a basic shower. The larger room was used for everything else. A rather ungainly, overstuffed plaid couch and an armchair covered by a crocheted Afghan served as the living room. A tiny table, covered by a red polka-dotted plastic tablecloth, stood next to the kitchen alcove. At the opposite end of the room, the study area consisted of a repurposed wooden door on trestles that served as a desk, and a bookshelf made of black plastic milk crates.

"As you can see, the décor is strictly student chic," said Marie-France.

They opened all the windows and stripped down to their underwear and T-shirts. Marie-France went into the bedroom and brought out a tall electric fan. Despite an annoying whirring noise, it did make the heat in the room a little more bearable.

"I didn't cook," said Marie-France, as she took a BBQ chicken out of the grocery bag and placed a plastic bowl of store-bought coleslaw on the table. There was also French bread, grapes, cheese, and a bottle of Rosé. They both plopped ice cubes into their wine.

"Thank you so much for setting up the interview at the Language School," said Elizabeth. "I really hope I can get a part-time job. On Tuesday, I have an appointment with an academic advisor at the University of Ottawa. It will be a busy week."

"Good! Get your life organised! So what do you think of the flat? It's no Taj Mahal!"

"As they say — location, location, location."

They talked all evening, not noticing the time. Marie-France told Elizabeth that she met a young man — a fellow law student, Benjamin — who lived across the river with his parents in Gatineau. He was still away, planting trees for the summer.

"What does he look like?" asked Elizabeth.

"Well... he's big and tall. He looks like an oversized teddy bear. I come up to about his armpit!" Marie-France laughed. "And he's not very talkative; shy, actually. And I really love him! And I know he loves me."

"You are one lucky girl!"

"How was your date with Alexander?"

"It was not really a date!" said Elizabeth. "It was a sort of 'thank you for your services' kind of supper. He was very nice, gallant, and almost warm at times. I used to think he was a snob. Now I don't quite know what to think. He keeps a distance — an emotional distance. It's like he's protecting some private, inner self."

"Poor little rich boy and all that. Bizarre family. Why wouldn't he be fucked up?"

"You would not believe what I found in Mathilde's boudoir... Oh, shit! I'm not supposed to talk about it. I signed a confidentiality agreement."

"Are you still paranoid? Agnew-Simpson is dead."

"Does the confidentiality clause still apply? Could the estate sue me?"

"For what? I already know that you were working on Madame's diaries."

"I also found some secret letters!"

"So, are you planning on selling them to the tabloids?"

"Oh, my god! I never thought of that!"

"Of what? Of selling them to the tabloids?"

"What if somebody finds the letters? The estate office may send people to do an inventory... Somebody could try to sell them... Oh, my god! Then everybody would suspect me!"

"What's so special about the letters?"

"Please, Marie-France, forget what I said. I've had too much wine!"

"OK! OK! But I don't understand a word of what you said. Alexander has access to all his mother's stuff. Let him handle it."

"I told Alexander about the letters, but what if someone finds them first? It will be such a shock!" Elizabeth gasped. "There might even be legal implications for him... Perhaps his inheritance... I have no idea..."

"You are not making any sense! Look at yourself in the mirror! You must still be recovering from shock! You get all worked up every time you talk about Mont Tremblant! Stay away! Time to move on!"

"I'm waiting for a phone call from Alexander. He offered me a short gig at Tremblant — organising Mr Ted's manuscript and stuff. I told him I'd check my schedule... I was going to say no and make up some excuse, but now I think I should go."

"There is no such thing as should! That place is toxic. They can hire someone else!"

"No, I'm the best person for the job. I know it sounds silly" — Elizabeth pulled a Kleenex from the box on the coffee table and dabbed her moist eyes — "but I feel protective of Mathilde. She was a naïve girl who fell in love. Her entire life was so unhappy. I don't want anyone getting their money-grubbing paws on her intimate letters. I don't want her pain splashed all over the tabloids, just to provide titillating entertainment for a public obsessed by celebrity gossip!"

"Lizzie! I've never heard you wax so eloquent!" Marie-France looked at her watch and said, "Look at the time! Go to bed! You have an appointment tomorrow morning!"

The following morning, as Elizabeth left the flat for her interview at the Language School, Marie-France called out, "You can take a short cut — walk right through the Rideau Shopping Centre. The Chateau Laurier Hotel is on the other side of Rideau Street. And don't be surprised that some classes are online tutorials. Did you bring all your documents?"

"Yes," said Elizabeth, and she lifted her elegant new purse. Elizabeth looked smart in her new black pants suit and patent leather pumps.

Elizabeth spent more than two hours at the Language School offices on the third floor of the Chateau Laurier. She filled in a stack of forms. She was interviewed by a very tall, thin woman with short black hair. Elizabeth wrote two exhaustive language tests in both of Canada's official languages. She would be contacted with the results on Friday. She returned to the flat and spent the rest of the day studying the Information Studies programme in preparation for her interview with an academic advisor. During the next few days, she completed the online application process, made an official request for her transcripts from Concordia University, and applied for a student loan. All this activity made her feel that she was finally taking control of her life. She looked at herself in the mirror and said, "I'm proud of you, Lizzie! Keep up the good work!"

That week, Marie-France and Elizabeth explored Ottawa: the flower-filled Byword Market, the Rideau Canal and Elizabeth's favourite, the National Gallery, that modern structure with green glass walls reflecting the nineteenth-century Parliament Buildings. She fell in love with the Group of Seven artists. Their northern landscapes were imbued with such an unmistakable Canadian spirit. One evening, they drove along Sussex Drive and took selfies outside the Prime Minister's residence and Rideau Hall. They stopped at a lookout to admire the view of the Ottawa River.

"This is so much fun; I'm a tourist in my own country," said Elizabeth, as she sent selfies to her sisters.

"Have you been inside the Parliament buildings?" asked Marie-France.

"No! I was sick during our high school trip to Ottawa."

Elizabeth booked a tour. It was summer, and Parliament was not in session. The marble corridors of the Centre Block Building were full of motley tourist groups, both native Canadians and foreign. All seemed to be more interested in taking photographs than listening to the guide recite historical facts. Inside the parliamentary library, Elizabeth felt as if she had entered a time machine and was transported back into the nineteenth century. It was a round room with vaulted, Gothic ceilings and a white marble statue of Queen Victoria in the centre. The walls were lined with gleaming white pine bookshelves with carvings of flowers and mythical creatures. As she walked out of the Parliament building and stopped at the eternal flame, her cell phone rang. It was Alexander.

"Elizabeth, sorry, I don't have time to talk, so I'll get to the point. Can you come to Mont Tremblant for a few days to help organise Ted's research? We could leave on Saturday morning."

"Yes, of course. I will be available, but for no more than a week. I may be starting a new job right after Labour Day, and if I do, I will have to attend some orientation sessions."

Alexander said he would pick her up at ten in the morning on Saturday. "I will drive you back whenever you say. I promise."

"In that case, I will text you Marie-France's address. See you on Saturday."

On Friday morning, Elizabeth returned to the offices of the Civil

Service Language School. She learned that she had passed both the English and the French language tests with flying colours. The school offered her part-time employment to teach French to unilingual civil servants. Elizabeth walked out of the Language School office with a bounce in her step. She smiled at everyone in the crowded elevator. Most smiled back. She made a mental note to take Marie-France out to dinner to celebrate! Elizabeth was still smiling as the elevator door opened on the ground floor of the Chateau Laurier. She stepped into the lobby and walked right into Stephen Turner. Elizabeth gasped and stood immobile. She was blocking the people rushing out of the elevator. She felt as if she had turned into a pillar of stone, with her feet firmly welded to the floor. Wide-eyed, she stared straight into Stephen's face. *It can't be! It's someone else.* But it was Stephen. He, too, looked stunned, eyes wide in disbelief.

Stephen recovered first. "Elizabeth!" His voice was a hoarse whisper. "What are you doing here?"

In the first instance, Elizabeth felt numb. She spoke mechanically, as if this was a casual encounter, as if she was answering an ordinary question. "I was at the Language School."

She felt his fingers dig into her upper arm. Her body felt limp. Like a rag doll, she let Stephen pull her out of the milling crowd around the elevator towards two red armchairs at the wall.

"I don't want to talk to you," she said, as she recovered from the initial shock. The next emotion was panic. It was as if Stephen triggered some flight instinct, and all she wanted to do was to run — to run as far away as possible. He continued to hold her upper arm in a firm grip.

"Elizabeth, I beg you! Please, let me say how sorry I am! So very, very sorry!" This pleading tone was something she had never heard from him before.

Elizabeth looked up at Stephen's face and in one split second registered all the minute, almost imperceptible changes in his appearance. He was still a very handsome man, although his cheeks seemed a little hollower, his nose slightly sharper, and the little furrows around his hazel eyes deeper. His wavy, brown hair, still combed behind his ears, was thinner, with grey tinges at the temples. Even his impeccably tailored suit did not seem to hang quite right.

As if reading her thoughts, Stephen said, "Yes, I know I've changed. Since Bangkok, my life has turned upside down. Laura left me, you know. She and Christine are now living in England. I'll be in Ottawa for another three years..." He continued to hold her upper arm. "Elizabeth, you are more beautiful than ever." He looked searchingly into her eyes and said, "I still think about you. I was devastated when I came back from home leave and they told me you were gone. I tried to reach you. Of course, I understand your reluctance to talk to me. I should have searched for you. But as God is my witness, know that I always loved you."

For a split second, Elizabeth wanted to believe him, fall into his arms, forgive him, and cry on his chest. Angry with herself, she said in a voice too loud for the lobby, "Why are you lying? I know you did not go away on embassy business before home leave. I saw you in Bangkok in December! I saw you at the Skytrain kissing Rajimi! Why are you still lying?" Elizabeth was surprised by the resolve in her tone.

Stephen looked surprised. Perhaps he expected to meet the Elizabeth he knew in Bangkok — naïve, gullible, compliant.

"You are a cad, Stephen — a cad and a liar!"

"Elizabeth! Do you think it was easy for me?"

"Let go of my arm before I make a scene."

He let go immediately. "Please," he whispered. "You are right. I behaved abominably. Do you think I did not suffer? At least let me tell you what happened. Do you want me to get down on my knees right here in the lobby and beg for your forgiveness? Let's go for a drink." Again he took her arm and tried to pull her in the direction of the lobby bar.

"No!" she gasped. "Let go of my arm!" Her voice must have been full of resolve, because he did let go. He tried to say something before she cut him off. "Do not ever bother me again!"

She would always remember the pained expression on his face as she turned away and ran. She ran as if she was fleeing for her life. Pedestrians on Rideau Street stopped and stared at her. With her heart pounding, she ran through the Rideau Centre, before she doubled over with a stabbing pain in her side. She reached the flat and collapsed on the couch. That is how Marie-France found her — curled up in a foetal position.

"What happened?"

"I ran into Stephen."

"Oh, no! Lizzie, you're not going to have another breakdown! You can't! I won't let you! You've just begun to turn your life around…"

"I've been lying here thinking about my own reaction," said Elizabeth, turning her face up from the pillow to look at Marie-France. Her face looked haggard and creased with pillow marks. "Don't worry. It's not as bad as before. I'm stronger now."

"I hope so," said Marie-France. "I hope your heart has more Teflon in it."

Elizabeth sat up slowly, with effort. "I feel so very, very tired — as if I spent the entire day hauling rocks."

Marie-France brought out a tray with a cold bottle of Rosé, glasses and ice cubes. "What happened?"

"I was coming out of the elevator at the Chateau Laurier. I was so happy. I will be teaching French part-time in September. Then the elevator door opened, and there he was. I felt such a range of emotions: shock, paralysis, anger, rage… I swear, if I had a knife or a gun, I could have killed him. But at the same time, and this is the weird part… I hate to admit it." Elizabeth took another sip of wine. "There was a part of me that wanted to throw myself into his arms and cry and…"

"Don't even say it!"

"It would have been so easy to forgive. I've forgiven Stephen before. In the past, it was as if I could stand any humiliation, any pain just to have this love."

"You are scaring me!"

"He helped me," said Elizabeth with a bitter smile. "I caught him in another bold-faced lie! He said he was surprised that I was not in Bangkok in January. 'I saw you with Rajimi,' I told him. He did not deny it. He recovered quickly and asked for forgiveness — he still loves me, you see. He thinks I should feel sorry for *him* because his wife left him. And what about Rajimi? For all I know, she could be here with him."

When they finished the wine, Elizabeth got up from the couch and said, "Come on, I'm taking you out for dinner. I want to celebrate."

"Celebrate? Don't you have to pack? Isn't Alexander picking you up early tomorrow?"

"Yes, but I want to thank you for everything you've done for me. I was planning on making it a celebration — the beginning of my new life," said Elizabeth without enthusiasm.

"Look, the celebration can wait."

"I need to go out. I need to see normal people, to forget…"

"Well, OK, let's go out. What about that pub down the street?"

"Sure, we don't have to dress up." Elizabeth splashed some cold water on her face.

At the pub, they ordered salads and more wine. Marie-France tried to distract Elizabeth. She talked about the Language School and teaching adult civil servants. She retold long-distance telephone conversations with Benjamin. Elizabeth tried hard to seem interested. Elizabeth paid the bill and promised to take Marie-France to a fancier place when she returned from Mont Tremblant.

At the flat, as soon as Elizabeth finished packing, she changed into a nightshirt and lay on the couch with eyes closed, pretending to be asleep. Like a broken record, every detail of her meeting with Stephen kept replaying in her mind. She knew herself well enough to expect a sleepless night.

Chapter 20

It was almost dawn when Elizabeth fell into a restless sleep. She awoke dreaming that a big black dog was nuzzling her arm. It was Marie-France.

"Lizzie, wake up! It's almost nine."

Elizabeth hid her face in the pillow. "Another five minutes…"

"Get up!"

Marie-France handed Elizabeth a mug of steaming coffee. "Put some ice on your face and wear dark glasses. Alexander will think you were partying all night!" Marie-France had one more bit of advice for Elizabeth before the hug at the door. "Just do your job with the books and manuscripts or whatever and get out of that mausoleum as fast as you can! And call me."

Elizabeth, suitcase in hand, went down to the sidewalk at precisely ten o'clock. She wore new, well-cut jeans and a long-sleeved white cotton shirt. Her puffy eyes were hidden behind huge black sunglasses. Elizabeth wished she hadn't promised Alexander she would go back to the mansion. She wished she could stay on the couch. She wished the meeting with Stephen had not upset her so much. The thought that Stephen was living in Ottawa, perhaps somewhere nearby…

What was she afraid of? That he would find her, or that she would…

"Right on time!" Alexander said, as he got out of a black Audi hatchback. He looked ready for a country weekend in his black chinos and black T-shirt.

I hope the glasses hide my sleepless night. "Did you buy a new car?" she asked. *Oh, god, will I have to carry on a civil conversation all the way to Mont Tremblant?*

Alexander placed her suitcase on the back seat. "I always rent cars. I'll be moving, so a hatchback is more practical."

Elizabeth had not seen him since their 'date'. She felt as if she was meeting not quite an employer but not quite a friend. She couldn't define her relationship with Alexander.

"How's the new apartment?" she asked.

"It's a condo on the Rideau Canal, not far from Carleton University. The designer says that the renovations are taking much longer than planned. But I told her, I am moving in September, ready or not! I dread her phone calls. My head is still spinning with all the decisions she insists I make — colour schemes, textures, Carrara or Calacatta…"

Boo-hoo-hoo. I wish I had your problems. "For some people, decorating a condo is fun."

"I told the designer not to bother me any more. Let her make the choices! What am I paying her for? But what have you been up to? How's the flat?" he asked, as the car turned towards the Macdonald-Cartier Bridge.

"The flat is cramped, hot, and stuffy, and the landlord is a bit of a nutcase. But it's close to everything. I've enrolled in some qualifying courses, and I've got a part-time job teaching French." *All in all, this was a great week, until I bumped into Stephen.*

"Good for you!"

The car turned east on Highway 50. The gentle motion and the purring of the engine lulled Elizabeth to sleep. When the car drove up to Mont Tremblant village, Elizabeth was awakened by the phone. It was Monsieur Gervais.

"Marcel, before I forget," said Alexander, "I spoke to Inspector Jolicoeur yesterday, and we made an appointment for two o'clock. Please ask Louise to prepare something light — you know, sandwiches. Nothing fancy!"

"Is Elizabeth with you?"

"Elizabeth is looking forward to seeing you," said Alexander.

"I feel so guilty, I meant to call," Elizabeth yelled, hoping Monsieur Gervais would hear her.

Alexander ended the call and said, "You can fill them in tonight. All this has taken a toll on both, especially Louise. They hoped to retire as soon as possible, but the estate office wants them to stay on for the transition."

"Couldn't you hire someone else to take care of the house? There must be agencies who handle this sort of thing."

"All that is in Jack's department now. He has taken over all the estate matters from his late father."

"But you're the heir. Don't you have a say?"

"I do not inherit the house…"

"What?" Elizabeth was incredulous. She turned to look at Alexander. "Did Mr Ted decide to turn the mansion into some sort of memorial library or…"

"Ted willed it to Dr Jordan."

"Dr Jordan?" Elizabeth was shocked out of her sleepy state. She felt her cheeks flush with anger. Whenever she talked about Dr Jordan to her sisters, she referred to him as *the creep from the crypt*. "What is he going to do with it?"

"He could turn it into a clinic! Or a bordello! Who knows?"

Elizabeth noted the contrast between her own outrage and Alexander's amused detachment.

"But it's your family home! Sorry, this is none of my business."

"Jack also said that Dr Jordan sent them a copy of the new will Ted signed less than a week before his death. I was going to treat this as confidential information, but according to Marcel, the whole village is talking about it."

Elizabeth was stunned. "I wonder whether he signed it at Dr Jordan's birthday party. Zsuzsanna made sure I was kept out of the study. Mr Ted certainly did not mention it. I saw no papers…"

"Jack says that in Quebec, one can download a blank will document from a government website and as long as there are two witnesses when it's signed, it is perfectly legal."

"But Mr Ted wasn't an ordinary Joe with a thousand dollars in his RRIF. His will must be extremely complicated."

"Apparently, the new will is one page long. I don't know the details. It was witnessed by a man called Vasquez, a lawyer, and by Mako. I'm not sure."

"It makes no sense. Mr Ted was furious when he left the party. The first thing he said when he got into the car was that he never wanted to see Dr Jordan again."

"Jack says that the estate office is considering contesting the new will. It is possible that Dr Jordan is merely creating mischief and wants to be paid off. Some estates prefer to pay off nuisance claims. I hope Dr

Jordan has deep pockets. Ted's lawyers could drag him through the courts for years."

Elizabeth was taken aback when she entered the kitchen. There was a hint of a shuffle in Monsieur Gervais's walk. Madame Gervais, impeccably groomed as always, looked smaller, her face paler under her perfectly coiffed grey hair. Elizabeth and Madame Gervais cried as they hugged.

Monsieur Gervais pumped Alexander's hand for a long time — his voice was hoarse and gravelly. "I never found the work tiring before," he said. "Now, it's too much for me."

"The house is so big. So many memories! I never had any problems with sleep before, but now…" Madame Gervais sighed.

M. Gervais's beeper sounded. "Someone is at the gate."

"It's Inspector Jolicoeur," said Alexander. "We'll meet in the study."

Elizabeth made her way to her bedroom. Everything was as she left it: the blue and white wallpaper, the little pots of violets, and the bed with the floral comforter. Looking at her own reflection in the bathroom mirror, she thought, *This is only for a few days. Whatever happens at the estate does not concern you! Don't become emotionally involved. Mind your own business!*

She went down to the second floor and opened the study door. She walked in with trepidation, as if expecting to see Mr Ted sitting at his desk in his rust tweed jacket.

She recognised the smell in the room — books, brandy, and furniture polish. The image of Agnew-Simpson's body lying prone across the desk flashed into her mind. She felt her knees buckle slightly and rushed out onto the balcony. She leaned over the stone balustrade and breathed deeply. The view was magnificent — a robust and rugged beauty — it reminded her of the Group of Seven paintings.

Alexander and Inspector Jolicoeur walked into the study. Inspector Jolicoeur was dressed in jeans and a shapeless light blue jersey shirt that hung loosely over his pendulous stomach. His walrus moustache turned up as he greeted Elizabeth. "Nice to see you again, Miss Burgess. I'm on my way to a family picnic," he added, to explain his casual attire.

"You've picked a perfect day. Look at this beautiful view!"

"Yes, it is beautiful. When I get stressed by my job, I escape into the wilderness. It's become a form of therapy." Then, turning to Alexander, "I won't take up much of your time. I thought I would fill you in on the latest developments."

Elizabeth looked at Alexander questioningly, not sure whether she should stay or leave. He caught her glance and said, "Inspector, I hope you don't mind if Elizabeth stays. I hired her as my assistant."

"No problem," said the inspector.

"Madame Gervais left us a trolley of sandwiches and goodies. What about something from the bar first?"

"Thank you. I had lunch, but would you have something cold to drink?"

Alexander walked over the wall of wooden panels. As if by magic, an entire wall slid open to reveal an enormous bar that stretched halfway across the room. There were dozens of bottles — mostly vintage scotches and cognacs on glass shelves illuminated by recessed lights. Elizabeth was dazzled. She had never seen more than one of the panels opened.

The inspector's eyes were bulging. "I'm not on duty, so I can have a beer — Molson if you have it. What an impressive bar! I did not see the entire bar during our first visit." Inspector Jolicoeur approached Alexander as he poured the beer into a crystal mug. "It makes me wonder what else we missed. May I see how the wall system works?" The inspector watched in fascination as Alexander turned a small carving of a beaver. The wall began to slide shut.

"What superb craftsmanship! Who could suspect that there is a bar behind this wall?"

Alexander opened the bar again, and Inspector Jolicoeur looked closely at the bottles.

"Some of these scotches are very rare indeed," said Alexander. "And look at the cognacs! I think there is one bottle here somewhere that is more than a hundred years old." Alexander picked up a bottle of Martell Cordon Bleu. "Ted certainly knew how to pick the best."

Elizabeth admired the rows of cut crystal: glasses for highballs, for whisky, for port, for liqueur. There were wine glasses of various heights, champagne flutes, and cut crystal snifters.

"Ted loved gadgets." Alexander turned the carved beaver in the wood panelling and the door slid shut. "My mother loved crystal."

"What an impressive collection," said the inspector. "May I sit on the straight-backed chair rather than on the sofa? It's my back," he said with a slight grimace.

Elizabeth could not help wondering whether the contents of the bar would also become Dr Jordan's property. She imagined the doctor sitting at Agnew-Simpson's desk, looking at the lake and sipping a vintage cognac from one of the crystal snifters. She cringed at the image.

"Elizabeth and I just drove up from Ottawa." Alexander pulled the food trolley over to the coffee table. "We have not had lunch."

Elizabeth had no appetite. Alexander filled his plate with croissant sandwiches and sat down under the wall of photographs showing three generations of Agnew-Simpson men. There was no photograph of Alexander on the wall.

Inspector Jolicoeur placed a manila envelope on the coffee table. "My final report is not ready, but I just received the toxicology results."

"Was it a stroke?" Elizabeth blurted out without thinking.

"No. The tests show that death was caused by the ingestion of a lethal dose of barbiturates."

"Barbiturates?" Both Elizabeth and Alexander stared at Inspector Jolicoeur in disbelief.

"Barbiturates and alcohol are a lethal combination. However, we did not find any barbiturates in any medicine cabinet or anywhere in the house. The only medication was for high cholesterol, prescribed by his Montreal physician. I spoke to Dr Robichaud, and he was unaware of any condition that would require barbiturates. By the way, barbiturates are illegal in Canada."

"What about Dr Jordan?" asked Elizabeth.

"Dr Jordan claims he was not Ted's physician. He told me he would never treat Ted because they were too close — almost brothers — and doctors do not treat their own relatives."

"Was my mother prescribed barbiturates?"

"I was not involved in your mother's case, but I went back over the files this morning and found no record of that drug. We now have Mr Agnew-Simpson's cause of death, but we may never know whether it was accidental or deliberate." Inspector Jolicoeur lowered his voice. "I am not convinced that I can prove either hypothesis."

"Ted was never one to take medication. He drank scotch and cognac for stress," said Alexander with a bitter smile.

"Statistically, drug overdoses are the preferred form of suicide in North America. Marilyn Monroe died of a combination of barbiturates and alcohol. In her case, the jury is still out. Was it an accident or deliberate? As for Mr Agnew-Simpson..."

"It is difficult for me to accept his death as suicide," Alexander interrupted.

"I agree," said Elizabeth. "He seemed so enthusiastic about the publication of his book, and the telephone was off the hook. Perhaps he was calling for help."

"Inspector, did you trace that call? Who was he calling?" Alexander looked intensely at the telephone as if it could give him an answer.

"He was not calling out, he was answering a call. The call was from a telephone booth at the CN train station in downtown Montreal. Unfortunately, that's a dead end. I wish I could tell you more. My wife tells me that I have become obsessed with this case. I wake up in the middle of the night, go to the computer, read and reread my notes. There is much that does not make sense to me."

Alexander's cell phone rang. "Please excuse me. I have to take this call." He went to the balcony and leaned over the balustrade.

Wearing jeans and a shapeless shirt, Inspector Jolicoeur no longer seemed intimidating. "You know, Inspector, after I came back from Thailand last January, I was not well — I have nothing to hide — I had depression. I spent about three months on my sister's couch. I watched the *Poirot* series several times."

"You must be quite an expert in using your little grey cells, Mademoiselle Burgess," said the inspector with a smile.

"No, no, that's not what I meant," Elizabeth laughed. "But have you ruled out murder? If someone rowed across the lake and threw a stone to kill the camera over the kitchen door, and then..."

Inspector Jolicoeur smiled as one would smile at a child who makes a naïve remark. "None of the indoor surveillance cameras show an intruder. Therefore, if it was murder, the only suspects are those who were in the house. The camera shows Alexander leaving well before Mr Agnew-Simpson's time of death. Who was left? You, mademoiselle, and the

Gervais couple. Did you murder your boss?" Inspector Jolicoeur looked at Elizabeth and smiled.

"Of course not," said Elizabeth, and she blushed. *He must think I'm an idiot.*

"So it must have been the Gervaises. What was their motive? Money? But why go through all the trouble at their age? Why not just retire?"

"I certainly did not mean to accuse them! I was reminded of a *Poirot* programme about a murder in a locked room."

"Mr Agnew-Simpson's study was not locked. There were no traces of barbiturates in the bottle of Courvoisier. The barbiturates were in the snifter. Mr Agnew-Simpson must have taken the tablets himself. Or, the murderer or murderers must have put the pills into the brandy glass without Agnew-Simpson noticing! Quite a feat!"

Elizabeth was irritated by what she perceived as the inspector's condescending tone.

Alexander returned from the balcony. "Again, my apologies. A call from England."

"Miss Burgess and I were discussing murder theories. I cannot figure out where he kept the barbiturates. We checked and double-checked the bedroom and the bathrooms. With your permission, I will send forensics to check the bar."

Then, leaving his glass of beer on the coffee table, Inspector Jolicoeur walked over to the desk and sat down. "I am Mr Agnew-Simpson. The telephone rings. I pick it up. Did someone call after I took the barbiturates? Before? If I took the barbiturates during the phone call, the pills must have been in… my coat pocket? A desk drawer? We turned the desk upside down. We found nothing. But now that I have seen the bar, can I assume that there are secret compartments in the desk, too?"

For the next few minutes, Inspector Jolicoeur and Alexander examined the desk, looking for secret drawers.

"The pills could have been stored in a pen," said Elizabeth, recalling an old movie.

They unscrewed all the pens on the desk and found nothing. Inspector Jolicoeur then inspected the carved beaver that opened the sliding bar. He came back to the desk and manipulated a similar carving. A hidden drawer slid open. There was nothing in it.

"I'll call our forensic experts," said Inspector Jolicoeur. "Perhaps they will find traces of barbiturates in this drawer."

Before he left, the inspector asked Elizabeth and Alexander to keep this information confidential. "There have been too many leaks and false rumours."

That evening, Elizabeth and Alexander ate supper in the kitchen. Elizabeth went down early to help as *sous-chef*. Her job was to place ice cubes in glass bowls of creamy *vichyssoise soup* and to tell Madame Gervais about her new life in Ottawa. Monsieur Gervais and Alexander walked in, discussing the logistics of moving Alexander's belongings. Alexander opened a chilled bottle of *Pouilly-Fuissé*. Madame Gervais was serving lake trout. They sat down to supper as a family. Madame Gervais peppered Alexander with questions about his new condo and offered to keep him stocked with his favourite foods.

"Louise, I will expect Federal Express deliveries of your quiches and *tourtière*," he joked.

Elizabeth listened to the easy banter of people who had known each other all their lives. *Alexander is like a son to them. And why wouldn't a poor little rich boy get attached to the staff? Father was distant and mean. Mother — loving but fragile.*

At the end of the meal, Madame Gervais reached across the table and patted Elizabeth's hand. "Everyone is gone. I don't feel safe here any more. Marcel, tell them about Dr Jordan. That man has the manners of a bulldozer."

"Dr Jordan called me several times and asked to visit the house. I suppose he is already making plans to turn it into some sort of convalescent home for his patients."

"And with Mr Ted not yet buried!" said Madame Gervais. "I don't believe that Mr Ted left him this house in his will. I just don't believe it."

Monsieur Gervais's cheeks turned pink. "I told Dr Jordan that I would not let him in unless I got express instructions from Alexander. Dr Jordan objected; he even raised his voice."

"That man has no shame!"

Alexander sat with his lips pressed firmly together.

"If Dr Jordan calls again, tell him that you take instructions only from the estate office. Give him Jack McDougall's number."

At the end of supper, Elizabeth felt very tired. The wine and the sleepless night had taken their toll. She skipped dessert, excused herself, and went upstairs. The day's events distracted her from the memories of Stephen. She was surprised to realise she hadn't thought about him all day!

Chapter 21

The kitchen smelled of croissants and coffee. Monsieur and Madame Gervais, wearing their Sunday best, were ready to leave for church.

"Has Alexander been down for breakfast yet?" asked Elizabeth.

"He's gone to Montreal," said Monsieur Gervais.

"You went to bed early, so he did not get a chance to tell you. Alexander got a call from a friend who will be passing through Montreal airport. He left at the crack of dawn."

"When is he coming back?"

"Today, although he didn't quite say."

They invited Elizabeth to come to town with them. No, Elizabeth would not change her mind. No, she lied, she was not afraid to stay in the house alone. She did not tell them about her irrational fear that Dr Jordan would crash his Aston Martin through the gate. Elizabeth was irritated that Alexander left without telling her. *Let's face it, Lizzie, just as you were warming to him, he treats you like hired help.*

Pouring herself a mug of coffee, Elizabeth sat by the picture window and looked out at the lake. It was a sad, dreary day. With no wind, the lake looked like a greasy mirror. She knew this view by heart: a steep rock face plunged straight into the water on the right. An anaemic pine tree that clung precariously to the slope. On the opposite bank, a pine forest descending to a shoreline strewn with boulders. The sky reflected varying shades of grey with intermittent blue patches, as if it could not make up its mind about what kind of day this would be.

She left the kitchen and crossed the vestibule to the ticking of the antique clock. She rode the elevator to the second floor and walked up to Mathilde's boudoir, conscious of every creak of the stairs. *Come on, Lizzie, let's not go all wobbly. The alarm is on.*

Mathilde's sitting room looked the same: white lacquered furniture and a pink chaise longue strewn with frilly pillows. She found the letters from Hassan in *La Princesse de Clèves*, untied the pink ribbon and laid them on the desk. There were six letters. She had read only the first four. The fifth letter was postmarked Casablanca, Morocco, 1977, the year Alexander was born. Elizabeth began to read:

My Life! My Soul!

I do not know how I will survive this summer without you. I cannot wait to return to university. I promised myself that I would never leave you again. I know you will ask me how I will perform this miracle. It pains me to admit that I am so dependent on my parents that I cannot even afford the price of an airline ticket. I plan to convince my father to let me stay and work in Montreal after the winter semester. He has contacts in Montreal, and perhaps he can help me find work in an accounting company. How can he be against my acquiring Canadian experience, so essential to my future career?

I have still not spoken to my parents about you. Just as your family, they are against my marrying outside my religion. My mother is kindness itself, and I know she can only want her son to be happy. I will find the right time to speak to her after she recovers from her illness. I do not doubt that she will love you when she meets you.

If only I could soar to you on a magic carpet or find a friendly dolphin who will carry me across the ocean. My beloved, know that as long as my heart keeps beating, even though you are not in my sight, you are in my heart. Even though I am silent, I am yours forever.

Hassan

Elizabeth stopped reading and tried to think of ways Hassan could have returned to Montreal. He could have stowed away on a cargo ship or... *Enough fantasies, Lizzie. What could a penniless, twenty-two-year-old student offer Mathilde?* She picked up the last letter, written a month after the one she had just read.

My treasure!

I love you too much to keep silent about the calamity that has befallen us. My eyes are full of tears as I write this. My beloved, I feel the pain I am causing you and my heart breaks.

My father found one of your letters and will not allow me to return to university next autumn. I begged, I cried — all to no avail. I locked myself in my room for two weeks. Every evening my father sat outside the bedroom door and talked to me. He said that he took no pleasure in interfering in my emotional life. However, as an older man, he claims to know that love is fleeting and that this period of darkness shall pass. He believes that we will both find happiness with spouses who share our respective religions and culture. I refuse to believe him. I will never stop loving you!

I cannot tell my mother about you because only now do I understand the severity of her illness. She will go abroad for treatment soon. She has asked me to accompany her.

I respect you too much to give you false hope. I wanted to tell you that I will find a way to be together; that perhaps in a few years after I graduate and become independent... Instilling such hopes would be dishonourable. I have no desire to tie you down. I can only promise you my eternal love.

Hassan

Elizabeth felt her eyes well up as she finished the letter. Her first impulse was to blame Hassan for not standing up to his father. But at least Hassan had the courage to tell the truth. It is no small feat for a young man to swallow his pride and admit to helplessness. She remembered Stephen and his lies. Stephen! What a spineless coward.

Elizabeth leaned back into the pink armchair. Was Mathilde pregnant when she read the last letter? Is that why she consented to marry Agnew-Simpson? What could Hassan have done had he known about the pregnancy? Nothing! If only a magic carpet could fly him across the ocean. But real life is no fairy tale.

Another girl may have sought an abortion. Elizabeth recalled reading that abortions, although illegal in Canada at the time, were not infrequent. Some girls disappeared for months to homes run by nuns. The babies were then adopted. In Mathilde's case, she was persuaded to marry a man she did not love to shield her devoutly Catholic family from scandal.

Was Mathilde even aware of how deeply Agnew-Simpson was wounded, once he realised he had been tricked? What about Mathilde? Did she understand what it meant to be in a loveless marriage? Elizabeth concluded that Mathilde's ill-fated love affair resulted in what Alexander called her 'fragility': the anxiety, insomnia and perhaps even sleepwalking.

Elizabeth pictured the portrait of the saintly Mathilde in the drawing room. The artist did not discern the pain behind her innocent blue eyes. He painted a generic portrait of a vacuous young woman — a Dorian Gray in reverse — and hid Mathilde's tortured soul behind the glossy veneer.

What about Hassan? How did his life turn out? Did Daddy really know best? Did Hassan embark on an illustrious career? Was he happily married with a brood of beautiful children? Did Hassan finally come to the conclusion that his wise old father was right? Elizabeth had a dim recollection of reading that the suppression of immediate gratification to achieve long-term interests was a measure of maturity. She wondered whether Hassan's mature decision brought him personal happiness. Then she remembered the euphoria of being in love with Stephen — the utter joy, the feeling that nothing else mattered. At that time, love controlled her completely and she could not even imagine life without Stephen. *But I can live without him now. So does this mean that Hassan's father was right?*

For some inexplicable reason, she recalled reading something from Freud in college. Once the pleasure principle is satisfied, it turns into mild contentment. Is that what happened to Stephen? His love for her faded, and addicted to intense pleasure, he found another high with Rajimi? She also remembered the pain of his betrayal and the deep depression that followed.

Elizabeth was roused from her thoughts when the porcelain clock chimed eleven. She looked down at the letters, the detritus of Mathilde's emotional life, and wondered how she would drop this bombshell on Alexander. She would accompany Alexander to the boudoir, show him the letters and leave. She would also have to think of something to say to prepare him for the shock.

Elizabeth heard faint voices coming from the lake. She could not see the entire lake from her vantage point and ran to Agnew-Simpson's study. She opened the glass door to the balcony and recognised Dr Jordan's voice. She felt her diaphragm constrict. Getting down on all fours, she crawled to the edge of the balustrade, pressing her body against the cold stone. *Am I ever a wimp! What can he do to me?* At that very moment, she heard Zsuzsanna's shrill voice.

"Yoo-hoo, Elizabeth! Yoo-hoo! What are you doing on your hands and knees? Have you lost an earring?"

Feeling ridiculous, Elizabeth stood up.

Zsuzsanna, feet bare, was carrying her high-heeled sandals in one hand and an oversized straw handbag in the other. She wore a striped, navy blue and white knitted top and navy slacks. A jaunty white sailor's cap balanced precariously on her lacquered blonde chignon.

Dr Jordan was tying the rowboat at the pier. He was dressed in black jeans and a long-sleeved black T-shirt. A black captain's cap covered his tar-black hair. Zsuzsanna waved furiously, and her full red lips stretched into a wide smile.

"I did not expect to see you here," said Zsuzsanna, and she craned her neck to look up at Elizabeth. "Please tell Alexander we are here."

"Alexander is in Montreal," Elizabeth shouted down to the lawn below.

Zsuzsanna turned to face Dr Jordan, who was walking up from the dock. "Tig, Elizabeth says that Alexander is not at home."

"What do you mean, not home? Where is he?"

"He drove off to Montreal early this morning; I'm not sure when he will be back."

"I'm sure he will be back soon. He did invite us. So lovely to see you again, Elizabeth."

"I have no idea when Alexander is coming back."

"Does he always inform you of his comings and goings? Where is Marcel?"

"In church."

"So they should be back at any moment."

"No, they usually have a big lunch with Madame Gervais's sister."

"Look, Elizabeth, I am developing a crick in my neck," said Dr Jordan. "We will wait for Alexander inside. I am so thirsty. You could at least offer us a glass of water. Come to think of it, I hope the champagne is still in the wine cooler in the bar. A glass of champagne on a Sunday morning?" He turned to Zsuzsanna.

"Oh, what could be more *civilisé*?" Zsuzsanna giggled, and began to walk towards the kitchen door.

"Monsieur Gervais told me not to let anyone in," said Elizabeth. "This is not my house and…"

"My appointment is with Alexander, not with Marcel."

"I'm sorry, Dr Jordan. I will have to check with Alexander," said Elizabeth, and she ran into the study.

Alexander did not pick up. She dialled Madame Gervais's sister's number. After six rings, no answer. She returned to the balcony. Dr Jordan looked irritated as he sat at the patio table. Zsuzsanna was whispering something into his ear.

Elizabeth composed herself and tried to look confident as she said, "Unfortunately, I could not reach anyone."

Dr Jordan got up and approached the balcony. "Elizabeth, we are all adults. Why can't I wait for Alexander in the study? What are you afraid of? Do you think I will abscond with the silverware?"

Zsuzsanna, her high-heeled sandals sinking into the grass as she came closer to the balcony, said, "My dear, the last time I was in the study, I lost an earring. It is very precious to me — belonged to my grandmother. Could you please let us in so I can look for it?"

"I will tell Madame Gervais."

"This is ridiculous! Would I be standing here if Alexander did not invite me?" asked Dr Jordan in a steely voice. "I spoke to Marcel. I would not be surprised if he did not transmit the message." Then, addressing Zsuzsanna, he said, "Marcel is a dangerous man! I know that he spreads all kinds of rumours about me. The latest gossip in the village is that I already hired a fleet of trucks to take away the valuables."

"I heard that you are planning to turn the mansion into a casino!" said Zsuzsanna.

Dr Jordan let out a guttural laugh. "Fools! Only stunted, envious minds could come up with this nonsense! Why can't they believe that I have humanitarian aims, that this will be a home for troubled young people? At some point, I will have to seriously consider suing for slander."

"I will try calling Alexander again." Elizabeth disappeared into the study. This time, Alexander answered, and Elizabeth began to talk at a breakneck speed.

"First of all, calm down," said Alexander. "Tell Dr Jordan that I will call him. Tell him there must have been some misunderstanding, and I will call him tomorrow." Alexander's voice did not betray any emotion.

"I will not open the door. When will you be back?"

"My friends' flight has been delayed. I will call you once the plane takes off."

"What if Dr Jordan insists on coming in?"

"He won't. Let's not blow this out of proportion. I didn't realise how much Dr Jordan frightens you."

Elizabeth returned to the balcony. "I just talked to Alexander — he says there must have been some misunderstanding. He will call you tomorrow when he gets back."

"A misunderstanding I can understand," said Dr Jordan. "But I am surprised at your attitude, Elizabeth! Such hostility! You treat me as if I am some intruder!"

Elizabeth retreated to the study and watched as Dr Jordan and Zsuzsanna rowed away.

She went to her room as soon as Dr Jordan left, took aspirin and went to bed. Her head was throbbing. The Gervaises returned at five in the evening. At six thirty, Elizabeth went down for supper. On Sundays, Madame Gervais usually heated up a casserole. Elizabeth noticed that they both looked very sad and very tired.

Monsieur Gervais poured himself a beer and said, "Suddenly, the whole family thinks we are millionaires. Yes, we will get a pension from a fund set up by Mr Ted. It's only fair — we served the family all our lives. And Alexander said that there is a bequest for us in the will."

"I hope it's enough to travel. Take a cruise, see the world!" said Elizabeth.

"Well, that's not what our relatives have planned for us," replied Monsieur Gervais. "Bernadette's children, her daughter Joselyn, the one who works at the Super C, wants us to open a restaurant so that she and her family can work there — as partners."

"They all have ideas how best to invest our money," said Madame Gervais. "Ideas galore — bed and breakfast, a pizza franchise, a daycare centre. They are all fighting each other to get their hands on our money. I am so tired!" Madame Gervais sighed deeply. "I just want peace and quiet."

"The only place that I want to see is Florida," said Monsieur Gervais. "I have never seen the ocean. And I would like to pick an orange from a tree and eat it."

"That sounds lovely!"

Leaving, Elizabeth kissed them both on the forehead. Inheritances, large or small, triggered human greed. Elizabeth did not tell them about Dr Jordan's visit. No need to upset them further.

Chapter 22

On Monday morning, Elizabeth found Monsieur Gervais in the kitchen, sitting alone at the oak table. His head was bowed low, and the corners of his mouth were turned down. She was about to say "a penny for your thoughts", but decided not to disturb him.

"Why didn't you tell us that Dr Jordan and that girlfriend of his tried to break into the house yesterday?" His tone was cold, almost hostile.

Elizabeth was going to reply with a cheerful, "And a good morning to you, too," but seeing a flash of anger in his eyes, she said, "Both you and Madame Gervais looked so tired and upset that I decided to wait till this morning."

Monsieur Gervais, his jaw clenched tight, turned away from Elizabeth to stare out the window.

"Dr Jordan said that Alexander invited him to come on Sunday morning. In fact, he said you passed on Alexander's message!"

"What?" shouted Monsieur Gervais, his cheeks turning bright pink. "I said no such thing!"

"I called Bernadette's number, but you were all still in church, so when I finally reached Alexander, he told me to say it was a misunderstanding. Dr Jordan got very angry, but I'm proud of myself. I stood up to him!"

Monsieur Gervais's face softened. "I am sorry I was not there to protect you from that demon."

"I admit that Dr Jordan frightens me, but I did not let him bully me!" Elizabeth sat down. Monsieur Gervais took her hand, squeezed it and said, "Dr Jordan is a dangerous man. Be very careful with him, Elizabeth!"

"He reminds me of Dracula from the old horror movies."

"That man has blood on his hands."

Neither Elizabeth nor Monsieur Gervais heard Alexander walk in. "Marcel, and who do you think Dr Jordan killed, apart from the odd patient?"

Monsieur Gervais did not smile at Alexander's joke. "I never told you this before, but I am sure that Dr Jordan is somehow responsible for your mother's death!"

Alexander sat down on the bench next to Monsieur Gervais and put his arm around his shoulder. "Marcel, I know that you loved my mother, but according to the police…"

"The police!" Monsieur Gervais's face became distorted with derision. "I don't know how, but he did it! Maybe he gave her hallucinogenic drugs, or…"

"Come on, Marcel!" Alexander's voice was soothing.

"I know one should not speak ill of the dead, but Mr Ted, he's responsible, too!"

Elizabeth felt her mouth drop.

"I never told anyone about what happened after Louise found Mathilde at the bottom of the stairs," Monsieur Gervais whispered. "Her eyes were open, but we couldn't wake her. I went back to the kitchen to call an ambulance. Then I thought that I should first tell Mr Ted. I went up to his bedroom. At the top of the stairs, I found Mr Ted's paisley robe and picked it up. Mr Ted was in his pyjamas, sitting on the floor in the corner of his bedroom, clutching his knees. He was babbling, his mouth was drooling. He kept repeating, 'It wasn't my fault! It wasn't my fault!' I couldn't get him back into bed, so I went to wake up Dr Jordan in the guest bedroom. That night, Dr Jordan brought Mathilde back from his clinic. She was there for a week. They all had dinner together in the study. When Mathilde went to bed, the men stayed up. Dr Jordan usually sleeps here when he has had too much to drink."

"What did Dr Jordan say when he saw my mother?"

"Dr Jordan looked devastated. He took Mathilde's pulse, then he shut her eyes. He said that although he was no forensic expert, in his opinion, Mathilde broke her neck as a result of the fall. Then we both went into Ted's bedroom. Mr Ted was still on the floor. He was shaking and repeating, 'It wasn't my fault. It was an accident. It was an accident.' Dr Jordan took one look at Ted and went to get his medical bag. Ted looked so pathetic that I took him in my arms and rocked him like a baby. That's when Ted started to cry and told me that he woke up in the early hours of the morning and saw Mathilde standing over his bed with a knife. He could not wrest the knife away from her. She seemed to have superhuman strength. He draped his robe over her shoulders and somehow managed to drag her down the hall. As they were passing the stairs, she attacked him with the knife. He pushed her away, and she fell down the stairs. As God is my witness, that is what Mr Ted told me. Then Dr Jordan came back and gave him an injection of some kind."

"Who called the ambulance?" asked Alexander.

"Dr Jordan called. The ambulance people called the medical examiner. They said that according to their protocols, the police were obliged to investigate. Dr Jordan told me to keep quiet about Ted's state of mind. He told me to say that Ted became so distraught that he had to be sedated. The police interviewed Ted only the next day, after they spoke to Dr Jordan. Ted was calmer by that time. Dr Jordan had given him more sedatives or something."

"What was Mother doing walking around at night?" asked Alexander, as he got up to pour himself more coffee.

"Did you not know that your mother was a sleepwalker?"

"Are you serious?"

"Yes, that's why Mr Ted installed surveillance cameras and alarms. One night, he looked out from his study window and saw her standing at the end of the dock. He woke me up, and we ran to her. Her eyes were open, and she told us she wanted to take a swim. After that, she began to visit Dr Jordan's clinic on a regular basis."

"I read about that incident," said Elizabeth. "Somebody who was probably in the house across the lake saw her on the dock and told a tabloid reporter. The reporter wrote that she was naked and that the witness heard a wolf howl. I thought it was nonsense. She must have been sleepwalking when she came into Mr Ted's room that night."

"This certainly puts a different slant on things," said Alexander. "Why didn't you tell me this before, Marcel? You did see me at the funeral."

"Because Dr Jordan said that if I told this to anyone, Ted could be accused of murder and Louise and I would go to jail for perjury!"

"Marcel, if you and Louise can be accused of suppressing information, so can Dr Jordan…"

"It doesn't matter any more. Mr Ted is dead. Yesterday, when you said that the police believe that Ted committed suicide, it all clicked. He killed himself because of his guilty conscience. Now I see why he left Dr Jordan this house. Dr Jordan was probably blackmailing him by threatening to tell the police that Ted pushed poor Madame Mathilde down the stairs."

"Marcel, I can't believe that Ted would harm my mother intentionally."

"He was often cruel to her," said Monsieur Gervais.

"Cruel, yes, but murder!"

Madame Gervais walked into the kitchen with a laundry basket full of wet towels. She took one look at her husband and said, "What is the matter with you, Marcel?"

"He is all right," said Alexander. "I really need Marcel today." Without uttering a word, they had decided to keep this conversation from Madame Gervais. There was no need to upset her.

"Marcel, bring cardboard boxes. I'll need you to help me pack and decide what to take to Ottawa."

"Is this really happening?" asked Madame Gervais in a quivering voice. "Last night I said I was eager to leave this house, but suddenly…"

"Have you ever heard the expression 'When one door closes, another opens'? You are about to start a new phase in your life, Louise. You will be free to travel, to see the world," said Alexander.

"All I want is peace and quiet," said Madame Gervais, as she walked outside with the laundry basket.

Alexander turned towards Elizabeth. "I spoke to Ted's publisher. Can you organise the manuscript materials and send them copies of Ted's electronic files?"

"What about the portraits?" asked Monsieur Gervais.

"I'll take my mother's portrait and a few personal things," said Alexander. "As far as the portraits in the study and all of Ted's other photographs, I'm sure the recipients of Ted's endowments will find suitable locations. I told the executors that I will definitely pilfer the library for books to add to my own collection."

Elizabeth realised that before Mathilde's diaries and personal effects were packed, she should warn Alexander about the probable emotional impact of Hassan's letters. "Alexander, could you please come to your mother's boudoir. I have something to show you."

"Sure," said Alexander, and he followed Elizabeth down the hall. As they were about to go in, Monsieur Gervais shouted down the corridor, "Show me what I need to pack. How many boxes will I need?"

"Elizabeth, can we do this later? I should organise Marcel first. Continue working on the history stuff."

"I placed some letters on top of the diaries on your mother's desk — the really private ones inside the *Princesse des Clèves* box. They could be…"

"Later," Alexander interrupted, and he walked briskly down the corridor towards Monsieur Gervais.

Elizabeth and Alexander did not meet again that morning. Everyone worked in different parts of the house. Elizabeth ate her baguette with pâté and cheese on the patio, then decided on a short canoe ride to clear her head. She could not stop agonising about whether Mathilde's death was an accident or Ted had pushed her deliberately. She remembered Madame Gervais's words on her first day at the mansion. Mathilde's fall was 'an accident — a horrible accident'. Elizabeth concluded that Madame Gervais was probably right.

Elizabeth continued to work in the study. She heard Alexander and Monsieur Gervais load the trolley outside Alexander's room. Then it became quiet. Elizabeth sat on the maroon love seat, stacking multi-coloured folders on the coffee table. Suddenly, the room became darker. Elizabeth looked out the window and saw a black cloud hide the sun. She did not hear Alexander walk into the room.

He sank into the love seat across from Elizabeth and leaned back into the maroon leather. Was it the light, or did his face look much darker? He closed his eyes and pressed his lips together. Elizabeth froze. Obviously, he had just read Hassan's letters. Elizabeth continued sorting. She placed a red folder on top of the pile closest to Alexander. He opened his eyes and swept the folders to the floor with the back of his hand. Elizabeth gasped. In the very next moment, Alexander was down on his knees, collecting the papers.

"I apologise," he said. "That was inexcusable." Then he got up and pushed open the bar and poured himself two fingers of scotch. "Can I get you something?"

"Sure, I'd love a beer."

Alexander poured a Heineken for Elizabeth and sat down.

Elizabeth said, "I was going to tell you about the letters. I should have prepared you for the shock."

"There is a lot to take in."

"I know."

They continued to sit in silence. Alexander finished his scotch and went back to pour himself another. "As a child, my mother told me that the Beaudry family have Indian blood and that one of my ancestors was a *coureur de bois* who married an Indian princess. I loved that story. I imagined my Iroquois great-great-grandfather hunting in the forest or fighting with his tomahawk. In my imagination, I saw myself fighting by his side." Alexander let out a deep sigh. "Should I now imagine my ancestor as an Arab sheik galloping on a steed, waving a scimitar?"

Elizabeth, her body rigid, sat and watched him.

Outwardly, Alexander remained calm. He did not look at her, preferring to focus on the whisky in his glass. Then he said, "I finally understand what Ted was saying during our last conversation."

"That's when you stormed out and drove to Ottawa?"

"Yes. That night, Ted was expecting his lawyer, Mortimer McDougall, for dinner. But McDougall had a heart attack. Perhaps he wanted the lawyer as a witness. Ted was really very drunk and kept repeating that he had my DNA as proof. I thought it was proof of my Indian blood. I misunderstood! He was telling me that I was not his biological son! He said I should change my name to Beaudry. Then he called my mother a slut. I stormed out. I resolved never to see him again."

"What do you know about how your parents got married?" Elizabeth asked.

"Not much. Come to think of it, I have never even seen any wedding photos. Mother never talked about it. All I knew was that she was a sad and unhappy woman. Poor, poor maman!"

"Alexander, after you drove off, I spent about an hour with Mr Ted. It was horrible. He fired me. He accused me of being a gold digger who was trying to seduce both of you. He actually told me that he had at one time considered marrying me because I am of child-bearing age."

Alexander took a deep breath and exhaled. Then he drained the whisky from his glass.

Elizabeth continued to tell Alexander the rest of her conversation with Mr Ted. "Mr Agnew-Simpson also told me that he always loved your mother. He told me that he wrote her a marriage proposal in verse. He believed that Madame Beaudry, your grandmother, tricked him into the marriage. He also told me that his own father was dead against it. To get his blessing, Mr Ted had to make one promise — he had to promise to remain faithful to his marriage vows. He was very proud of himself for keeping his word."

"Too bad. I would have preferred that he reneged on the promise and divorced my mother."

"Ted once told me that he was a man of honour, who took full responsibility for every decision he made. I guess after your mother died, he was free of his vow, and maybe, he tried to get some sort of perverse revenge through you. We are always taught to keep our word, to abide by vows. In this case, I think everybody would have been happier if Mr Ted broke his marriage vows or if Mathilde got a..." Elizabeth choked on the last word.

"Were you going to say, got an abortion," said Alexander with a wry smile.

"Your grandmother probably assumed that Mathilde would grow into the marriage and that Ted, who adored Mathilde, would accept the child as his own. That would have been a happy ending. Madame Beaudry and Hassan's father had much in common. Love is fleeting, while marriage is about family, security and respectability."

"I would like to find Hassan," said Alexander.

"Without a surname?"

"How many Hassans were studying at the University of Montreal in 1976 to '77? I will hire an investigator and see what he finds."

"My father abandoned my mother with three small children when I was a baby. My father is living somewhere in the Maritimes, but I have no desire to find him."

They continued to sit in silence as the sky outside grew darker.

"Elizabeth, I will call Louise and tell her to send my supper to my room on a tray. I am not in a very sociable mood tonight," said Alexander, and he walked out of the study.

Elizabeth sat, looking at the files on the coffee table. *I want to go home! I've had enough.*

Chapter 23

Elizabeth spent most of Tuesday morning in the first-floor library, copying Agnew-Simpson's manuscript onto electronic files. She brought her work to the study, where Alexander was seated at Agnew-Simpson's desk, sorting papers. The floor around Alexander was littered with stacks of files and papers.

"I promised the publisher I'd sort as much of the book-related stuff as I could," said Alexander. "The estate office hired the Gervais couple for the transition."

"Alexander, I know you invited Dr Jordan tonight. Do I have to be here?"

"Having a witness wouldn't hurt. Unless, of course, you mind terribly."

"What does he want?"

"Probably something about the will." Alexander continued to sort files. "Dr Jordan was Ted's lifelong friend, so I do want to be civil to him."

At five thirty, Elizabeth heard Dr Jordan's Aston Martin drive up to the front door. When she went down to the study, she found Dr Jordan on the balcony, leaning over the balustrade. Alexander stood next to him, ramrod straight.

"Elizabeth, my dear..."

A wave of revulsion swept over Elizabeth, and she could not even fake a smile.

"You seem so afraid of me! I'm quite harmless, I assure you." Dr Jordan took her hand and brought it to his cold lips. Elizabeth felt a frisson of disgust, as if her hand had been licked by a cold, slimy lizard. "Alexander, this young lady did not even let me into the house last Sunday! Treated poor old Zsuzsanna and me as if we were highway robbers!"

"What can I get you, Tig?" asked Alexander.

"Scotch — lots of ice."

Alexander looked at Elizabeth. "Sherry," she said.

"My dear." Dr Jordan took Elizabeth's elbow to guide her inside. "I don't understand. Why this hostility?"

"On the ride home from your birthday party, Mr Ted said that he never wanted to see you again."

"Is that all?" asked Dr Jordan with a shrug. "Ted and I did have disagreements from time to time. The mutual sulking usually never lasted more than a week." Dr Jordan let out a deep sigh and placed two fingers under his tinted glasses, as if to wipe away a tear. He took Elizabeth's elbow to guide her towards the love seat corner, where Alexander had placed their drinks on the coffee table.

"How many evenings of my life did I spend in this room?" Dr Jordan turned to take in every corner. He sat down on the love seat under the wall that just yesterday had displayed photographs of three generations of Agnew-Simpsons. Alexander's image was conspicuously absent.

"I see the photographs are gone, but their lives are immortalised thanks to Ted's history book." He raised his glass. "To Ted! Eternal memory!" Then he glanced at his watch. "You will excuse me if I come straight to the point. I came here to talk about a private matter." He looked questioningly at Elizabeth. "It's about Ted's will."

"Elizabeth is my personal assistant. You can speak freely."

"The whole village knows about the will," said Elizabeth, and she realised that she had overstepped the bounds of propriety.

Alexander put down his drink and looked at Elizabeth with surprise.

Dr Jordan's black eyebrow shot up over his tinted glasses. "You are extremely well informed, my dear." His syrupy tone became icy as he stared directly at Elizabeth. "Well, since we are all being so frank, may I ask whether you have an expectation to be remembered in Ted's will? Ted told me that he was very satisfied with your... services."

Elizabeth's face turned crimson as she registered the double entendre. She turned to Alexander, but his expression was inscrutable as always.

Elizabeth did not answer the question, but said, "Why was Mr Ted so upset when he left your birthday party? On the ride home, Mr Ted did not behave as if he had just made you the beneficiary of his will. And he called that Señor Vasquez a gangster in a pin-striped suit!" Elizabeth's voice was overly agitated.

"Ah, Señor Vasquez! He's a lawyer, based in Miami. The Quebec government provides such lucrative tax incentives in the Mont Tremblant region that the expansion of my Wellness Centre has attracted international interest. And as everyone in the village knows" — he looked point-blank at Elizabeth — "I am in dire need of investors."

"But why did Mr Ted call Vasquez a gangster, and why was Mr Ted so upset when he left your party?" She realised that it was not her place to interrogate Dr Jordan in such a brazen tone. She did notice that Alexander looked at her with consternation.

"My, my, but we are curious!" Dr Jordan seemed more amused than offended. "Let me clear the air. It was all an unfortunate misunderstanding. Señor Vasquez's English leaves much to be desired, and Ted got the impression that I presented him as the largest investor in my Wellness Centre. I did not, and Señor Vasquez certainly did not form that impression! Ted over-reacted — he does that when he has one too many. With absolutely no basis, he accused Señor Vasquez of being involved with the Columbian cartels. I became very angry. After all, Ted had embarrassed my guest, in my home!"

"Why did this Vasquez witness the will?" asked Elizabeth. She could not control the belligerence in her voice.

Dr Jordan seemed not to notice. His voice was soothing. "Ted and I prepared the will some months ago. Ted signed it that night. Since Señor Vasquez happened to be at my party, I asked him to witness the new will. And when Mako walked in with the *hors d'oeuvre*, he inadvertently became the second witness. Mystery solved!"

Alexander looked at Elizabeth. "I can certainly see this."

Dr Jordan continued, "I have nothing to hide. Ted forgave my prior debts, he willed me this mansion, and he left me ten million dollars from his estate." Dr Jordan turned to Alexander. "I hope that these generous bequests have not cut too deeply into your legacy. I do know that Ted was a multi-millionaire, so I assume there is more than enough for both of us."

"I have absolutely no interest in Ted's legacy. In fact, I know nothing of Ted's finances or the provisions in his will."

Dr Jordan leaned forward. His body was still for a moment. "Does this mean that you will not contest? What about this house? You must be attached…"

"No, I do not plan to contest any part of the will." Alexander spoke in a firm, cold voice.

Dr Jordan, stunned, collapsed onto the back of the love seat. He recovered quickly and said, "Thank you! My patients thank you. I will name this rehabilitation centre in honour of your late mother. I treated her, too, you know. Such a lovely woman." Dr Jordan suddenly stopped talking, overcome by emotion.

Alexander looked very uncomfortable. He pushed the tray of canapés towards Dr Jordan. "May I suggest the salmon pâté? Louise makes it herself."

Dr Jordan picked up the canapé, put it on a napkin, then placed the napkin on the coffee table.

"May I refresh your drink?" asked Alexander.

"I have to get back. I need to talk to Mako." Dr Jordan rose to leave. "That young man is the bane of my existence!" Dr Jordan shook Alexander's hand. "I thank you from the bottom of my heart!"

Why can't I buy any of his Mr Nice-guy routine? He is such a phony! Can't Alexander see it?

Turning towards Elizabeth, Dr Jordan said, "I am so very, very sorry that my pride prevented me from calling Ted after the party. I will regret it until the end of my days."

Dr Jordan was about to kiss Elizabeth's hand, but she pulled her hand back abruptly. "Good night, Dr Jordan," she said, and walked away.

"Dr Jordan. I will walk you to your car." Alexander took him by the arm and they both left the study.

Elizabeth, left alone, asked herself whether her intense dislike of Dr Jordan coloured her conclusions about his motives. *Why can't I accept his version of what happened in the study the night of the birthday party?*

Alexander returned, and without a word, he poured himself another scotch and more sherry for Elizabeth. "Why were you rude to Dr Jordan?" To her relief, his tone was neutral.

"I am very sorry I embarrassed you. I don't know what came over me. It's just that I have this gut feeling that Dr Jordan is evil."

"A gut feeling! Do you actually believe that Ted could be coerced into doing what he didn't want to do? Let alone sign a will?"

"All I know is that Dr Jordan is a liar and that he insulted me."

"How did he insult you?"

Elizabeth thought she perceived a condescending tone. "He said that Mr Ted was very satisfied with my services. Did you not hear the double entendre?"

"No. Why can't you accept the statement at face value? Ted was satisfied with your work! That is all he meant. Elizabeth, you are overly sensitive. Don't be. You are hurting yourself."

"I am very, very sorry. I will make a point of keeping my mouth shut. In any case, I will probably never see Dr Jordan again."

"It's our last night here, and Louise made her *pièce de résistance* — *Canard à l'orange*." Alexander took the tray of uneaten canapés, and they left the study.

"Didn't Dr Jordan like my food?" asked Madame Gervais.

"Dr Jordan had to rush off to talk to Mako," said Alexander.

"That Mako is dangerous!" said Monsieur Gervais. "I hear he's been bragging about selling information to some tabloid! He claims he can unmask Mr Ted's murderer and earn lots of money!"

"Marcel! Please! No village gossip tonight!" said Madame Gervais. "I don't want you to ruin everybody's appetite. Alexander, did you know, Bernadette tells me that my family is distantly related to Madame Jolicoeur. Her name is Jeanine. Apparently, she is not quite five foot tall. It always amazes me that tall men marry tiny women."

"And these tiny women usually terrorise their husbands," said Monsieur Gervais, and he winked at Alexander. "Do they live in St Agathe?"

"Not in the village itself — on the road to Gerard's farm. We've passed it many times; it's the house with all those painted dwarfs. Bernadette says that Madame Jolicoeur knits or crochets all day. The house is full of handmade doilies, tablecloths, even curtains."

"I noticed that the inspector wears hand-knitted ties," Elizabeth added.

"It always amazes me," said Alexander with a smile, "that in the country, everyone knows everything about everyone. Oh, yes, Inspector Jolicoeur promised to call me when his final report is ready."

They all savoured the duck, and Madame Gervais received many compliments. Alexander also made her happy by recalling past Christmas parties when the house was full of Beaudry relatives.

"We used to decorate the vestibule with wreaths and garlands. We had music and dancing. I loved the sound of children's laughter all through the house." Madame Gervais took out her handkerchief.

"And I used to cut down such a huge tree," said Monsieur Gervais.

"We will always have those memories," said Alexander.

The following morning was full of frenetic activity. Alexander and Monsieur Gervais packed and repacked Alexander's car. Some boxes were destined to be shipped to his Carleton office, some to his condo. Another pile of boxes, for the publisher of Agnew-Simpson's books, would be sent separately.

"You will have to come back," said Monsieur Gervais. "I haven't even started with the trunks in the attic."

"I don't know," said Alexander. "Once the semester begins, I'll be super-busy."

The goodbyes were tearful. Alexander was returning to Montreal for a few days for meetings. Elizabeth was going back to Catherine's apartment to pack before the final move to Ottawa.

Alexander was on his car phone most of the way to Montreal. He talked to the publisher. There were angry calls from his designer complaining about the contractor, and angry calls from the contractor complaining about the designer. Elizabeth dozed most of the way.

Alexander only had enough time to carry Elizabeth's suitcase to the front door of Catherine's apartment building before the honking started. A hurried hug.

Inside Catherine's apartment, Elizabeth felt a surge of relief. *I can forget about Mont Tremblant! I am about to step into my shiny new life.*

Chapter 24

The next few days spent in Catherine's apartment were filled with frenetic activity: packing, banking, enrolling in qualifying courses at the University of Ottawa, and reviewing the materials for orientation week at the Language School. Elizabeth bought a bed — online — and hoped it would fit into the Ottawa flat.

Elizabeth's sisters and Marie-France held a farewell dinner at a Chinese restaurant.

"I want to raise a toast to Lizzie and wish her luck! My baby sister survived a very tough year and landed on her feet," said Amanda, raising her glass. "Success in your studies! And while you're at it — look for a suitable man."

"To your success!" said Catherine. "Go for the degree and ignore Amanda! Men are a dime a dozen!"

"To Lizzie!" They all raised their glasses.

"Thank you. I certainly have no intention of letting you down. I was getting too obsessed with all the stuff happening at the estate. I feel as if I've escaped from prison, and I'm finally breathing freely. No more heartaches, suicidal bosses, or musk-smelling creeps."

The following morning, Elizabeth's luggage was crammed into Marie-France's car. They did not stop talking all the way to Ottawa.

Orientation at the Language School took place in the second half of August, and by early September, Elizabeth settled into a routine. She divided her time between studies at the university and part-time teaching at the Language School. Her schedule was brutal — long days and sometimes even longer nights. Whenever she walked past the Chateau Laurier Hotel, she experienced a faint dread. What if Stephen was lurking in the shadows? That part of her life was over — the memories all packed away. They did not hurt any more.

One evening, Elizabeth's cell phone rang as she was finishing a spaghetti dinner with Marie-France. "Alexander, how nice to hear from you." Elizabeth smiled as she made her way to the overstuffed armchair.

While Elizabeth was on the telephone, Marie-France cleared the table and washed the dishes. When the call ended, she plopped herself on the couch and asked, "Come on, what did he say? I want every detail!"

"Alexander said that Inspector Jolicoeur called about the toxicology tests. They had to do a second set of tests that should be ready by the end of this week. Inspector Jolicoeur wants to see us both again before he submits his final report. The inspector asked Alexander to drive up to Mont Tremblant next Sunday. It would be a one-day trip — in and out."

"Why you?"

"Maybe he suspects I poisoned Mr Ted."

"Don't be silly! So, are you going?"

"I told Alexander I'll call him back tomorrow. Alexander's completely swamped — teaching a new course, and then the continuing condo nightmare. He doesn't really want to go, but he thinks he should. Can I refuse? Can one refuse to be interviewed by the police?"

"I don't know. But if you do go, it will give you a chance to hang out with Alexander. I always hoped that you two would become an item. He is so handsome."

"Yes, but…"

"But what?"

"He's very nice to me, but… he never made any moves. I feel like there is an invisible wall between us. Maybe I'm too ordinary for him. I never went to finishing school."

"Finishing school! Seriously? But are you attracted to him?"

"I do like him very much… I was in love with Stephen, remember. Alexander is nothing like that."

"Look, forget I brought it up. You should go out with Ben and me once in a while. Come and meet our friends." Marie-France got up to make them both some herbal tea.

"Not yet. I told you, I really owe it to myself to do well this first semester. I can barely balance studying and teaching."

"You really need some R and R. Look at yourself in the mirror — bags under your eyes, at your age!"

Later that evening, Elizabeth telephoned the estate. She had promised to keep in touch, and at the same time she was curious about what the Gervais couple knew about the investigation. Monsieur Gervais was overjoyed to hear her voice. The estate office hired him to do an inventory of the contents of the house. He was expected to email photographs and to input an inventory of household belongings into a master catalogue. He said he was embarrassed to admit that he could not fathom the mysteries of the computer.

"One of Bernadette's daughters, Claudine, who works as a part-time secretary to the local notary, tried to teach me. She gave up. We split the job — she does the computer work."

Madame Gervais snatched the telephone away from her husband and bombarded Elizabeth with questions about life in Ottawa. Then it was Elizabeth's turn. She asked about Inspector Jolicoeur. No, he did not get in touch with them. With tongue in cheek, she asked whether Dr Jordan sent a moving truck to take away all the valuables.

"No, but that Dr Jordan should get out of the country! They say that he owes money to the Mafia, and the Mafia does not forgive or forget! Then there's a new will…"

Monsieur Gervais took the telephone away from his wife. "Let me explain what is happening with the new will. Louise will get it all muddled. Apparently, the will had not been notarised, but that in itself is not a problem. In Quebec, a will signed by two witnesses is perfectly legal. However, since Mr Ted died so soon after signing the new will, the estate office decided to contest it. Why a new will?" asked Monsieur Gervais. "Something smells fishy! If you ask me, Mr Ted was murdered. I don't know how they did it, but Dr Jordan owed money to the Mafia and they probably wanted Mr Ted dead so that Dr Jordan could inherit his money!"

"You've lost me," said Elizabeth. She did not contradict Monsieur Gervais. Here in Ottawa, these issues no longer seemed important. She remembered the tabloid article insinuating that Alexander stormed out of the mansion because he killed his own father.

Speaking rapidly, Monsieur Gervais continued, "Elizabeth, please forgive me, but I think I should tell you. That horrible online tabloid wrote about you! What, Louise? Louise says it's called *Gossip Queen*. Everyone in the village is talking about it, but Louise and I don't believe a word.

Please, Elizabeth, don't take it seriously. It's nonsense. I think I know who is spreading all these rumours. It's that Mako. He sells lies to anyone who will pay. The bartender at the Crazy Caribou is Bernadette's granddaughter's boyfriend. He heard Mako talking about you."

"But he doesn't even know me!" Elizabeth exclaimed. "He probably makes up stories."

"That would not surprise me," said Monsieur Gervais.

When Elizabeth put down her cell phone, she asked Marie-France, "Want to catch up on the latest gossip?" She walked over to the far end of the room and opened her computer.

"Monsieur Gervais said something about some gossip tabloid — apparently, they mentioned me."

"Wow! You're famous," said Marie-France.

"I really shouldn't even bother to read it."

There was an email from Inspector Jolicoeur inviting her to come to the estate with Alexander. She replied that she would. Then she found the latest edition of *Gossip Queen* and began to read out loud.

"'*According to sources close to the family,* Gossip Queen *has learned that Mr Agnew-Simpson signed a new will shortly before he died. Why? And who is the beneficiary?*'"

"Wasn't Alexander the heir? So was he cut out of the new will or what?" asked Marie-France.

"I don't know the details," said Elizabeth. "I never felt comfortable asking Alexander about his inheritance."

Elizabeth read, "'Gossip Queen *has no opinion on the death of Mr Agnew-Simpson. We are publishing the letter below solely as our contribution to the search for truth:*

"*The Musings of an Armchair Detective. Dear editor, As a resident of the Mont Tremblant region, I am concerned about the competence of our police. Agnew-Simpson was found dead in his study. Was it death by natural causes, suicide, or murder? The police claim they are still waiting to verify test results. Does this mean they suspect foul play?*

"*Accurate forensic analysis is essential, but it can only answer how and not who or why? Inspector Jolicoeur must know that Mr Agnew-Simpson signed a new will shortly before his death. I have heard it on good authority that Alexander Agnew-Simpson was disinherited. I would* not be surprised if the beneficiary is Elizabeth Burgess, the pretty young assistant hired only this May.

"Who had motive, opportunity and means to kill Mr Agnew-Simpson? According to the police, we can cancel out Alexander. The police confirm that he left the mansion hours before his father died. What about Miss Burgess? And must I state that I am not accusing her of murder. This is merely speculation by an armchair detective. Elizabeth Burgess lived in the mansion where Mr Agnew-Simpson died. The study door was always open. How hard could it be to purchase poison in our drug-soaked society?

"Since her arrival, Miss Burgess achieved extraordinary control over her boss. She succeeded in isolating him from his friends. An example of her power was witnessed by more than a dozen guests at the birthday party of Mr Agnew-Simpson's best friend, Dr Tig Jordan. All eyebrows were raised as she literally dragged Agnew-Simpson out of the doctor's house. I can only marvel that such a seemingly naïve and pretty young woman could have turned her boss into a besotted old man. I would not be surprised if she manipulated her boss into making her the beneficiary of his vast fortune. To my knowledge, the police are not even pursuing this line of investigation. As in their inquiry into the mysterious death of Madame Agnew-Simpson, they can't see what is right under their noses.'"

Elizabeth could read no further; she felt her throat constrict as if some invisible hand had choked off her breath. She sat gasping for air. Marie-France looked visibly shaken; her permanently rosy cheeks turned pale. She shut off Elizabeth's computer and led her away to the armchair. "Sit down, let me get you a glass of water." Elizabeth gulped the water.

"No one takes this crap seriously, Lizzie. Anyone who knows you would never believe it," she said in a shaky voice. "Let's go to bed. I have an early class."

Elizabeth did not go to bed; she continued to sit in the armchair, overcome by helpless rage. Who was this Armchair Detective? Mako sold stories to the tabloids. It must be Mako! All night the desire to confront Mako was like a fly buzzing about in her brain. She could not swat it away! Before dawn, she gave herself a pep talk. *OK, Lizzie, enough wallowing in self-pity. Do something!* She fell asleep sitting in the armchair.

"Why did you sleep here?" asked Marie-France as she nudged Elizabeth awake.

"What time is it?" Elizabeth was suddenly panic-stricken. "It's OK, my first class is at eleven."

Marie-France rushed off to university. Elizabeth made herself a strong cup of coffee, showered, dressed and waited until nine a.m. to call Alexander.

"Hi, Alexander, I hope this is not too early. I have a huge favour to ask. I know how busy you are, but this is really important. I need your help."

"What happened? You sound upset."

"I am upset! I just sent you an email with a tabloid article implicating me in Mr Ted's death. I've been defamed. I definitely want to go to Mont Tremblant with you. But as a personal favour, I would like to go on Saturday instead of Sunday."

"What? I don't understand! Calm down! What happened?"

"Read the article I sent you!"

"Let me open my computer." After a few minutes of silence, Alexander said, "Aren't you taking this a bit too seriously? It's just a tabloid!"

"Too seriously!" Elizabeth was almost shouting. "The tabloid spilled a bucket of slime over my head. This kind of slime sticks forever. I have to fight back! I have to confront the accuser!"

"Before you do anything else, let me consult my lawyer." Alexander sounded calm and reasonable.

"Well, I don't have a lawyer." *Sure, for you rich people, it's always 'let my accountant, let my lawyer, let my decorator handle it'.*

"Wait till I talk to Jack. I'll send him the article and ask for his comments. He's swamped, but I am sure he will look at it. Off the top of my head, I would say that there were no direct accusations and hardly anyone sues tabloids."

"I want to find out who wrote that letter!"

"And then what?"

"I don't know! All I am asking is that we leave for Mont Tremblant on Saturday instead of Sunday."

"Why?"

"I think I know who the source is!"

"Who?"

"Mako."

"Dr Jordan's assistant? What possible reason would he have? Why not Dr Jordan himself? Or Zsuzsanna? Or some busybody from the village?"

"Mako hangs out at the Crazy Caribou bar on Saturday nights, and according to Monsieur Gervais, Bernadette's grand-daughter's boyfriend, the bartender…"

"Who is Bernadette?"

"Bernadette is Madame Gervais's sister. The bartender's name is Richard, but everybody calls him Rocky. Rocky told Monsieur Gervais that Mako is always there on Saturday nights and that he sells gossip to reporters."

"All that is fascinating, but…," said Alexander.

Elizabeth did not register his incredulous tone, and continued, "We could drive up on Saturday afternoon. Pick me up at… say, at four p.m. We would go straight to the Crazy Caribou bar, and I could talk to the bartender and then confront Mako."

"Elizabeth, why don't we call Inspector Jolicoeur and ask for his advice."

"Great idea! Yes, please, invite the inspector to join us at the bar, but before Mako arrives so that I could…"

"Elizabeth, you are far too excited…"

"Alexander, please, please! I'm begging you! I have been treated unjustly before, and this time I will not behave like a doormat! This stuff is on the web — it can ruin my life!"

"I can't see how…"

Elizabeth's voice broke in sobs. "You have an army of expensive lawyers and assistants. I only have myself!" Elizabeth froze when she realised that perhaps she sounded hysterical.

To her surprise, Alexander said, "Well… I could try to rearrange things… but…"

Elizabeth did not let him finish the sentence. Still sobbing, she said, "Thank you, thank you, Alexander. I'll be waiting for you downstairs. Call me before you leave."

Elizabeth ended the call and sat for a full minute with her teeth clenched and her eyes shut tight. She sat expecting Alexander to call back at any moment and say that he could not go after all. She knew that she was imposing on Alexander. What exactly did she hope to achieve? Did she expect Mako to confess to the defamatory letter? She wanted to drag Mako by his hair, to drag him to the police station, and force him to write a retraction. For a split second, it occurred to her that she was allowing her rage to dominate the faint objections emanating from a barely audible voice of reason. "Why not wait for advice from the lawyer or Inspector Jolicoeur?" asked the voice. But Alexander had already agreed to go on Saturday, so what was the point of turning back?

Chapter 25

"I hope you're feeling better," said Alexander, as he placed Elizabeth's overnight bag into the trunk of his Audi.

In the cold light of day, Elizabeth wondered whether she had over-reacted by asking Alexander to drive to Mont Tremblant a day before planned. But in the next moment, she remembered the gratuitous lies in *Gossip Queen*. Like a flash flood, her outrage drowned out any lingering doubt.

"I feel guilty for dragging you into this," she said. "I must have sounded pretty hysterical on the telephone yesterday. I hope you're not mad at me."

"You were very upset. Perhaps you're taking this too seriously?" Alexander turned away from the wheel to look at Elizabeth. He saw her jaw clench and eyes well up. "Forget I said that."

They drove on in silence. Once on the highway, Elizabeth, exhausted from the emotional turmoil, fell asleep and woke up as the Audi approached the Crazy Caribou. It was six forty-five p.m.

"I forgot to tell you," said Alexander, "Inspector Jolicoeur can't make it tonight. His daughter is coming from Montreal; it's her birthday, so they're having a big family celebration. We will see him tomorrow."

The Crazy Caribou was a log chalet at the edge of the ski resort. A statue of a tipsy moose, holding a bottle of beer, welcomed visitors at the door. There were not many patrons — four young men dressed in leather jackets were drinking at the bar, and a few young couples in jeans and hoodies were laughing at a table in the corner. During the winter season, the bar catered to the après ski crowd. Summer brought a steady clientele of cottagers and tourists. The last week of September was slow. More tourists would arrive later, when the Laurentians turned into a blaze of orange, red, and gold. Rather than the table next to the picture window overlooking the lake, Elizabeth chose the one with a parking lot view. Suddenly, a chilling thought — what if Mako doesn't show up? *How could I be so sure that Mako would be here on this particular Saturday night?* Elizabeth felt her face turn red.

A bored-looking young waitress in black leggings and lumberjack boots placed menus on the table.

"I'm starving," said Alexander, perusing the choices. "I can't say I'm tempted by the poutine or the Buffalo wings, though."

"They have French onion soup *au gratin*."

"Right, and would you like to share the *charcuterie* plate?" After a quick glance at the wine list, Alexander said he would stick to beer. Elizabeth ordered a small carafe of the white house wine. *Maybe the wine will calm me down.* Alexander kept texting as they waited for the food. She drank the wine too quickly. They ate the onion soup in silence. It turned out to be very good. When the charcuterie platter arrived, Alexander asked about her university courses. *He's just making polite conversation.* Her answers were stilted. She kept looking out at the parking lot. *What if Mako doesn't come tonight?*

They were still eating when a biker walked into the bar. Elizabeth paid little attention as he sat down and talked to the bartender, a corpulent young man with a mop of curly, brown hair. Elizabeth did not look at the biker again until she heard laughter. There was something familiar about that biker's voice. Where had she heard it before? When the bartender moved to the cash register, the biker turned to face their table.

He looks a little like Mako. The flash of recognition was like a jolt of electricity. It was Mako! The colour must have drained from her face, because Alexander asked, "Elizabeth, are you all right?"

The last time Elizabeth saw Mako was at Dr Jordan's party, when he was dressed in a silk pyjama-style outfit and embroidered Chinese slippers. This version of Mako wore black motorcycle boots and a black leather jacket with a red dragon on the back. A heavy metal chain looped down one leg. Black eyeliner gave him a menacing, ghoulish look. Elizabeth's mouth dropped. She gasped audibly. Alexander looked at her with eyebrows raised. Elizabeth pointed her index finger to the bar. "Mako!" she mouthed.

Mako looked around the room. He noticed Elizabeth and Alexander. Without a moment's hesitation, he walked over to their table. Gone was the subservient attitude and exaggerated manners Elizabeth witnessed at the party. This Mako looked self-confident, even aggressive, as he stood before them, feet wide apart.

"Elizabeth, nice to see you again. You must be Alexander. We have not actually met, but I certainly know who you are! I'm Mako. I work with Dr Jordan."

"Nice to meet you," said Alexander, rising to shake Mako's extended hand. "Sorry, I don't recall your last name."

"The name on my birth certificate belongs to my Japanese foster mother. You see, I was born out of wedlock. My mother was the daughter of a high-ranking samurai. She died right after I was born. My biological father never acknowledged me."

Elizabeth stared at Mako, eyes bulging. Then she looked at Alexander, her face a question mark. Alexander's expression remained neutral. There was an awkward silence. *Mako, didn't you tell Zsuzsanna that your mother was a famous Mexican soap opera star? Which version of your ancestry should we believe?*

"You were born in Japan?" Elizabeth asked in a hoarse whisper. She did not know what else to say.

"Yes. Haven't the Gervaises filled you in?"

Elizabeth could not quite remember whether Monsieur Gervais told her that Mako was part Mexican or part Inuit.

"Please join us." Elizabeth moved to give him room on the bench.

Mako sat down and snapped his fingers. The waitress rushed over, and he ordered another beer, a bottle of Canadian Club, and three shot glasses.

"And how did you come to Canada?" Elizabeth asked. She asked mechanically, without thinking, as if she was waiting for the former Mako, the gentle Mako wearing embroidered slippers, to step out of this biker disguise. It did not happen. Tough-guy Mako poured a shot of whisky and moved it towards Alexander. Alexander pushed it back. Elizabeth also declined. Mako drank the whisky and then took a long gulp of beer from the bottle.

"Yes, I was born in Japan. It's a long story, but I'll keep it short. Dr Jordan is my biological father, although, of course, he denies it."

Elizabeth and Alexander looked at each other, eyes wide with surprise. Mako seemed oblivious to their stunned reaction and continued in a matter-of-fact tone. "He was doing post-doctoral work in Japan in a super-secret American facility. Even the CIA did not know about it. They recruited Asians, brainwashed them and sent them to China or North Korea as spies, or assassins, or whatever. I used to think it was all science fiction bullshit, but after seeing that *Jason Bourne* movie, I changed my mind. Dr Jordan must have used some of those same techniques to treat the addicts at his clinic."

"Did your mother come to Canada with you?" Elizabeth asked, trying to keep Mako talking while she figured out how to turn the conversation to the article in *Gossip Queen*.

"No! I just told you, she died after I was born. Dr Jordan sent me off to some remote Japanese village and paid a village woman to look after me. Then the old lady died, and he brought me to Canada. I think I was seven or eight. After that, it was all foster homes. I was always running away and getting into trouble. When I landed in a juvenile prison, Dr Jordan brought me to his clinic."

Elizabeth was at a loss for words. There was no bitterness in Mako's tone, no appeal for sympathy. Elizabeth looked across the table. Alexander was concentrating on his bottle of beer, lips shut tight.

"Everybody always asks me how I know that Dr Jordan is my biological father. So I always say: he brought me to Canada and he subsidised me all my life. But of course, that was before. Now that he's bankrupt, he stopped paying my salary! So what kind of loyalty does he expect from me now?" Mako looked at Elizabeth and Alexander as if he expected understanding. "People think that the clinic is making all kinds of money with all the cured addicts and facelifted ladies, but no, it's a bottomless pit. He kept borrowing and spending, borrowing and spending! And on top of that, Dr Jordan claims he's royalty!" Mako's face turned into a mask of derision. "He says he has to maintain a lifestyle befitting his noble status." Mako laughed out loud. It was an unpleasant, grating sound. "His motto is: Why die without debts?" Mako muttered what sounded like obscenities under his breath. "I should have my DNA tested and sue him," Mako continued, and he gulped down more beer. "But what good would that do me? I'd probably be last in a long line of creditors."

"How is Dr Jordan coping?" asked Elizabeth. *Why are you asking, Lizzie? Get him to talk about* Gossip Queen*!*

Mako had no intention of keeping quiet. "Tig turned into a basket case. I guess he didn't expect the estate office to contest the new will! He should have stuck to the old one. According to the new will, apart from the mansion, he would also get a big chunk of change. And I mean big! Like Agnew-Simpson's estate, and all those fancy lawyers were going to let him have a nickel." Mako's speech was now slightly slurred. "Stupid bugger! I told him — declare bankruptcy! He said that if he did, he'd be signing his own death sentence. So, how is he coping, you ask? He started to take a lot of liquid medication, if you know what I mean."

"Does Dr Jordan really have so many debts? Can't he ask the bank for an extension?"

"This is not some student loan!" Mako sneered. "You met Señor Vasquez at the party. Don't be fooled by the pin-striped suit. He represents some bad *hombres*." Mako lowered his head and whispered, "The Cartel!"

"Are you sure that's not just gossip?"

"Dr Jordan cured the drug-addicted son of a cartel member. His mistake was that he borrowed money from the kid's father. Did he expect the gratitude to last forever? As they say, no good deed goes unpunished. Right after the party, Señor Vasquez gave him some sort of ultimatum. Those cartel guys don't fool around." Mako poured himself another shot of whisky and did not offer any to the others at the table. "You know, I'm leaving! Tonight! What kind of loyalty does Tig expect? It would be different if he acknowledged me as his son." Mako took a long slug of beer.

"Let's have one for the road." Mako poured another shot of whisky.

Both Alexander and Elizabeth shook their heads.

Alexander's phone rang. He picked it up, and his face lit up in a smile. Elizabeth had never seen this smile before. For a brief second, his dark eyes became a warmer brown.

She could not explain why she felt a twinge of... A twinge of what? Jealousy? He had never smiled at her like that!

"I'll take this at the bar," Alexander said, and he walked away.

"So what brings you back to Tremblant? Come to collect your loot?" Mako asked Elizabeth with a sneer.

Elizabeth ignored the churlish remark and asked point-blank, "Have you read *Gossip Queen*?"

"Sure, everybody around here reads it, especially when they write about our neck of the woods. Who doesn't like juicy gossip? They certainly did a number on you," he said with a wicked smile.

"I'm taking this libel seriously. Do you know who wrote that letter?"

"Could be one person or a bunch of people. All kinds of media guys started snooping around after Madame Agnew-Simpson died in what they call 'mysterious circumstances'. Boy! Did the village ever become famous that summer! Some reporters promised to pay good money and handed out business cards left and right. People began to send them stuff. Most of it was probably made up. But who cares?"

"I care," said Elizabeth. "When the tabloid publishes a letter claiming that I manipulated Mr Ted into making me the beneficiary of the new will, that is defamation!"

"So how does it feel to be a multi-millionairess?" Mako smirked.

"Mako, you know that it's not true; you witnessed the new will."

"Yes, I signed as a witness. But I didn't actually read the will." Mako squinted his left eye and raised an eyebrow. "Or did I? Don't remember. Señor Vasquez was a witness, too. Ask him!" Mako chortled as if he had said something witty.

Elizabeth was shocked at Mako's surliness. She looked across the room at Alexander. He was deeply engrossed in conversation. His back was turned.

"Do you know who is feeding them these lies?" she asked Mako.

"No idea. I think I did meet someone from *Gossip Queen* a while back. I may even have his card somewhere." Mako put his hands into his jacket pockets as if looking for something.

"If you know someone, could you give me his or her name?"

"What's in it for me? Why should I?" His tone was now openly hostile. "If it's not true, you should hire a lawyer and sue them. Why don't you call up *Gossip Queen* yourself and ask about their source?" Mako laughed. It was a joyless, wicked laugh.

Elizabeth was paralysed by his hostile insolence.

At the bar, Alexander was paying the waitress. When he returned to the booth, Mako said, "We've been talking about *Gossip Queen*. Did you happen to read that article where they accused you of killing your own father? Are you going to sue?"

"I don't pay attention to nonsense." Alexander's face maintained its customary sphinx-like composure, although his lips seemed to press together more tightly.

"I heard that you were disinherited by your old man. Bum rap. I feel for you, man. You and I are in the same boat."

Alexander's face became darker. Elizabeth held her breath, unsure of how he would respond. "I don't think so," said Alexander. His tone was calm. Elizabeth thought she discerned more than a hint of condescension.

"Oh, really? So you're OK, financially? So your mother must have been rich, too, eh? Did you know that everyone in the village is talking about how your father disinherited you because you don't look like him?"

"I don't look like my mother either," said Alexander.

With an insolent sneer on his lips, Mako said, "You probably don't even know who your real father was."

Elizabeth let out an involuntary gasp.

Alexander replied with dismissive sang-froid. "Are you interviewing me for *Gossip Queen*?"

"Great idea for the next issue!"

This is getting unpleasant. "We should be going," said Elizabeth, and she picked up her purse.

Mako didn't stop talking, and blocked her attempt to exit the booth. "Poor old stupid Tig. For some crazy reason, he believed that his best friend, Ted, would leave him everything — that is, until this foxy lady beat him to it. It must have been easy for you, with your big blue eyes." Mako lightly cuffed Elizabeth under the chin.

Alexander leaned forward and grabbed Mako by the arm. "Don't touch her."

"Alexander, isn't Inspector Jolicoeur expecting us? Let's go," Elizabeth lied, hoping that the invocation of the inspector's name would dampen Mako's belligerence.

"Why so soon? Let's have one for the road."

"Should you be driving?" Elizabeth asked Mako.

"I'm used to it." Mako downed another whisky. "Time to get outta Dodge! Dr Jordan is dead to me now. In more ways than one. Dead as a door nail." Then he rose and bowed deeply in the Japanese fashion. "Have a pleasant evening."

Mako scattered bills over the bar and waved to the bartender. Elizabeth continued to watch as he entered the parking lot and got into Dr Jordan's black Aston Martin. The tyres screeched as he drove away.

Elizabeth broke their stunned silence. "He's had too much to drink! Monsieur Gervais told me that Dr Jordan forbids him to drive the Aston Martin."

"Does Mako strike you as someone who does what he's told?"

"He could easily kill someone. Should we call the police?"

"I know you don't like Dr Jordan, but he was Ted's best friend, and I think I should call him first. Do you have his cell number?"

"No, I don't."

"I know how you feel about Dr Jordan, but I want to stop at his house and tell him that Mako is driving drunk. It's on our way. You won't need to get out of the car."

As they drove to Dr Jordan's clinic, Elizabeth said, "I can't get over how wrong I was about Mako. At the party, he was so sweet and gentle. I thought that Monsieur Gervais must have been wrong about him. You know how they gossip in the village. I guess I just can't read people."

"I know almost nothing about his background," said Alexander. "As a teenager, Mako was a patient at the clinic. Did Marcel tell you about the scandal?"

Elizabeth shook her head.

"It must have been more than seven years ago," Alexander continued. "A young female patient was raped. Dr Jordan settled out of court. That definitely contributed to his financial troubles. There was talk that Mako was the culprit."

Elizabeth felt uneasy as Alexander drove up to the sprawling bunker-style house. Further up the hill, the lights outside the clinic illuminated the white van and a few cars in the parking lot. The door to the triple garage was open. There were no cars inside.

"Maybe he's out," said Elizabeth. "Did he forget to close his garage door?"

Alexander rang the doorbell for several minutes. There was no answer. He walked into the open garage. Elizabeth got out of the car and followed. Her fear of staying alone in the dark outweighed her abhorrence of Dr Jordan. The door to the kitchen was ajar. A sliver of light. Once inside, Elizabeth recoiled from the faint scent of sweet, cloying musk incense. The outdoor lights around the infinity pool projected a hazy glow into the living room.

"Dr Jordan? Are you home?" yelled Alexander. The door to the study was wide open. "Dr Jordan?"

Alexander stepped into the study. He found the switch. They both gasped. Clad in a black silk Japanese kimono, sitting upright in a chair behind the desk, was Dr Jordan's headless torso. The front of the kimono was wet, and the entire desk glistened with blood. Dr Jordan's severed head was placed in front of the torso — upright on the desk — facing the door. The eyes were bulging. The mouth was open in a final scream of terror.

The ornate Japanese scabbard that hung on the wall behind the desk was missing. An unsheathed sword lay across the desk. Elizabeth gagged as she felt bile rise up to her throat. Knees weak, she staggered into the living room, where she collapsed onto the couch. She heard Alexander call 911.

The rest of the evening was a blur. A figure in a white suit gave Elizabeth some pills and a glass of water. Elizabeth slumped on the couch, and was vaguely conscious of police and people in white suits going in and out of the study. At the opposite end of the room, Alexander spoke to Inspector Jolicoeur. Before Elizabeth fell into a deep sleep, she wondered why their voices seemed muffled.

Chapter 26

The next morning, as Elizabeth began to emerge from a state between sleep and consciousness, she saw — or dreamed she saw — hovering over her bed, Dr Jordan's severed head, mouth wide in a soundless scream. The hair at the nape of her neck stood on end. She pulled the blanket over her head. When the terror abated, she opened her eyes and saw the familiar forget-me-not pattern on the wallpaper. The relief was euphoric! Fully clothed, she was lying on the blue and white comforter. Someone had covered her with a white woollen blanket. She was in her room at the mansion.

A gentle knock on the door. "Elizabeth, are you up? It's ten o'clock." Madame Gervais, immaculate as ever in her white apron, sat down on the bed. Elizabeth put her arms around her and cried. Madame Gervais rocked her gently.

"A good cry always makes a girl feel better, doesn't it? Are you hungry? Alexander and Inspector Jolicoeur are in the study. I prepared coffee, sandwiches and muffins. Can you join them? Are you up to it?"

"I'll wash my face and come right down," said Elizabeth, wiping away a tear running down her cheek. Elizabeth had to force herself to get out of bed. *You've got no choice, Lizzie. Get the police interview over with and get out of here.*

Inspector Jolicoeur was dressed casually, in baggy jeans and a long-sleeved plaid shirt.

Is that your Sunday attire, Inspector, or are you going fishing after the interview? Constable Fortin, wearing a uniform and a smile, sat at Agnew-Simpson's desk, typing on his portable computer.

"Good morning, mademoiselle," said Inspector Jolicoeur. He motioned Elizabeth to the maroon love seat. "I am sorry you had to see the gruesome scene last night. I hope you are feeling better. Unfortunately, this interview can't wait."

Alexander stood over her and squeezed her shoulder. "You look so much better! Would you like some coffee?"

Elizabeth accepted a mug. "It feels like a bad dream. When can we go back to Ottawa?"

"Let us finish this quickly," said Inspector Jolicoeur, and he moved his tape recorder across the glass coffee table.

"First, I will repeat what I told Alexander. The second toxicology report confirmed the findings of the first. Mr Agnew-Simpson died of barbiturate poisoning. I am in the process of writing my final report. Both the prosecutor and I agree. Suicide."

"I still find it difficult to believe." Elizabeth felt too tired to argue.

"The final ruling will be made at the inquest. And now, we have a new case — a clear case of murder."

"Yes, it must be murder. Dr Jordan could not have cut off his own head," said Elizabeth, and in the next instant, hoped that the inspector would not notice the sarcasm. *Be polite, Lizzie!*

"Alexander filled me in on what happened, but I would like to ask you a few more questions." Inspector Jolicoeur asked her to describe Mako at the Crazy Caribou. Elizabeth went into great detail about Mako at the bar and at Dr Jordan's birthday party. He also asked what Mako said about the cartel and whether she spoke to Señor Vasquez at the party. The interview lasted almost an hour. When it was over, she felt as limp as a rag doll.

"Constable Fortin will prepare your statements," said Inspector Jolicoeur, as he shut off the tape recorder.

Alexander rose and offered everyone a drink.

"I will decline on behalf of Constable Fortin as he's driving, but I certainly would appreciate a Molson's," said the inspector.

Everyone opted for beer. Elizabeth was dying to tell the inspector about her new theory — a theory that emerged spontaneously after the meeting with Mako. She now felt a strong compulsion to test it on Inspector Jolicoeur.

"Mako told us that Dr Jordan once worked in a super-secret CIA hospital in Japan where they researched programming human beings."

"Elizabeth," said Alexander, "can we believe anything Mako said? He seems to have a creative imagination."

"That information can be checked. If it is true, can't we assume that

Dr Jordan used some of those same techniques on the addicts in his clinic? What if he was able to somehow programme or hypnotise Mr Ted into committing suicide? I once saw a film about that. I think it was called…"

"*The Manchurian Candidate*," Alexander completed the sentence. "Do you think that Ted's death was a case of life imitating art?" Both men smiled.

"Please don't make fun of me. It's a legitimate theory."

"Yes, Miss Burgess, a theory. Police investigators are trained to base their theories on concrete evidence; however, prosecutors insist on facts that will stand up in court." The inspector spoke softly, as if explaining something to a child. "Unfortunately, your theory has no basis in fact."

"Facts can be discovered by using one's intuition. Perhaps prosecutors have no imagination!" Elizabeth was irritated by the condescending smiles.

"Miss Burgess, I assure you that you would not want to be arrested by an imaginative policeman or brought to trial before an intuitive judge."

Another put-down. Why can't the inspector admit it is possible? Elizabeth remained defiant. Her face became pink, and her voice quavered. "Yes, some people may not see the connection between the dots."

"And what are these dots, may I ask?" The inspector's smile was gentle.

"Elizabeth, please! Calm down; you are still in shock," said Alexander.

"Tell me, Miss Burgess, what dots do you see and how do you connect them? I am really interested."

"I just thought that with all the recent deaths in Mont Tremblant, could we not assume that they are connected? Madame Mathilde, Mr Ted and now Dr Jordan? It can't be a coincidence!"

"How do you think they are connected?"

Elizabeth was about to say that *he* was the detective, and therefore *he* should find a connection, but Alexander interjected before she could speak. "Inspector, Elizabeth is a great admirer of a famous detective, Hercule Poirot. If Poirot were investigating, he would have called together all the suspects, and using only his little grey cells, he would lay out the devilishly convoluted plot and name the murderer! No loose ends — all neatly packaged with a bow on top."

"Yes," said Inspector Jolicoeur, "Agatha Christie mysteries are like games or puzzles. Her novels are reassuring in their predictability. I think they are popular because they tap into a deep-seated human need for order and clear links between cause and effect."

"I agree," said Alexander. "There is a human tendency to fear the chaos of a random universe. Due to the multiplicity of disparate variables, people often cannot understand the complexity of a phenomenon. That is why many find comfort in conspiracy theories. Bad things happen because of the machinations of evil men plotting in smoke-filled rooms. Let's take Ted's death, for example: people will want a clear cause and effect. If the cause is ambiguous, there will be no shortage of theories that provide an esoteric, yet psychologically satisfying solution."

Elizabeth assumed that Alexander's words were addressed to her. *Thank you, professor! I gather that I have just been relegated to the category of simple people who need simple answers.*

Inspector Jolicoeur addressed Elizabeth. "Miss Burgess, I am intrigued. Tell me how you connect the dots. Deaths in the same house may very well be related or unrelated — a coincidence. I believe that Madame Agnew-Simpson slipped and fell down the stairs. An accident is something that is unpredictable and can happen to any of us at any time. Therefore, perhaps it is more frightening than murder."

"Mother did have a history of sleepwalking and other nervous disorders," said Alexander. "The gossips in the village would prefer to tie Ted's suicide to my mother's death. I heard one rumour that Ted committed suicide because of a guilty conscience for having pushed her down the stairs. I believe that Ted did commit suicide. Why? We will never know."

Elizabeth could not stop herself from objecting to Alexander. "Why is it so difficult to imagine that Dr Jordan somehow programmed Mr Ted to commit suicide? He told me himself that he used hypnosis on his patients. I am not searching for a cause and effect; I am only trying to connect the dots. Otherwise, Mr Ted's death makes no sense at all." Elizabeth could not control the nervous excitement in her voice.

"Miss Burgess, the operative word in your theory is 'somehow'. That is simply not good enough. Dr Jordan was in Montreal the night Mr

Agnew-Simpson died. In any case, since Dr Jordan is no longer with us, this is all moot. I suggest that we put your theory to rest." The inspector got up and walked over to the desk, where Constable Fortin had finished printing the statements.

"I suppose it will be easy to prove who killed Dr Jordan. Mako must have left fingerprints on the sword," Elizabeth mused out loud. "I still don't understand why he chose to kill him in such a gruesome way."

"Could it have been the cartel?" asked Alexander. "The estate office was contesting the new will and were bound to start digging around in his affairs. So the cartel got rid of him, like an inconvenient loose end."

"Could be," said the inspector, and he put his notes into his briefcase.

Alexander continued, "What do you think of the staging of the crime scene? The body was sitting upright in the chair. The grotesque positioning of the head! Did Dr Jordan obligingly sit still in his chair and wait while the killer raised the sword?"

"There were probably two killers." Elizabeth could not restrain herself. "One could have been pointing a gun at him while the other one chopped off his head from behind."

The inspector did not look eager to pursue this discussion. Constable Fortin was packing his computer and the recording device. The inspector asked Fortin to meet him downstairs.

"There could have been more than one killer. However, in police work, we try not to get in front of the facts. Best wait for the forensics."

Elizabeth, despite herself, interjected. Her tone was very agitated. "The samurai sword! Is there some kind of symbolism here? What if Mako's Japanese family took revenge and…"

Alexander interrupted. "That would mean that Mako's imaginary family sent a samurai, or perhaps some ninja killer, to avenge the seduction of the Japanese maiden almost thirty years ago."

Elizabeth was hurt by Alexander's sarcasm. *OK, Mr Smarty-pants professor. You don't have to make me sound so stupid.*

"Dr Jordan and Mako could have had a mundane argument — say, over money. Mako became furious and grabbed the first weapon available," Alexander concluded.

"The sword in the study was decorative," said Inspector Jolicoeur. "It would have to be razor sharp to sever the head so cleanly. The cartel would have sent a professional with a gun."

The inspector looked at his watch, walked over to the desk, and picked up the printed statements. "Let's see what we have here," he said, as he scanned the top sheet and passed it to Alexander. He handed the second sheet to Elizabeth.

"You can read them at your leisure and ask Monsieur Gervais to bring them to the station or simply fax them to me."

Alexander walked the inspector to the front door.

When he returned, Elizabeth was still sitting on the couch, reading her statement. "I need another beer before we go," said Alexander, and he opened one of the hidden bar panels. "Want one?"

They sat opposite each other and read, and then signed their statements.

Elizabeth broke the silence. "When we met Mako at the bar, Dr Jordan must have already been dead. But Mako behaved as if nothing had happened. He spoke about him in the present tense."

"Yes." Alexander looked at his watch, finished his beer and got up. "Let's go! I have to be in Ottawa this evening."

The farewells with the Gervais couple were subdued. Madame Gervais was disappointed that Alexander would not stay for supper, and forced him to accept a bag full of sandwiches. On the long ride to Ottawa, neither spoke. Elizabeth dozed and opened her eyes only when the Audi passed the exit to Gatineau on the Quebec side of the Ottawa River.

"By the way," asked Alexander, "do you still want me to talk to my lawyer about the defamation in *Gossip Queen*?"

"Could you, please?" said Elizabeth. "I don't know how it works, but perhaps the estate office could issue some sort of statement to the effect that I am not the beneficiary of the new will."

"I'll ask. But I won't have time to call before Tuesday."

"I hear one voice in my head telling me to stand up to the gutter press, and another one is telling me that it would be a useless exercise."

Alexander did not reply. It was already dark as the car crossed the bridge to Ottawa. "I have to prepare a lecture for tomorrow. I'll be up late tonight."

Elizabeth kept quiet until the car stopped in front of her flat. She rushed out, grabbed her overnight bag before Alexander could take it, and said, "You are not allowed to park here! The bag's not heavy! I'll take it up myself. Go!"

"I'll call you," he said. "Take care of yourself!" He gave her a friendly hug and got back in the car.

Chapter 27

Elizabeth rushed into Marie-France's arms. "I'm home! Our gorgeous flat! Our beautiful shabby chic!" Elizabeth twirled around the room.

"Why all this euphoria? When you phoned this morning, I was worried that you were depressed again. Your mood swings like a yo-yo! What happened?"

"As I was coming up the stairs, I realised that I am now a new and improved version of the old me. I'm tough. I've seen a dead body and a headless corpse! It has to be blue skies from now on!"

"Don't bad things happen in threes?" asked Marie-France.

"Yes. I guess. Stephen." Elizabeth raised her index finger. "Mr Ted," she said, and raised her middle finger. "And now Dr Jordan — three. Don't you think I have fulfilled my quota?"

"If such a law exists, you certainly have!" Marie-France laughed. "Are you hungry?" She opened the refrigerator door. "I have some leftover spaghetti Bolognaise. Or I can fix some Rice-a-Roni."

"Madame Gervais gave me sandwiches." Elizabeth placed the bag on the kitchen table and took out plates from the kitchen cupboard. "Any wine?"

Marie-France opened a bottle of cheap *Chianti* that Benjie had brought. She found a bag of chips.

Elizabeth told the entire story — from the meeting with Mako at the bar to the horrible sight of Dr Jordan's headless body. Marie-France sat with her blue eyes bulging and mouth open, interjecting with questions from time to time.

"A sword! The head next to the body! Did you sleep at all last night?"

"Somebody gave me some pills — tranquillisers, I guess."

Marie-France poured Elizabeth another glass of Chianti and said, "Let's not talk about any of that. Tell me about Alexander. Any developments?"

"No."

Marie-France looked very disappointed.

"Think about it. Every time I meet Alexander, somebody dies. Not terribly romantic. Also, I still can't figure him out. I used to think he was a snob or super-reserved. Then we went on the boat ride, and he opened up about his mother, and I thought he'd warmed up. When he helped me out of the boat, I was conscious of the touch of his hand. After Stephen, I thought I had developed an allergy to men, but…"

"Next time, I hope you meet in some romantic setting. Isn't he supposed to ask you out for dinner?"

"I hope so. At that dinner in Old Montreal, he didn't seem so cold. We walked back to the car, and when I stepped off the kerb, he took my hand. I liked the feeling, but I'm not sure I want to risk having my heart broken again. I told you, he's never made any moves…"

"Maybe you haven't noticed, or…"

"He kissed me goodbye once. I was crying, so he held me and kissed my forehead like a child or his sister. I know he likes me, but I feel like there is some invisible wall between us."

"You said that he's very reserved. Just think of what he's been through — moving back to Canada, losing his parents, a new job. And he's teaching a new course."

"Don't forget his condo woes."

"Sorry to bring this up, but have you ever considered that he may have a girlfriend? Did he have someone in England? You told me yourself that he disappeared from Mont Tremblant to meet someone flying in from London."

"He's never mentioned anyone specific. But there was a phone call recently. He smiled. It was a special kind of smile that I never saw before. Never mind. Look, I suddenly feel so very, very tired."

"Let's go to bed. I have to be up at seven."

Alexander did not call on Tuesday, as he promised. He called the following week. He apologised for the delay and said he had only recently tracked down the right lawyer to ask about suing *Gossip Queen*. He told Elizabeth that it would be very costly and could take years. "And about your other question — the estate office does not issue statements about the contents of wills."

Elizabeth had half expected this. With no money and with no guarantee of winning in court, what could she do? Elizabeth thanked Alexander and asked about news from Mont Tremblant.

"Mako is still at large. According to Inspector Jolicoeur, there is a market for luxury cars in Africa and Asia. Usually, these cars are sold to middlemen, who ship them out from the port of Montreal. Sorry, I have to go, my class is about to begin."

Elizabeth was surprised at her own equanimity. She was so absorbed by her teaching and studies that the recent horrific events dissolved in the whirlwind of her busy life. She did not meet Alexander again until late October, when he called out of the blue and said he was nearby. He apologised for the spur-of-the-moment invitation and asked if she was free for drinks at Zoe's in the Chateau Laurier Hotel. "You live close by, can you drop over?"

"When?"

"Today, at five p.m. I'll give you a rain check for a real dinner. I have to be at the Faculty Club tonight."

Elizabeth had been avoiding the Chateau Laurier Hotel since her encounter with Stephen. She was haunted by the irrational fear that Stephen was hiding in the shadows and could step out at any moment. *Don't be silly. I'm sure he's forgotten all about you by now. He's probably into his latest conquest.*

Elizabeth walked into Zoe's, an elegant bar with high ceilings and gleaming marble walls. The atmosphere was sedate — a few middle-aged ladies were finishing their afternoon tea. Alexander was at a table by the window. He put down the book he was reading, stood up and waved. He looked very handsome in a soft, rust-coloured suede jacket and black turtleneck.

They greeted each other with light kisses on the cheek.

"I apologise for the last-minute invitation, but I was here for a meeting. Since you live nearby…"

A waiter in an impeccably white shirt and bow tie approached their table with a tray. "I haven't had lunch today. I hope you don't mind; I ordered some *amuses geules*. Otherwise, I might faint." He laughed. Elizabeth had not heard him laugh before.

The waiter put down a wooden serving board with artistically arranged cold cuts, pâtés and cheeses. A sliced baguette, a ceramic pot of herbed butter, and a crock of olives already stood on the table. "I ordered a bottle of *Pouilly-Fuissé*, but would you prefer something else?"

"The wine is fine. Thank you."

"How have you been?" he asked, as he slathered pâté on a piece of bread.

"Busy! Exhausted! I hope to be accepted into the Information Systems Programme next semester. I must say I am proud of myself. For the first time in my life, I feel as if I'm in control. I have three more years at the University of Ottawa, then I will do a work/study stage somewhere." Elizabeth continued to talk about the programme, and at the same time she noticed that there was something different about Alexander. What was it? He said he was overworked, yet his eyes and skin glowed. He looked more handsome.

"Any plans for the holidays?" he asked.

"I'll be back in Montreal for Christmas with my sisters. I haven't seen them since August! And you?"

"I was away so much that I've drifted apart from my Beaudry relatives. Of course, I am always welcome for Christmas, particularly by Uncle Jean's family. But this year, as soon as I plough myself out from under the pile of student papers, I'm going away. To Morocco."

"You found him!" Elizabeth exclaimed with enthusiasm. *That's why he looks so happy. He's found his biological father.* "You must be so excited!"

"Yes, and frightened."

Elizabeth felt her heart rate quicken. Since she was the one who discovered the letters, she felt an almost proprietary interest in Alexander's heritage. "How did you find Hassan?"

"I hired an investigator. It took him a few months. Hassan lives in Casablanca and occupies an important post as a regional administrator in the Finance Department."

"Does he have a family?"

"Four daughters. His wife died of breast cancer a few years ago."

"I am so excited for you! Have you spoken to him?"

"No, and I am not sure that I will. How can I ring the doorbell and say: 'Here I am, the son you did not know existed; my mother was the woman you abandoned'?"

"But he did not know she was pregnant."

"Will he want to see me? Will he want his daughters to know about me? How do I know how he will react?"

"Perhaps you can discreetly approach him through his relatives or friends, or... Look, I don't know what I am talking about. I know you will find a solution. If you do meet him and if it does go well, please send me a photograph. I mean it."

"Of course! I will always be grateful that you showed me the letters." Alexander smiled at Elizabeth and reached across the table to squeeze her hand.

Elizabeth felt herself blushing. She changed the subject. "Have you heard anything about Mako? Why is it taking so long to find him?"

"Inspector Jolicoeur suspects that he's probably sold the car, so he has money to live on, and perhaps he's already left the province. Oh, I also have news about Marcel and Louise. They want to move out of the estate right after Christmas. Even with all the security, they were pretty shaken up by Dr Jordan's murder."

"I don't blame them." Elizabeth cut off a slice of cheese. "So, do you inherit the mansion now? How does this work, with Dr Jordan dead?"

"I hope not; otherwise, *Gossip Queen* will start accusing me of killing both my father and Dr Jordan! Some of the lovely people in the village will organise a lynch mob!" Alexander's smile was sad. "I suppose they can't imagine that I was never in Ted's will."

"What?" The surprise spread over Elizabeth's face.

"No one needs to know about my relationship to the estate. I'll tell you in confidence. The bulk of Ted's wealth is in the corporation. God only knows what goes on there and who stands to benefit! All above my pay grade! Ted transferred his personal fortune to the Agnew-Simpson Endowment Fund. Best idea he ever had. An awful lot of universities will be thrilled."

"And you?"

"My mother's family made Ted sign a prenuptial agreement with a guaranteed trust fund for any future children. Uncle Jean's investment company still manages my assets. I am very comfortable."

Elizabeth was impressed at the shrewdness of the Beaudry family.

She now understood why Alexander was amused by those silly tabloid reports accusing him of patricide. Elizabeth was surprised at his candour. She had not expected him to confide in her.

"I am curious; who inherits Dr Jordan's house, clinic, and spa?"

"Haven't the foggiest. Probably the creditors. Let the lawyers figure it out."

"You are absolutely right!" said Elizabeth. "I want to forget about Mont Tremblant! I want to get on with my life!"

"To you, Elizabeth, to your success!" Alexander raised his glass.

"And best of luck in Morocco!"

They clinked glasses.

"So, where will you be in Morocco?"

"Casablanca, but I would like to visit Marrakesh if it works out."

"Casablanca! Humphrey Bogart! Ingrid Bergman!"

Alexander's phone rang. "Yes, I'll be there," he said.

Elizabeth noticed or thought she caught a hint of that soft smile again.

"Elizabeth, I know this is rude, but my ride to the faculty dinner will arrive early. My car is being serviced. I am so sorry."

Elizabeth was disappointed. *So he met me as a courtesy to fill me in on his trip to Morocco. Weren't we having a lovely conversation? I was really enjoying this. Wasn't Alexander enjoying it, too? He doesn't seem sorry to leave. He seems to want to rush off to his boring faculty dinner.*

Alexander got up and went to the bar to pay the bill. When he returned, he said, "I am so sorry, I still owe you a real dinner, but I spend most of my evenings preparing for lectures. I am embarrassed to admit I'm one lecture ahead of my students. We will definitely go some place nice before I leave. Please stay and finish the wine."

"I certainly won't let the wine go to waste," said Elizabeth. "Have fun at your faculty dinner."

"Fun at a faculty dinner?" Alexander was about to bend down to kiss her on the forehead, but Elizabeth stood up and hugged him.

The waiter poured her the last of the wine. As she picked up the glass, she noticed Alexander's book lying on the white tablecloth. Taking the book and her purse, she ran out of the restaurant, through the lobby to the main entrance. The front doors were blocked by a busload of American tourists, all carrying shopping bags. Elizabeth caught sight of Alexander getting into a grey Honda Civic. She saw a glimpse of the driver's profile. The young man had thick, wavy, honey-blond hair. *His hair looks sculpted. He reminds me of a Greek statue. What is it called? 'The Discus Thrower'.*

Elizabeth did not return to her table to finish the wine. Still holding the book, she walked home. She would call Alexander about the book tomorrow.

Chapter 28

Elizabeth continued the grinding routine of teaching and attending classes. By the middle of November, the pace quickened, and the stress became almost unbearable as assignments, research projects and corrections all came due. Alexander did not call. From time to time, she wondered how he was doing. *He's snowed under, just like I am.*

One Saturday morning in late November, Elizabeth and Marie-France drove to a big box store to buy groceries and a microwave oven. The old, scruffy microwave, with brown stains inside, had died a natural death, but Angel refused to replace it.

"So, young lady, am I supposed to replace all the property you destroy? I replace it, you break it! No, I will not buy a new microwave! You will buy *me* a new microwave! That is only fair!" Angel's face became red, his black eyes bulged, and he sprayed spit as he talked.

Marie-France could not convince him that she had leased a furnished apartment and that the microwave was the owner's responsibility. A long screaming match followed. Marie-France finally conceded.

Elizabeth tried to console her. "You lost the microwave war with Angel! Stop agonising about it! He's not worth it!"

"I'm taking the microwave with me when we move out!" said Marie-France. As an act of defiance, she stopped her car on the street in front of the flat. "There's no way we're going to carry the groceries and the microwave along that frozen driveway!"

"Salt costs money!" Elizabeth imitated the landlord's voice. "Let's be quick; maybe he won't notice."

"I don't care if he notices! I will park the car in the back after we carry all the stuff upstairs! I don't care what he says!"

They trudged up the stairs, hauling their purchases. Elizabeth put down the bags of groceries and rummaged through her purse, looking for her keys.

"This thing is heavy," said Marie-France, as she put the microwave box on the floor. "Next time, let's get a place with an elevator."

"I agree." The voice was low and husky. It came from the alcove next to the front door. A woman stepped out of the shadow. She had flaming red curls that cascaded down to her shiny red nylon jacket. Her tight purple slacks were tucked into red vinyl boots with two-inch spiked heels. She was heavily made-up — blue-shadowed eyes with thick false lashes, and bow-shaped crimson lips. She reminded Elizabeth of a campy female impersonator. Both women shrank back at the sight of this grotesque figure.

"Aren't you going to let me in, ladies?"

Marie-France had the presence of mind to panic first, and pulled the gawking Elizabeth inside. Before they could close the door, the woman pushed the box with the microwave over the threshold and stepped inside. She was holding a switchblade knife in her hand, which was manicured with long, red fingernails.

Elizabeth froze in terror. Marie-France pulled her cell phone from her purse.

"Sweetie, please give me that phone. That is, if you want Elizabeth to go on breathing!"

Wrapping an arm around Elizabeth's upper body, the woman placed the knife at Elizabeth's throat.

We should both yell bloody murder. Someone will hear us and call the police. I should scream! Why can't I?

"How do you know my name?" asked Elizabeth, her voice quavering.

"We've met before."

Elizabeth was incredulous. *I've never met anyone like you.*

"What do you want?" asked Marie-France.

"What does everybody want, sweetheart? Money, of course." The woman spread her thick red lips into a wide smile.

"I have about fifty dollars in my wallet," said Marie-France.

"Miss, whatever your name is, I don't need bus fare. I'm not even going to march you to the nearest ATM and take your paltry savings. I've been trying to find Alexander. Now, *he's* got serious money."

She knows Alexander? Who is she? The woman was holding Elizabeth from behind. The arm felt strong and muscular. *And the voice! Where have I heard it before? She knows Alexander, too! It can't be.*

Mako? Mako in drag?

"Mako?" Elizabeth tried to turn around, but felt the hold tighten, and the knife sting as it pushed into her neck.

"Who's Mako? My name is Gilda."

She recalled Mako as the subservient servant wearing red embroidered slippers, the biker, and now this... this... *Another personality? Another incarnation?*

"How did you find me?"

"It was easy. I called Madame Gervais and said I was a friend passing through Montreal and that I really wanted to get in touch with you. I told her we've known each other since kindergarten and how we used to be in Girl Guides together. She was moved to tears and gave me your address and phone number. I really enjoyed our girl-to-girl chat. I asked her for Alexander's number, but her husband came in and told her not to give information to strangers. She actually apologised to me! But Elizabeth, darling, you must have your boyfriend's number."

"Alexander is not my boyfriend!"

"Why pretend? No need, now that Daddy's dead! Al must be so scrumptiously, filthy rich! Yum!" Mako licked his lips.

Mako guided Elizabeth over to the couch and sat her down. "I phoned all the universities in Ottawa. There is no Professor Agnew-Simpson at any one of them. Are you sure he's a university professor and not a high school teacher? Has Al been lying to you? But never mind! You know, I could go for Al myself. I like intellectual types. They tend to be gentler."

Elizabeth felt the pressure of the knife. She felt a trickle of warm blood oozing down her neck. *He would kill me without flinching!* A wave of panic swept over her.

"Alexander is in my cell phone contacts. It's Saturday. Maybe he's gone away for the weekend."

Mako grabbed her purse, took out her cell phone and called Alexander. He left a message in a flirty voice. "Hello, Al, my name is Gilda. I'm at your girlfriend's place. I thought you should know that I've got my knife at Elizabeth's throat. Such a beautiful, delicate, white throat! In fact, I must have pushed a wee bit too hard! She's bleeding a little. Wait, I'll lick it off." Mako removed the knife and licked Elizabeth's throat as she squirmed. "So, Al, please call back; unless, of course, you have no objection if I get rid of her. Then I could be your girlfriend." Mako giggled and put down the cell phone.

"No problem, ladies, we wait. And why not make ourselves comfortable?" Then, looking straight at Marie-France, Mako became aggressive. "What's your name, fatty?"

"Marie-France."

"OK, go sit on that armchair. Elizabeth and I will make ourselves comfortable on the couch."

"I have to go to the bathroom," said Elizabeth.

"Good, we can all go together. We're all girls here."

Elizabeth cringed, as Mako said, "You go first, fatty."

Marie-France dutifully walked to the bathroom, pulled down her jeans and sat on the toilet seat while Mako stood at the doorway with the knife at Elizabeth's neck. Then it was Elizabeth's turn, while Mako held the knife at Marie-France's throat. Mako placed Elizabeth on her knees in front of him while he pulled down his purple slacks to reveal black lace panties. He sat down on the toilet seat like a woman. Elizabeth felt nauseous as she heard the trickle of urine in the toilet bowl.

On the way back to the living room, Mako stopped and told Marie-France to open the refrigerator.

"Got any beer? No? How disappointing. OK, now bring in the groceries from the landing."

Marie-France did as she was told.

"Show me what's in the shopping bags. Olives, sliced ham, cheese, French bread! Oh, goodie! A bottle of *Cabernet Sauvignon*! A twist-off! Now pour me some wine. You've only got one bottle, so forgive me if I don't share."

Marie-France, moving slowly, placed the food on the coffee table and opened the wine bottle.

"Now go to the closet and find me two scarves." Mako instructed Marie-France to tie Elizabeth's hands behind her back.

He checked for tightness. Then, placing the knife on the coffee table, he tied up Marie-France and pushed her into the plaid armchair.

"Now, let's relax," said Mako, and he removed his red jacket to reveal a purple turtleneck sweater and a prominent bust. He sat down on the couch beside Elizabeth and took a long gulp of wine.

"Mm... Heaven!" He looked at his watch. "What's with your boyfriend? Doesn't he care about you?"

"What do you want from Alexander?" asked Elizabeth.

"It shouldn't be too difficult for him to get... say, a hundred thousand dollars to keep you safe. On second thought, that sum is insulting! You are worth more than that! At least five hundred thousand."

It was uncanny, but Elizabeth and Marie-France could often read each other's thoughts. Elizabeth recognised the look on Marie-France's face — panic.

He's crazy enough to kill us both if Alexander doesn't pay him. Does he expect Alexander to just go up to the teller and withdraw five hundred thousand dollars from his chequing account? Is Mako so naïve or so unfamiliar with banking practices? Maybe he saw that movie where the bank manager goes to the vault and fills a gym bag with wads of cash. Is that what he thinks Alexander can do? Why is Alexander not calling back? Has he heard the message? Has he called the police?

Did Alexander think it was a crank call?

"Can a bank give Alexander so much money all at once?" Elizabeth asked.

"Shut up!"

Better keep my mouth shut. Mako's had more than half a bottle of wine. Will he be mellower? More aggressive? Does he even remember that he was once that polite young man in embroidered slippers?

"Gilda, do you know Dr Jordan?" Elizabeth asked. Would this approach transform him into the gentle version of Mako?

"Yes, I've been to his clinic. I'm planning to get some work done on my body soon!"

"Did you know Dr Jordan's dead?" asked Elizabeth.

"Yes, I was there when it happened."

"You were?" Elizabeth felt her diaphragm tighten. She looked at Marie-France, who sat up in the armchair, eyes bulging.

"Yes, I was there. I was there with my cousin." Mako's tone became casual as he reclined on the couch and admired his long red fingernails. "His nickname is Stomper. One tough dude!"

"You were there when Dr Jordan was killed?" Elizabeth asked again, her voice suddenly hoarse.

"Ya, sure! I saw Stomper kill him!"

Elizabeth gasped. "Why? Was it a robbery?"

"You're very inquisitive!" Mako gulped more wine. "OK, why not? So, while we're all waiting for your gallant knight to gallop to your rescue, I'll tell you the story. Actually, Stomper didn't really mean to do it. At first, that is. I mean, he didn't even plan it. He was sort of fond of the old goat in his own way. It all started when Dr Jordan caught Stomper going through his desk. Stomper found the combination to the safe, written in a little black notebook that Dr Jordan kept hidden in some secret drawer. But Stomper had time to memorise the combination. All he planned to do was take the money from the safe and split."

"I thought that Dr Jordan was bankrupt." Elizabeth blurted this out without thinking.

"So did Stomper! But one day, he sees Dr Jordan stuff wads of cash into the safe. Rumour had it that Dr Jordan was laundering money for some drug lords. Private airplanes brought in rich ladies needing facelifts, and some say they also brought in drugs. I mean, like who would have thunk it?" Mako rolled her eyes. "Anyways, so that day, the day Dr Jordan died, he was actually supposed to drive to Montreal. But when Stomper goes into the study, he sees the old guy asleep at his desk — obviously dead drunk. The old geezer had his mouth open, and his head was thrown back over his chair." Mako fell back against the couch to illustrate the pose. "So Stomper tiptoed up to the safe and tried to open it. But he couldn't, and got really mad. The old guy must have changed the code after he caught Stomper snooping around his desk. So Stomper goes all crazy like and starts looking for the little black book. And guess what? It's lying right there on the desk! And would you believe it, the old code is crossed out, and the new code is written in. So Stomper grabs it and almost jumps for joy! I watched as he tried to open the safe. It didn't work the first few times, but then presto! Alakazam! Open sesame!

"Well! Would you believe the safe was empty? There was only some letter in an envelope. The money must have been shipped off to wherever. Anyways, I have never seen anyone get mad like that. He looked like he had steam coming out of his ears. So Stomper grabs the sword hanging behind the desk. He used to like to pretend he was a samurai and practised with it. He loved that sword — he oiled it and kept it razor sharp. It gave him some sort of thrill. So Stomper takes the sword in both hands and walks up to the sleeping old guy, and with one swing, lops off his head. I kid you not, he did it in one swing. Swoosh!" Mako laughed.

"The blood shot out of his neck like a fountain! There was so much blood! So the head falls on the floor. I can still remember the sound of the thump." Mako made a squeamish face.

"The head bounced! Really gory! I almost barfed. But Stomper, he's OK with it, and says that the guy got what he deserved."

Elizabeth and Marie-France sat mesmerised by the horror story.

"So we were about to leave, and I says, 'So, are you going to leave the head lying on the floor?' The guy deserves some dignity! I mean, really!" Mako rolled his eyes. "So Stomper picks up the head and says, 'Where do you want me to put it?' So I says, 'Put it back on the body where it belongs.' So Stomper picks it up by the hair and tries to stick it back. But it keeps falling on the floor. I swear I couldn't have done it. I mean, like, it's somebody's head!" Mako made a squeamish face. "So, finally, I says, 'Stop it!' So, he picks up the head and puts it on the desk next to the body, facing the door. So we both look at it and start to laugh! Well, it was kind of funny in a gruesome sort of way. Stomper enjoys that kind of stuff — he likes really gory horror movies. He watches them and laughs his head off. So, anyways, we took the Aston Martin. Like, we had to get out of Dodge! Stomper drives like a madman. I swear I was scared shitless." Mako drank more wine.

"Does he still have the car?" Elizabeth was not sure what she wanted to accomplish by asking questions. Mako had just confessed to murdering Dr Jordan as the Stomper personality, and this Gilda personality could kill them both without a second thought. *Why did I ask him about the car? Shouldn't I try to convince him not to kill us?*

"No way! Stomper sold it to some guy who specialises in hot cars. He knows him from juvie. The money was fun while it lasted. When it was gone, would you believe that Stomper actually tried to pimp me out? Like who does he think he is? And then he dumped me!"

Mako sighed deeply, wiped away an imaginary tear and gulped the rest of the wine. "But he did tell me all about you and your rich boyfriend. I really don't think it's fair that some people have so much and others have to live on the streets. I was in foster care with the family of some sort of a preacher. He made me go to church and all that. God knows why I still remember this, but didn't Jesus say that it is easier for a camel to go through the eye of a needle than for a rich man to get to heaven? So I guess Jesus didn't really like rich people. So it must be OK to take their money. It's only fair!"

Mako poured himself the last drops of the wine. "What's with your boyfriend? Doesn't he answer his phone?" Mako looked at Elizabeth and raised one painted, black eyebrow.

Elizabeth did not answer, but her body tensed as she heard that familiar rasping sound of a faulty muffler. It could only be Angel's old, green Chevrolet, with rust stains painted over in a colour that did not quite match the original, and scotch tape pasted over a crack in a side window. The women tensed and exchanged frightened looks. *Angel will see Marie-France's car on the street. He will have a fit.* They both froze in anticipation as Angel's car stopped in the driveway. Marie-France's cell phone rang.

"It must be the landlord. I'm not allowed to park in front of the house," said Marie-France.

Mako rose and went to the window to look out onto the street. Angel was standing on the sidewalk, holding his cell phone to his ear. The Angel of Doom yelled so loudly that everyone in the room heard his rant. "Move that car this very minute!"

Mako put the cell phone next to Marie's-France's ear.

"I can't right now," said Marie-France, casting a frightened look at Mako. "I'll do it later."

"What do you mean, later?" yelled Angel. "I'll call the police. I'll call them this very minute! If you think I will pay…"

"Our landlord has this thing about parking on the street. He really will call the police!"

"Oh, yeah!" said Mako in a masculine voice, and he took the cell phone away from Marie-France. "Look, you old fart," he shouted. "Leave the lady alone, or I'll come down and cut your heart out! We're leaving in a few minutes anyway, so keep your lid on, you fat bastard!"

Mako put down the phone and said, "We're getting outta here. Get your purses! And don't forget your credit cards and bank cards. You'd better pray Alexander calls soon, sweetheart!"

They were all astounded when they heard stomping up the stairs. It could only be Angel! Elizabeth knew that Angel was not a man to be intimidated. He would never let some university kids defy him! By refusing to move the car immediately, Marie-France had crossed Angel's red line.

"Who do you think you are?" yelled Angel, bursting through the open door. "You can't talk to me like that!" For a second, he stood with his mouth open; then, pointing his cell phone at Mako, he shouted, "Who is this whore of Babylon?"

In his Gilda splendour, Mako was standing in front of the couch, bending down to look for the knife that was somewhere on the coffee table. Perhaps the wine slowed his reflexes, because Elizabeth saw Mako fall back as Angel pushed him down. Angel's short, squat body pinned Mako to the couch. Despite her tied hands, Elizabeth bent over to bite Mako's ear, but only succeeded in pulling off his wig. Marie-France got up from the armchair and stomped her foot on Mako's red vinyl boot.

Mako, now wigless, struggled and cursed. Without a wig, his garish make-up made him look both frightening and ridiculous.

"I already called 911!" yelled Angel.

Perhaps Mako could have wriggled out, but Angel managed to grab the knife from the coffee table. From the look of rage on Angel's face, it was clear that he would not hesitate to use it.

Elizabeth's phone rang. It was from Alexander. With her hands still tied, she could not answer it.

Then came the wailing police sirens. It was the most beautiful sound Elizabeth had ever heard. The rest of the day was a blur. There was the sound of stomping police officers running up the stairs, and Mako's enraged screams as they led him away: "I'll kill you, Elizabeth! I'll kill you!"

When Mako was gone, the wave of relief rushed through her body and left her so weak that it was difficult to lift the glass of water offered by a young female police officer. She sat on the couch, hugging Marie-France and crying. Then they both thanked Angel and told the police he was their hero. Between sobs, they recounted what happened.

"Is there anyone you can call to spend the night with you?" asked the police officer.

"We have our Guardian Angel downstairs. We feel safe," said Elizabeth. She and Marie-France never imagined that Angel would turn out to be their saviour. Angel seemed to grow a few inches. He preened in front of the policemen, his shoulders back and chest forward. He looked almost handsome.

Chapter 29

That night, Elizabeth dreamed she was running for her life, chased by a woman with flaming red hair. She awoke paralysed by fear. She turned her face into the pillow to stifle the image. *Who could blame me for staying in bed all day? Lizzie, you were kidnapped at knifepoint by a madman in drag. Oh, shit, I have to go to the police station.* She looked over to Marie-France's empty bed and heard the shower. *Of course, Wonder Woman hasn't gone all wobbly. Shape up, Lizzie! You're not the same person you were last year.* Slowly, she forced herself to get out of bed.

By nine a.m. as she and Marie-France were on the way to the police station, Alexander called. Elizabeth did not pick up. He called again when she was reading her statement. She did not pick up. *Why don't I want to speak to him? Why do I feel as if he let me down somehow? There's no rational reason to blame him for not picking up his phone when Mako called. How could he even imagine...? I'll call him later.*

Leaving the police station, Elizabeth went to the library to prepare for her exam on Tuesday afternoon. She felt a steely resolve not to let the Mako incident interfere with her studies. *Your future depends upon it, Lizzie!* She shut off her cell phone and forced herself to cram all afternoon.

As she walked into the flat that evening, she bumped into Marie-France, who was on her way out.

"Where were you? Alexander came over just now. He has been calling you all day. He's very worried. Why didn't you call him back?"

"I was studying for my exam on Tuesday! I don't need any distractions."

"Alexander told me he drove over here last night, just as the police were taking Mako away. He recognised Gilda as Mako, so he was asked to go to the police station. It was late when he came back, and our lights were out."

"He called me repeatedly today, but I did not pick up."

"I don't understand your sudden hostility towards Alexander."

"I'm exhausted. I'll eat, then I'll study some more."

"Why don't you call Alexander?"

"Please!" Elizabeth almost shouted. "Don't tell me what to do!"

"OK! OK! I'm having supper with Benjie." Marie-France looked at her watch and ran down the stairs.

Elizabeth did call Alexander. She tried to sound cool and casual. Alexander told her that on Saturdays, he plays racquetball in the afternoon and then swims laps at the university pool. He went out to a pub with a colleague and did not turn on his cell phone until he was paying the bill. That is when he called the police and came right over.

"How were you to know there would be a crisis?" Elizabeth said. She did not ask whether he would have tried to rescue her had he known about the kidnapping earlier. She realised that there was no rational reason why Alexander should have acceded to Mako's demands. After all, they were not related, and she was not even his girlfriend. And yet, she was conscious of some faintly defined wish that, like a knight in shining armour, Alexander would have galloped to her rescue and freed her from the clutches of the evil Mako. *Honestly, Lizzie! Stop with this fairy tale bullshit! There are no knights in shining armour!*

"It must have been terrible! How are you feeling?"

Elizabeth said she was fine and that she was studying for an exam. He must have sensed the coolness in her voice. "You sound very tired," he said. "I will let you concentrate on your studies."

"Oh, does Inspector Jolicoeur know about what happened?" Elizabeth asked.

"Yes, I called him last night from the police station. He told me he is coming to Ottawa on Tuesday morning. He plans on calling you. I'm inviting you both to dinner. I'll text you later."

Elizabeth made herself a pot of strong coffee and crammed till she fell asleep on the couch. Marie-France came home at midnight and pushed Elizabeth into bed.

At six p.m. on Tuesday, Elizabeth walked into the Unicorn and Lion pub. She was in a good mood, confident that she had done well on the exam.

Alexander looked very smart, dressed in a black turtleneck and a brown suede jacket. He put down his cell phone and rose to hug her.

"After all you went through, you did not miss your exam! I know you must be exhausted, but you look so good!"

Elizabeth slid into the booth, which was upholstered in green plaid. "You know, it's strange — yesterday I was totally wiped out, but now I feel euphoric. It's probably some kind of primitive, physiological survival response. Wow, I survived! It could also be relief that the exam is over."

"You know, I feel responsible. You were a target because of your connection to the Mont Tremblant estate." He reached across the table and squeezed her hand. His hand felt warm and reassuring.

Yesterday's resentment melted away. *He must care, at least a little bit. I can feel it in his touch.* Elizabeth squeezed his hand in return, looked straight into his eyes and said, "I'm sorry I did not call back yesterday. I am really touched by your concern. You know how much you mean—"

Looking embarrassed, Alexander turned his eyes away. "The Quebec police will charge Mako with murder," he interrupted. "Mako confessed in front of two witnesses to killing Dr Jordan. Case closed!"

Why did he interrupt? Does talking about my feelings make him uncomfortable? Did he think I was about to confess that I'm in love with him or what? Why did I even bring up my feelings? Idiot!

"What's the matter?" he asked.

"I don't know... I'm happy, sad, and confused all at the same time. What were you saying?" Elizabeth's smile was sad. *Forget about any budding romantic nonsense, Lizzie! Don't embarrass yourself!*

"Mako will be required to undergo a psychological assessment. It could very well be that he will not stand trial. I've read that most criminals single-mindedly pursue their own interests with no sense of social conscience or empathy for their victims. However, in order to stand trial they should know the difference between right and wrong," he said, as a young waitress wearing a plaid miniskirt and black knee socks approached their table. Elizabeth ordered a glass of white wine. Alexander chose beer on tap. He told the waitress that they were expecting another person.

"Inspector Jolicoeur seems to be running late. He was at the Ottawa police station most of the day." Alexander looked across the restaurant.

"Well, speak of the devil."

A puffing Inspector Jolicoeur walked into the pub. He left his hooded parka in the coat check room. His navy-blue blazer must have been purchased when he was at least one size thinner. He also wore a navy blue knitted tie. There was a broad smile under the walrus moustache. He waved, bought a beer on tap at the bar, and came to their table.

"I don't have much time," he said. "My wife is expecting me. She doesn't like being left alone for the night." He sat down next to Alexander.

"Elizabeth! I'm so sorry you had to go through such a horrible ordeal. But because of you, we now have Dr Jordan's murderer. I can't imagine how terrifying it must have been for you and your friend! You behaved heroically!"

"I'm just glad it's over. I want to forget all about it as fast as I can."

"Thank goodness your landlord proved to be such a tough guy. At least you did not have to wait for Alexander to rob a bank to get your ransom."

This was the very question that Elizabeth had been afraid to ask — a perfect opportunity. "What would you have done, Alexander, if Mako had asked you for a ransom?"

"I don't know!" Alexander seemed amused by the question. Elizabeth leaned forward; she did not want to miss a word of Alexander's reply.

"I'd call my Uncle Jean, who handles my trust fund. I'd call the lawyers, my accountant, the police... I don't even know for sure how much money I have. I get a monthly allowance from the trust. Did Mako think that I keep bags of cash under my bed?"

"Here's to our fearless Guardian Angel. He literally saved our lives," said Elizabeth, and she raised her glass.

The inspector took out his notebook. "I don't have much time, so, with your permission, I will get right down to business. I've read the transcript of your police interview. Can you tell me what Mako said about Dr Jordan's safe after he opened it?"

"I don't remember his precise words. I think he said the safe was empty. He said that on a previous occasion, he saw the safe was stuffed with wads of bills."

"It was not quite empty," said Inspector Jolicoeur.

"Ordinarily, I would not disclose the details of a case. As you know, our police station leaks like a sieve. You may have read about the scandal in the newspapers a few years ago. Our district chief retired, and the SAQ executives at head office ignored the union's recommendation and appointed an outsider — from Montreal. All hell broke loose. The new chief was harassed, orders were ignored, and dead cats were left at his front door. After a year, the poor man resigned and moved away. But the genie was out of the bottle. Discipline was never entirely restored, and we still have serious leaks. Everyone in the village already knows that Dr Jordan was decapitated. And yesterday, I heard that someone started a rumour that the police lost Dr Jordan's head!"

"What was in the safe?" asked Alexander.

"It was a letter. According to village gossip, the letter is Dr Jordan's confession. He admitted to being Mako's biological father, among other things."

"What?" Alexander and Elizabeth exclaimed in unison.

"I took the original letter for safekeeping. Not strictly by the book, but at least it won't appear in the *Gossip Queen*," said the inspector, and he took out an envelope with an embossed Sureté de Quebec logo. "This is a copy. It's addressed to you, Alexander."

"To me!" Alexander's olive complexion became a shade paler.

"I read it," Inspector Jolicoeur continued. "Apologies, but this is a murder investigation."

Alexander placed the letter into the breast pocket of his suede jacket.

The young waitress approached to take their orders. Elizabeth ordered fish and chips, while the inspector and Alexander both opted for steak and kidney pie.

During the meal, Inspector Jolicoeur asked questions about the attempted kidnapping. Then he told them about Dr Jordan's connection to drug smuggling.

"Vasquez is well known to our American colleagues. He is a Miami lawyer and a front for a Columbian cartel. We suspect that the private planes that brought rich ladies to Dr Jordan's cosmetic surgery clinic also smuggled in drugs, and money was laundered through Dr Jordan's clinic. The clinic is only one of the cogs in the wheel of an intricate drug-smuggling network."

"I know that Mako confessed, but is it possible that he was hired by the cartel? That Dr Jordan with his debts and mismanagement became a liability and the cartel wanted to install a new front man?" asked Alexander.

"Yes, I suppose... However, I doubt it. The cartel uses its own killers. The SAQ drug division is investigating, and forensic accountants are going over the clinic's books." Inspector Jolicoeur stopped talking to take a call on his cell phone. "Ten minutes," he said. "That was Constable Fortin; he's finished at the Ottawa station. He's on his way to pick me up."

"Was Zsuzsanna involved in the murder or the drug smuggling?" asked Elizabeth.

"I would like to interview her. She seemed to have left town in a hurry — right after Dr Jordan's murder. She told some people that she had been invited to visit friends in Florida. Her cell phone has been disconnected. No dessert for me," he told the waitress standing at the table. He took out his credit card, but Alexander objected.

"Please, I invited you, Inspector!"

The inspector rose and shook hands with Alexander and Elizabeth. "I'll keep in touch," he said, as he walked to the coat check room.

When Inspector Jolicoeur left the pub, Elizabeth looked at Alexander and said, "Are you all right?"

He raised his head and looked at her with sad eyes. "Why would Dr Jordan write me a letter? I feel the envelope scorching my ribs."

"It's none of my business, but considering what I already know about your family, can you share the letter with me?" Elizabeth asked.

Alexander did not answer, and sat looking down at the table. Finally, he said, "I suppose I'm afraid to open it. It could be something completely harmless, banal or... I don't want any more unexpected revelations about my family."

He sat looking into his glass of beer for what seemed a long time, then he looked up at Elizabeth and said, "Perhaps sharing will make it easier." He took the envelope out of his jacket pocket. The letter was written in long-hand, in a script that resembled Gothic.

"To Alexander. To be opened after my death."

"Rather melodramatic," said Alexander, and he began to read out loud. "Alexander, You are probably wondering why this letter is addressed to you. The answer is simple. I have known you since your infancy, and you are one of a few people I still feel close to. I lost my parents when I was still a teenager, and due to my lifelong friendship with Ted, I created the illusion that your family was also mine.

"This letter is a confession. Why, you may well ask? I will try to explain. As a child, I went to church every Sunday with my Bulgarian grandmother. I can still remember the heavy smell of incense and the flicker of candles under the dark icons. Several times a year, I would confess my horrible sins: I stole my friend's marbles, I lied to my teacher about my homework... I confessed to an old Orthodox priest with a long white beard. After my confession, the priest muttered prayers and placed a cloth of gold brocade over my head. Then I kissed a large golden cross. Finally, he would bless me and tell me that God absolved me of my sins. I believed that the warm wine I drank from the golden cup was the blood of Christ, and the morsel of unleavened bread was the body of Christ. To this day, I remember the feeling of lightness and joy I always felt after this ritual: my sins were absolved and I was pure.

"I have long since stopped believing in God, but inexplicably, I now feel the need to confess. Perhaps, in the dark recesses of my soul, I have a dim hope that He exists after all and that He will accept this confession, forgive my horrible sins, and I will stand before Him clean and pure. How silly! Alexander, I do not expect anyone to forgive me or even understand me. I know I will be killed soon. The people I became entangled with are ruthless and merciless. I accept my imminent death as a form of punishment for my earthly sins, as a restoration of some kind of cosmic equilibrium. Is that what they call justice?

"For most of my adult life, I have been secretly in love with your mother. I cared for you, I still care for you, because she loved you. Ted was often unkind to you both because he must have suspected... In his heart, he knew that he was not your biological father. He was tormented, but remained madly in love with her. Ted was unable to forgive her, yet he could not let her go. He became cruel, and she suffered in silence. When Mattie's bouts of depression became more frequent, I convinced Ted to move to the Mont Tremblant estate to treat her in my clinic. In reality, this was a ploy. I wanted to be near her. To have her to myself, at least at the clinic. It did not matter that Ted was my best friend and that she took her vows seriously. I was totally obsessed, even though I knew that she felt only friendship for me.

"She would stay at the clinic, usually for a week. At first, I treated her insomnia and sleepwalking with drugs. However, I could not control myself; often, when she was in a drug-induced sleep, I entered her room and held her in my arms. These were moments of utter happiness. I never violated her in her sleep; I wanted her to give me her love willingly."

Elizabeth gasped as Alexander dropped the sheet of paper. When he continued to read again, his voice became a whisper as he struggled with his emotions. *"I began to hypnotise her into believing that she was madly in love with me. When she awoke in the morning, she had no memory of our nights of passion."* Alexander crumpled the letter. His face became dark, and he pressed his lips together so tightly that they almost disappeared. "If he was alive now, I would kill him myself."

Elizabeth felt sick to her stomach. "I always knew that man was evil." She reached across the table, picked up the crumpled sheets and flattened them with her palm. "Alexander, would you mind if I read it?"

Alexander nodded.

Elizabeth read: *"You must feel anger and disgust. My obsessive love for Mattie is not an excuse. Confessing these sins does not lighten their despicable nature. I also want to clear up my role during the night Mattie died. I brought her home from the clinic, and Ted and I both had a lot to drink at supper. I stayed in the guest bedroom. Later that night — around three in the morning — Ted rushed into my room. He was panic-stricken, babbling, and barely coherent. He found Mattie standing over his bed with a knife raised over him. She was sleepwalking. He placed his robe around her shoulders and led her back to her room, but at the top of the stairs, Mattie turned and tried to stab him. They struggled, and she fell down the stairs. When I examined Mattie, she was already dead! I wanted to cry and howl at the moon. 'You pushed her! You killed her!' I hissed at Ted. 'No, no, it was an accident!' Ted wailed. I decided then and there that I would make him pay. I convinced Ted that he would be the prime suspect. I promised to protect him from the police. He was so grateful! He lent me money..."*

Alexander interrupted. "Stop! I need to catch my breath. How can it be? How could Uncle Tig, the same Uncle Tig who found quarters behind my ears, who brought me books and toys...? How could he...? He was playing a role... He was actually trying to seduce my mother the whole time! How much more is there?"

"Another full page."

"Let's get it over with," said Alexander.

Elizabeth returned to the letter. *"And finally, my last confession. Mako is my biological son. I broke my Hippocratic Oath — I slept with a patient at a psychiatric hospital where I was an intern. No excuses. Her name was Uki; she was an Inuit from Kujuuak. She was on the mend, young, pretty, and lonely. She fell in love with me. I thought I loved her, too. When she was released, I promised to fly to Kujuuak that summer and bring her back. Then I received a letter telling me that she was pregnant. I made up excuses for delaying my trip. I sent money. The baby, Mako, was about one year old when I told her that I was not coming. She committed suicide, and Mako was left in the care of his alcoholic grandmother. Some years later, I received a call from a social worker. She arranged to have Mako brought to Montreal. I never did develop any real paternal feelings for him. He lived with a succession of foster families. Mako was born a sociopath! He is the punishment for the sins of my youth.*

"So many other sins, although I'm not sure that bad management is a sin. I should have declared bankruptcy, but my pride would not allow it. I borrowed from the cartel, and they turned my clinic into a centre for drug smuggling and money laundering. It is a wonder that the police were in the dark for so many years.

"As an adult, I lived outside the bounds of conventional mortality — I lived as if everything was permitted. Why do I return to outdated concepts of right and wrong? Why do I write this confession? Yes, I have confessed, but am I really repentant? What if this confession is a lie, too?"

Elizabeth stopped reading and looked up at Alexander. His demeanour remained expressionless, as he held the remains of a tattered, red napkin in his fist.

"Let's go," he said. He took back the letter, called the waitress, and paid the bill. They drove several blocks to Elizabeth's flat in silence. He got out of the car and walked Elizabeth to the steps of the flat. "Good night, Elizabeth," he said, and turned away.

Elizabeth could not fall asleep. She thought it must have been excruciating for Alexander to listen to Dr Jordan's confession about his mother. *Poor, poor, Mathilde — so beautiful and so unhappy. Except for that brief love affair and her love for Alexander, her life was full of pain! And I was right about Dr Jordan; he really was a monster! But why did he write that confession? Was it really a confession? Did he write it in case — in case God really does exist?* She faintly remembered a line in the letter — something to the effect that perhaps the entire confession was a lie. But why lie about Mathilde? Did he make it up to hurt Alexander? Didn't he say that Alexander was the only person he cared about? Was that a lie, too? What if he invented the whole story to get back at Mathilde for repulsing his advances? His revenge was to cause pain to her beloved son? No, that's too sick! Too weird! Or not? *Enough psychobabble, Lizzie! You're overexcited and tired! Go to sleep!* Elizabeth lay awake until dawn.

Chapter 30

December turned out to be dreary, overcast and cold. The sun disappeared from the sky, and as it seemed to Elizabeth, from her life as well. Apart from her commitments at the Language School, every day meant either a deadline for an essay or a test. The nightmares she experienced after the kidnapping were less frequent, although those that she remembered always came just before dawn. Once she dreamed that Gilda, in a red chiffon ball gown, was chasing her through Rideau Mall. Elizabeth begged pedestrians to protect her, but they all walked away. She woke up out of breath. On another occasion, she dreamed that as she walked into her flat, she saw Dr Jordan's headless body sitting in the armchair. She awoke shaking in terror. Elizabeth stopped telling Marie-France about the nightmares to avoid endless advice about seeing a counsellor. Her sisters, particularly Amanda, called every day for a week after the attempted kidnapping.

"No, I am not going to have another depression! I don't have time for depression! I'm too busy!" Elizabeth told Amanda. "I have to finish this semester! I have to do well!"

"Are you sure you can do it without any counselling? Please get some help!"

"Stop treating me like a victim! I'm OK!"

Somehow, Elizabeth managed to keep all the balls in the air. One evening during exam week, both Marie-France and Elizabeth came back to the flat exhausted. They opened a can of beef and vegetable soup and made ham and cheese sandwiches for supper.

"If we live through this week, we both deserve medals," said Marie-France. "I will probably collapse after my final exam."

"I forgot how people live if they're not working and studying all the time."

"I'd love to go skiing," said Marie-France. "I want to be on top of a hill on a sunny day and look at snow-covered wilderness. Vast, peaceful, pristine…"

"And the air — so crisp, so invigorating! Last summer at the estate, I really loved being out on the lake in the canoe. Water and sunshine — so therapeutic!"

"Did you canoe with Alexander?" asked Marie-France. "By the way, how is Alexander?"

"He hasn't called. It's the end of the semester for him, too. He probably associates me with all the recent horrors. Why would he want to revisit all that?"

Elizabeth did not tell Marie-France or anyone else about Dr Jordan's letter to Alexander. She felt very protective of information concerning Mathilde's tragic life. "Last I heard, Alexander's going to Morocco for Christmas."

"Really! Why Morocco?"

Elizabeth was discreet about Alexander's private life. She would tell Marie-France the real purpose of his visit to Morocco after Alexander's return. "Maybe he likes couscous! He probably wants to go somewhere very far to get away from it all."

"Did he invite you to go with him?"

Elizabeth blew up. "Why would he? Stop insinuating that we are an item. He considers me a friend. That's all!"

"OK! OK! No need to get mad!"

Elizabeth did not finish her sandwich. She rose abruptly, put her dishes into the sink, went to the makeshift desk across the room, and began correcting tests.

Alexander did call later that week. He said he had only a few minutes to talk and was off to Casablanca on 20th December.

"That's in two days! I guess I won't see you again this year. You promised me that photograph! Remember?"

"It's not something I can control, but I certainly hope that I will be able to send it." He wished her Happy Holidays and said that he would be back in Ottawa the first week of January.

When she put down the telephone, she thought that she detected a certain nervousness in his voice. *Sure, he must be anxious about whether his father will even want to see him. I hope he's not still upset about Dr Jordan's letter. Although how does one get over something like that?*

On 22nd December, Elizabeth and Marie-France packed the Mini Cooper and drove to Montreal. Marie-France would spend Christmas with her brother. Elizabeth was looking forward to seeing her sisters and to a week of rest.

Elizabeth opened the door with her own key and walked into Catherine's apartment. She pulled up the Venetian blinds to let some faint light into the dark living room and picked up Catherine's clothes scattered over the blue velvet couch.

Catherine woke up as Elizabeth tiptoed into the bedroom. "You still sleep till noon!" Hugs, kisses, tears and laughter. Elizabeth made coffee, and they sat down on the couch, knees curled under, and caught up. Catherine had no regrets about dropping out of sociology at Concordia University, although she found the computer diploma programme extremely challenging. "I'm not sure I will enjoy working with computers; I'm more of a people person."

"But at least you won't be working nights and weekends."

"I guess I could get used to normal hours. It's a practical diploma; I still have time to decide what I want to do when I grow up," she said, and she began to laugh. "This is my first vacation in god only knows how many years. Oh, by the way, we are expected at Amanda's tomorrow. She and Rob are driving to Kingston the next day to spend Christmas Eve and Christmas Day with Rob's family. Amanda asked us to bring a dessert."

The sisters took the commuter train from the Vendome Station and arrived at Pointe-Claire fifteen minutes later. They walked the four blocks to Amanda's little white clapboard cottage. Amanda, perfectly groomed as usual, greeted them in a dark brown velvet lounge outfit and matching patent leather flats. She air-kissed her sisters without smudging her lipstick and guided them into the small, white living room.

"I just bought this leather sofa at Mobilia," she said. "Isn't it gorgeous? Genuine Italian calf! I couldn't resist it. When I told Rob how much it cost, he gagged on his coffee. We had this huge fight, so I'm paying it out myself."

"Why the bare white walls?" asked Catherine. "It looks like a hospital."

"I don't want to hang up anything tacky, so I'll wait until I can afford something decent."

The adjoining dining room had a glass table and six white leather chairs. The galley kitchen was all white with modern cabinets and new shiny chrome appliances.

"We postponed our Mediterranean cruise to do a mini-makeover in the kitchen. The expansion will have to wait. I won't show you the rest of the house. It hasn't been done yet."

"And where is your lord and master?" asked Catherine.

"He's at his company's Christmas party. He was miffed that I didn't go. I told him that I have family obligations, too." Amanda's tone emphasised the extraordinary sacrifices she was willing to bear for the sake of her sisters.

Turning to Elizabeth, Amanda asked, "So how's life in the nation's capital? You practically never phone."

Elizabeth had warned them that she did not want to discuss anything to do with the kidnapping or the Mont Tremblant estate. Elizabeth began to describe her courses, while Catherine opened a bottle of white wine. Amanda led them into the living room and placed supermarket sushi on the glass and chrome coffee table.

"Have you met anyone yet?" Amanda interrupted Elizabeth.

"Who has the time?"

"Make time! Go to the places where rich men hang out. Do you know how the wife of that millionaire... what's his name... met her husband? She took tennis lessons and spent a lot of time at the club's pool in a bikini. She got her man."

"It's winter," said Catherine.

"So, do you still have your skis? You don't even need skis. Go for the après ski and hang out at the ski bar."

"I'm concentrating on getting a degree!"

"Hey, I haven't skied in years," said Catherine. "Why don't we go on a ski trip? I know where I can get a cheap room up north. We have to have some fun during the holidays."

"Sure, but ask Marie-France first — she's the one with the car."

As they sat down at the glass dining table decorated with a silver wreath centrepiece, Amanda explained that she had worked half a day and did not have time to bake a whole turkey. She served a turkey roll, the kind that goes from the freezer to the oven. It was accompanied by canned cranberry relish, lumpy mashed potatoes and a frozen vegetable medley. The gravy and stuffing came from packets.

"We'll have to get up at the crack of dawn to drive to Kingston tomorrow — Rob's whole family is gathering, and we have to help his parents," Amanda explained with a yawn.

The sisters took the hint and did not overstay their welcome. Amanda drove them to the train station. Once seated in the empty car, Elizabeth put her head on Catherine's shoulder. "I feel so alone."

"Am I invisible or what?"

"I didn't mean it that way! It's just that it doesn't feel like Christmas. As I was sitting at Amanda's glass table, I remembered Grandma's tablecloth with the little embroidered poinsettias and the smell of roasting turkey. And the *Buche de Nöel* and those cookies shaped like Christmas trees we used to decorate with green frosting and silver sprinkles."

"And on Boxing Day, Grandpa used to take us tobogganing on the mountain," said Catherine.

"When you get married, I'll be completely alone."

"First of all, I'm not getting married. Moving to the suburbs is not exactly on my to-do list!" Catherine hugged her sister.

For the next two days, Elizabeth and Catherine stayed in the apartment, lounging around in pyjamas, binge-watching Netflix and eating pizza.

On Boxing Day, Marie-France drove up in her Mini Cooper. Her brother had installed a new ski rack, so they managed to get to the Laurentians without losing a ski.

The cheap accommodation turned out to be a cosy little inn built in the Alpine style — all lacquered logs. An orange vinyl couch stood in front of a massive stone fireplace in the communal living room. The owners, a middle-aged Austrian couple, included breakfast and a hearty supper for their twenty-five guests. There was an open bar. Catherine had managed to reserve a room with two bunk beds, only because of a last-minute cancellation. The inn was twenty minutes from the ski hill — in Mont Tremblant.

Chapter 31

On 25th December, Elizabeth had phoned Monsieur and Madame Gervais to wish them a Merry Christmas. They were now the proud owners of a cell phone. From the sound of voices in the background, she knew that they were at Bernadette's for a big family dinner. They insisted that she visit them for lunch during her ski vacation. Elizabeth was reluctant but agreed, not wanting to offend them.

As expected, the Mont Tremblant weather was sunny but freezing. The wind cut through the woollen ski mask, and Elizabeth put Vaseline on her nose. On the third day of skiing, Elizabeth bought a half-day ticket. Monsieur Gervais, driving his golden Impala, picked her up at the base of the ski hill. On the way to the estate, he told Elizabeth that the couple would leave the mansion in January. The inventories were done. Papers and books were shipped off and the tedious process of settling the estate was almost over. Alexander had pushed the estate office to expedite Agnew-Simpson's bequest to the couple.

"Louise is not looking forward to living with her sister. It's fine for Sundays, but she is used to being her own mistress. We would like to buy a little house in the village. By the way, I ran into Inspector Jolicoeur at the hardware store the other day, and I told him you were coming for lunch. He asked to drop by. He wants to talk to you. I hope you don't mind."

Elizabeth did mind. *What could he want from me? The murder of Dr Jordan solved itself. Guardian Angel caught Mako. The police would never have found Mako in his Gilda disguise.* "I don't have much time," she said. "I have to meet my sister in the parking lot at four."

As Monsieur Gervais drove the car into the private road lined with tall pine trees, Elizabeth remembered that day in May when the colonnade of trees reminded her of an honour guard. Under the grey December sky, amid the white snow, the mansion looked stark and foreboding. But the joy in Madame Gervais's blue eyes was warm and welcoming. Elizabeth felt guilty about her initial reluctance to visit them. They had been so kind. She couldn't have survived without them.

The kitchen smelled of good food — pea soup, apples, and a faint hint of cinnamon.

"You need something warm after skiing in such arctic weather! I made a *soupe aux pois*, a *ragoût de boulettes* and apple pie. Marcel is happy, too, because I have not been in the mood for cooking. You look so lovely, Elizabeth; I thought that you would lose weight after your ordeal."

"I've had a rest during the holidays, and I am trying to put all the horrible events behind me. Let's not talk about it. What about you? Why don't you start your retirement with a trip to Florida? Sunshine! The ocean!"

"Alexander offered to send us on an all-expenses-paid vacation. I don't know! I never travelled."

"What about a Caribbean cruise? My sister Amanda has been on a cruise, and she says that everything is taken care of, so you could relax completely!"

"I'll think about it. I would like to get away from the village. I can't go to the grocery store without having to listen to all kinds of nonsense."

"I'm sure the village gossip is as colourful as ever."

That must have been the cue Monsieur Gervais was waiting for. "Elizabeth, did you ever see the star Dr Jordan wore around his neck? It was a pentagram — it's the Devil's symbol."

"I don't remember. I saw a gold chain, but it was always under his shirt."

"And that witch of his, that Zsuzsanna... My cousin's daughter was her cleaning lady. She saw a cross with a snake entwined around it on Zsuzsanna's dresser!"

"Marcel, why do you repeat such nonsense? Elizabeth will get upset."

"These are solid facts! Elizabeth should know! Yvette, that's Bernadette's daughter, who cleaned Dr Jordan's house, she saw the pentagram..."

"Marcel, Yvette didn't actually see it. Gerard, the orderly, who was asked to clean the study after they took away Dr Jordan's body, he saw it and told Yvette."

"Yes, that's right," said Monsieur Gervais. "The pentagram must have flown off Dr Jordan's head when Mako chopped it off."

Elizabeth squirmed at the memory. Monsieur Gervais did not notice, and continued, "I think it's obvious, it was a satanic ritual killing. That's the only logical conclusion!"

"I find that difficult to believe," said Elizabeth, suppressing her discomfort.

"You have to admit that the murder scene was staged, and the body was posed. According to Gerard, someone traced 666 in blood on the desk, right next to his severed head. And the police found all kinds of satanic paraphernalia in his study — a goblet with an image of a goat, and a large golden cross with a snake entwined around it."

"Monsieur Gervais," said Elizabeth, "Alexander and I found the body. I didn't see anything like that."

"But you were in shock! How closely did you look?"

"Marcel!" said Madame Gervais. "Enough!"

Elizabeth changed the subject. "And what will happen to the clinic and the patients?"

"The cosmetic surgery clients — no problem — with all their money they can go wherever they choose. But the addicts and mental patients who weren't picked up by relatives were kicked out to god knows where. The bank will probably auction off the entire complex," said Monsieur Gervais.

"Please! It's time for you to get away from all this! Please, take a vacation in the sun!"

As they were finishing the apple pie, Inspector Jolicoeur arrived. He asked to speak to Elizabeth in Mr Ted's study. With only the desk and two chairs, the study looked cavernous.

Elizabeth walked up to the glass doors to look outside. She had not seen the lake in winter. It was covered by a blanket of dull snow under a dreary, leaden sky. The fir trees looked haggard as they stood alone or in clusters, waiting for spring. *And I'm different, too. Last winter, I was a basket case, just back from Bangkok, still agonising over Stephen — thinking my life was over. Don't worry,* she addressed the trees, *your spring will come. Life will bloom again.*

"I know you have to be back at the ski hill this afternoon," Inspector Jolicoeur interrupted her thoughts. He was wearing baggy jeans and a hand-knitted, navy blue sweater with lime-green Christmas trees. This could only be a creation of the prolific Madame Jolicoeur.

"Yes, I have to meet my sister soon," she said, looking at her watch. "I was happy to see Monsieur and Madame Gervais, but I felt very uncomfortable listening to the bizarre rumours about Dr Jordan's death. I am trying to forget about all that horror."

"What can you do about village gossip? Ignore it! Mako is behind bars, and you can be sure that he will never threaten you again! You will probably be required to testify at the inquest and at the trial — if there is a trial."

"Are you saying that Mako may be placed in a psychiatric institution?"

"I don't know. Perhaps he will plead insanity. In any case, he will have to be assessed. Miss Burgess, I wanted to talk to you because of something you said during our first interview. I am reviewing my final report for the inquest into Mr Agnew-Simpson's death. It is coming up in January, and I want to make sure I have covered everything as thoroughly as possible."

Elizabeth approached the desk. It looked like an orphan in this enormous room — smaller than she remembered. She touched the carved beaver head on the false drawer. She gave it a turn, and the secret drawer slid out.

"Finding this was a lucky break," she said.

"Yes, it was. The presence of barbiturates in the drawer, however, only explains the location of the pills. It does not rule out suicide."

"And you are absolutely sure that it was suicide?" asked Elizabeth.

"Based on the facts, I am reasonably sure. Although my gut tells me that I may have overlooked something... Something I cannot quite figure out."

"So you do not deny the role played by intuition. Last time we spoke about it, I thought you dismissed it as nonsense."

"I recently read something interesting about intuition, although I'm not sure I understood it correctly. According to neuroscience, our choices about everything we do are made by billions of split-second calculations in our brains. Intuition is a shortcut — a form of instant pattern recognition based on past experience. I certainly do not discount intuition,

Miss Burgess. It is definitely useful, provided it can lead to evidence that can stand up in court."

"Well, my intuition tells me that it was murder by telephone. Unfortunately, I can't prove it."

"My wife and I watched *The Manchurian Candidate*. We both enjoyed it. However, I could not present the film as evidence without being laughed out of court. I would need proof — physical proof of some kind." Inspector Jolicoeur leafed through his notebook. "What was it you said about your feeling that someone was listening to your telephone calls? Was it based on anything specific?"

"I always heard a click when I picked up the phone. I don't know whether that means anything. Although, once I told my sister that my boss was intimidating but not an ogre. I don't remember the context, but the next morning, when I went into his office, Mr Ted laughed and said that he was not an ogre. Of course, it could have been a coincidence. But if he was recording conversations — where is the equipment? The police must have scoured the entire house."

As Elizabeth spoke, the inspector walked up to the panels hiding the bar. He pushed the carved beaver head in the decorative frieze of the wainscoting. The panels slid open, revealing bare shelves.

"Mr Agnew-Simpson certainly liked secret drawers and hidden panels." He stood looking at the wall, then turned to Elizabeth and said, "Perhaps we missed something. Let's look."

"What should I look for?"

"Try manipulating carved beaver heads in the frieze on your side of the room."

Elizabeth made her way down one side of the study wall. At the end of the room, at the spot where the mobile bookshelf once stood, she turned a carved bear's head and heard a creaking sound. A latch was released, and a panel slid open to reveal a small white door.

The inspector lowered his head and stepped into a recording studio. Elizabeth was slack-jawed. There was a console with knobs, lights and piles of disks stacked on shelves.

"Elizabeth, please pick up the phone and call someone," said Inspector Jolicoeur. Elizabeth called Amanda and left a message, then returned to find the inspector seated on a metal stool in front of the console. One of the lights was flashing red. He pushed a button. They listened to a recording of her message to Amanda.

"That explains the click," she said.

The inspector fiddled with the buttons as they listened to fragments of recorded conversations — Madame Gervais talking to her sister, Elizabeth and Catherine, Agnew-Simpson and his lawyer.

Her next thought came like an electric shock. "Who called Mr Ted just before he died?"

"Who, indeed? Give me a few minutes. I have some experience with tapes."

The inspector manipulated other buttons. Elizabeth shivered as she heard Agnew-Simpson's voice. "Tig, I do not want to talk to you! How dare you try to get me into bed with that gangster?"

"What gangster?"

They both recognised Dr Jordan's voice.

"The one from the Columbian cartel!"

"Señor Vasquez? Really, Ted!"

"He's a gangster in a Brooks Brothers suit! And furthermore, I have had enough of your blackmail…"

"I resent your choice of words, Ted. May I remind you that I have always had your best interests at heart? Have I ever breathed a word about that night when Mattie…"

"It was ruled an accident!"

"That is not why I am calling. I am calling to say goodbye."

"Are you going away?"

"No, Ted. It's sunset time, Ted. Sunset time. What time is it, Ted?"

"Sunset time," said Agnew-Simpson. His voice sounded hollow.

"What time is it, Ted?"

"Sunset time."

"I presume you are drinking cognac?"

"*Courvoisier.*"

Elizabeth detected a slowness and a metallic tone in Agnew-Simpson's voice.

"Find your pills… How many pills do you have, Ted?"

"Four."

"Take the pills. Now drink your cognac. It's sunset time, Ted. Sunset time. Have you taken the pills?"

"Yes, I have."

There was a long silence, then hoarse breathing, and the sound of the telephone receiver falling on the desk. Elizabeth felt bile rise to her throat. "Sunset time is the trigger phrase!" Elizabeth's face turned pale. "This proves murder! How can anyone doubt?"

Inspector Jolicoeur did not reply. He played the same conversation over again and said, "We have to carry out a forensic analysis of the tapes before we come to a definitive conclusion."

Elizabeth objected. "But if a judge heard Dr Jordan on tape, what other conclusions…? Isn't this proof positive that Dr Jordan hypnotised Mr Ted?" Didn't Inspector Jolicoeur hear the same tape she did? Wasn't Dr Jordan telling Mr Ted to take alcohol with barbiturates? Wasn't it a lethal combination?

"How would Dr Jordan explain this conversation on a witness stand?" asked the inspector.

"The tape is self-explanatory…"

"Could he not deny any knowledge of barbiturates and insist that the pills he referred to were mild sleeping pills or…?"

"Why are you trying to defend Dr Jordan? Anyone can see…"

It was Inspector Jolicoeur's turn to interrupt. "When I was studying at *Collège Classique*, the Jesuits taught me that Cicero, a Roman philosopher and lawyer, never lost a court case. Why? Because he spent so much time studying the counter-arguments of his opponents. I also try to anticipate what could be presented in Dr Jordan's defence if he was still alive. I have to admit that I have no idea how vigorously the department will investigate the tapes, given that Mr Agnew-Simpson and Dr Jordan are both dead." He took out his cell phone and called the station.

Elizabeth, very disappointed, walked over to the balcony window to calm down. Inspector Jolicoeur finished his conversation and approached her.

"Tell me, Miss Burgess, why do you reject suicide? Why is it so vital for you to believe that Mr Agnew-Simpson was hypnotised?"

Elizabeth based her view on a conversation with Agnew-Simpson on his philosophy of life. "I don't think that Mr Agnew-Simpson would want to be remembered as someone who committed suicide. I think that for him, suicide would mean giving up, an acceptance of defeat. He always wanted to be in control."

"One could argue that suicide was one way of taking control by deciding to end his life."

"No," Elizabeth objected. "He would want to be remembered for his books on Canadian history, for his academic endowments — he was not afraid to accept responsibility for all his actions. For Mr Ted, suicide would mean acting in bad faith — a cop-out."

It was three thirty. Elizabeth had to get back to the ski hill.

On the ride back with Monsieur Gervais, Elizabeth said she had a nasty headache. Thankfully, he did not ask any questions about the interview. He was anxious to return to the mansion to meet the forensic team. Elizabeth skipped dinner with Catherine and Marie-France. Nor could she sleep. She resolved that the memories churned up by Inspector Jolicoeur would not ruin the last days of her ski vacation. *You are going out on the slopes tomorrow, Lizzie. Let the cold wind blow away the cobwebs!*

The next day was 31st December. Elizabeth skied most of the day. They were planning to celebrate New Year's Eve with the other skiers at the inn. First, the hosts served a hearty supper of goulash soup, roast pork, red cabbage and mashed potatoes. Later, sitting by the enormous roaring fireplace in the shared living room, sipping a sweet, mulled wine, Elizabeth valiantly tried to keep awake. She lost the battle and went to bed before midnight. Catherine and Marie-France did not.

Chapter 32

On 1st January, Elizabeth awoke to the click of her cell phone under her pillow. It was an email from Alexander. He wished her a Happy New Year. There was a photo attached. Quietly, so as not to wake her roommates, Elizabeth climbed down from the upper bunk, and throwing her ski jacket over her pyjamas, crept down the wooden stairs to the hazy lounge that still smelled of stale beer. At seven in the morning, no one had cleared away the beer cans, plastic glasses, and greasy flakes of chips scattered all over the communal living room. She sat on the orange vinyl couch across from the fireplace, where faint wisps of smoke hovered over black embers. Only then did she open the attached photograph.

Alexander stood next to a man of similar height and build. The older man was handsome, with short, black hair tinged with grey at the temples. Both wore jeans and white shirts. They were surrounded by four girls, aged from about ten to twenty. The two eldest wore hijabs; the others had straight, shoulder-length hair. All were smiling. They were standing in a Moorish courtyard, beside a fountain decorated with blue tiles. The implicit message in the photograph was unmistakable — Alexander had been welcomed into Hassan's family. Elizabeth was so excited that she jumped off the couch and decided to call Alexander. Her heartbeat quickened as his phone rang — three, four, six times. Right before she was about to hang up, Alexander picked up.

"I just got your email and photo!" she said breathlessly. "I am so happy for you! Tell me, how did you meet Hassan? How did he react?"

"And a Happy New Year to you, too!" Alexander laughed out loud. "What did I do? I sent someone with a letter. I wasn't sure what to expect. I would not have been surprised if he refused to see me. But Hassan was overjoyed. He had no idea... I will tell you all about it when I get back. I can't talk now; we are all going to meet some relatives."

"But at least give me a few facts. What does Hassan do? What about his wife?"

"Hassan works as a Deputy Minister of Finance in the regional government. His wife died of breast cancer four years ago. My four half-sisters literally smother me with attention. They are all coming to Canada this summer. Sorry, Elizabeth, I'm keeping everyone waiting. I promise you a really nice dinner when I get back!"

"One last question. When are you coming back?"

"On the sixth, with Air Canada, through London."

Elizabeth put down the phone with tears in her eyes. *Alexander sounded so genuinely happy!* Ever since she opened the letters and read about Mathilde's ill-fated love affair, she had felt emotionally involved. *If there really is a heaven, I hope that Mathilde is looking down at Alexander and Hassan's reunion. After everything she went through, is this what they call poetic justice?*

By noon, the car was packed, and the skis tied to the rack. Catherine was dropped off in front of her apartment in Montreal. Still exhausted from skiing and dancing at the New Year celebration, Marie-France struggled to stay awake as they drove to Ottawa.

"I am so stupid! Why did I schedule my private tutorial for tomorrow? We could have slept in Montreal." They drove in silence, drinking coffee to stay awake. Elizabeth kept thinking of Alexander, but she did not want to talk about him. She would ask him for permission to tell his story after they met. She hoped he would invite her for dinner soon.

As the car turned off Trans Canada to Highway 417, Elizabeth said, "You know, I haven't spent Christmas with my sisters since before I left for Thailand, and I don't even remember the last time I went skiing. This will be my last vacation for a long, long time." Elizabeth had been accepted into the Information Studies programme, and for the next several years she expected to be tied to a gruelling work and study routine. She looked forward to it — confident in her own strength.

"Just think of where I was last January. Just back from Bangkok — a total basket case. I can't believe that I'm the same person."

"It's like you ran a gauntlet of terrifying ordeals — murder, suicide, kidnapping. I'm proud of you, Lizzie! You survived!"

Elizabeth began to sing at the top of her voice: *"I did survive. I didn't crumble; I didn't lay down and die. Oh, no, not I!"* Marie-France joined her for a rousing chorus of Gloria Gaynor's hit song.

"For some reason, I just remembered a fairy tale Mother used to read to us. I can visualise the book — it was old and tattered. I think she bought it at a garage sale. The hero was called Ivan, a peasant boy. For reasons I can't remember now, he aspired to marry a princess. To achieve his goal, he had to go through a series of ordeals set by an evil sorcerer. First, he had to jump into a cauldron of boiling milk, then into a cauldron of boiling water, and finally into a cauldron of ice-cold water. Ivan conquered his fear and performed this feat."

"So what is the moral of this fascinating story?" asked Marie-France.

"He was transformed into a prince and married the beautiful princess. So what about me? Don't I deserve some sort of reward?"

"You survived your ordeals! Isn't that enough?"

"No! I want a reward! And what about you, what are you looking forward to in the new year?" asked Elizabeth.

"I'm so looking forward to seeing Benjie again. I really missed him! He spent the Christmas holidays working as a bartender and skiing in Banff."

"When is he coming back?"

"On Saturday. I'll meet him at the airport. Wanna come?"

"Is Saturday the sixth? Alexander is also coming back on the sixth. From London."

"Check the arrival time of Alexander's flight. You could surprise him at the airport."

"Alexander did not ask me to meet him, but... but if I'm already at the airport with you..."

"Actually, Benjie asked me to bring you."

"What?"

"He wants to introduce you to a new friend he met at Banff. His name is Scott, and he's an engineering student at Carleton."

"Like I need a blind date! No, thanks!"

"Why not? Don't be so anti-social! Benjie showed Scott a picture of us skiing at Mont Tremblant. Scott was so smitten, he asked to meet you."

"He must be a real loser if he needs help meeting girls."

Chapter 33

On 6th January, Elizabeth and Marie-France arrived at the Ottawa airport early and stood looking up at the arrivals screen. There was a fifteen-minute difference between the arrival times of the London and Calgary flights. Benjie's flight was to arrive first.

Elizabeth's heart sank. She was looking forward to seeing Alexander again. She hoped that all the horrors were behind them. Who knew what the new year would bring? She regretted that she would miss Alexander's arrival.

But right before their eyes, the arrivals screen began to change. The Calgary flight would be late. Elizabeth smiled as she realised that Alexander would arrive first. To kill time, Elizabeth and Marie-France went to the café next to the gate. They nursed cappuccinos and stared at the messages on their phones.

"You'll probably bump into Alexander," said Marie-France. "I wouldn't be surprised if it will be different between you two now. You have both adjusted to life in Ottawa. All the crimes are solved…"

"What do you mean, solved? Inspector Jolicoeur — and don't get me wrong, the man is far from stupid — but he is no Poirot! Mako confessed to the murder of Dr Jordan. He confessed to us both, remember! Inspector Jolicoeur did not have to strain any of his little grey cells."

"What about Mathilde?" asked Marie-France.

"It was an accident! Why is that so hard to believe? Mr Ted loved her all his life! He really did!"

Marie-France was sceptical. "And Mr Ted's death?"

"The only useful thing the inspector ever did was to find the secret tapes. I'm sure that in his heart, Inspector Jolicoeur agrees with me that Dr Jordan hypnotised Mr Ted into committing suicide. Dr Jordan confessed to Alexander that he used hypnosis on poor Mathilde. Why not on Mr Ted? But the inspector claims he can't prove that in court — even with the tapes. I disagree, but who am I? Nobody! Don't forget that Inspector

Jolicoeur is not an independent detective with unlimited resources — he's a bureaucrat. He works for bosses who are more like bean counters than Poirots. The bean counters decide on how much money to allocate to an investigation. The January inquest into Mr Ted's death will rule it a suicide! Everybody will be happy. All neat and straightforward. No convoluted plot!"

"I'm disappointed," said Marie-France. "I like convoluted plots and twist endings."

"What about those rumours? Was it Dr Jordan's or Mr Ted's death that was supposed to be some sort of satanic ritual murder?"

"Please! Have you been reading *Gossip Queen*? Isn't it amazing, here we are in the twenty-first century, but so many people still believe this satanic ritual nonsense? What does this tell us about people?" asked Elizabeth.

"Well, I read somewhere that our brains are still wired to the Stone Age. So we may send men into space, but psychologically, we haven't really evolved that much. That article also made a connection between herd mentality and gossip. I don't quite remember the details."

"I guess we are not exactly rational creatures," said Elizabeth. "That's why tabloids make so much money. But going back to Mr Ted, I also suspect that he was hypnotised into signing the new will at Dr Jordan's birthday party. Of course, I can't prove that either."

"What does Inspector Jolicoeur think?"

"I have no idea. Inspector Jolicoeur told me that the police are investigating the connection between Dr Jordan's clinic and the cartel's drug and money-laundering operations. But he also said that this was outside his jurisdiction, so he's not even involved. I think that Dr Jordan had a debt to pay to the cartel. That's why he invited Señor Vasquez to witness the new will. He miscalculated. The cartel pressured him into getting rid of Mr Ted to get their money back as quickly as possible."

"I guess we will never know for sure." Marie-France looked at her watch. "Time to move on, Lizzie! It's a new year, time to turn a new leaf. Why not rewind your relationship with Alexander?"

Elizabeth wondered. Perhaps, just perhaps, Marie-France was right. She liked Alexander very much. Would this feeling blossom into something more? She pictured her heart as if it was encased in stone.

Were there any tiny cracks through which tender shoots could sprout?

Marie-France picked up Elizabeth's hand and looked into her palm. Imitating a foreign accent, she said, "I am a fortune teller, and I see your future. I see... I see... I see a man in your life... He will be tall... Wait a minute... No, medium height. With blue... No, with brown eyes. You will meet him very soon, very soon."

Both Marie-France and Elizabeth exploded in peals of laughter. Elizabeth stopped laughing and said, "You know, with all the recent turmoil, I don't think I gave my feelings a chance. Maybe now..."

Marie-France squeezed Elizabeth's hand.

A steady flow of passengers began to stream through the arrivals gate. Elizabeth looked up and saw Alexander. He looked tanned and relaxed as he pushed a luggage cart loaded with large suitcases and a small rolled-up carpet. Elizabeth was sitting behind a column. She rose and was about to call out his name, but sat down again. Alexander could not see Elizabeth from his vantage point, but he stood close enough that she could clearly see the expression on his face. He was obviously waiting for someone and smiling. Elizabeth gasped as she recognised the person approaching Alexander. She had christened him Discus Thrower. He was the handsome young man with honey-blond locks and an athlete's build, who drove Alexander to the faculty dinner from the Chateau Laurier. Alexander took Discus Thrower by the arm and whispered something into his ear.

Elizabeth had never seen such a warm glow on Alexander's face. There was such intimacy in the way Alexander straightened the lapel of his companion's safari jacket. How could she not see it before? *Alexander is gay!* In the first instance, this realisation was paralysing. Elizabeth felt breathless, as if the wind had been knocked out of her. She watched as Alexander and Discus Thrower walked away, shoulder to shoulder, pushing the baggage cart and talking.

"What's the matter? You look like you've seen a ghost," said Marie-France.

"Alexander." Elizabeth pointed to the arrivals section. Her voice was a whisper. "Alexander is gay."

"What! How did you suddenly come to this conclusion?"

"Look!" Elizabeth pointed to the passengers walking towards the exit.

Marie-France turned around in her seat, but could not find Alexander in the crowd. "So he went to Morocco with a friend or a colleague. So what?"

"I saw the way Alexander looked at him. His face was positively radiant. He's never looked at me like that."

Marie-France was at a loss for words. Elizabeth was silent, then said, "You know, honestly, I wish him happiness. He deserves it."

"I hope you're not too upset... But you may be wrong."

"I did think about the possibility of something more between us. Maybe I wanted to be in love again; but now it all makes sense. He was always very polite, but there was no flirtation. We were friends. He will always be my friend. I really do like him very much!"

Marie-France was going to say something, but bolted out of her chair and ran to the arrivals section. There was Benjie, carting his luggage and skis. She had to jump up to kiss him. Benjie guided Marie-France away from the throng. Elizabeth waited for the exuberant welcome to die down before she walked up to the couple.

"Let me introduce my friend, Scott. Can you give him a lift to his Carleton dorm?" asked Benjie.

Elizabeth had not noticed the young man in the beige parka. Scott was of medium build with curly brown hair and soft brown eyes. *He has full lips and a gap between the two front teeth. Not totally unattractive.* Elizabeth continued to examine his face, perhaps too intently. She noticed that Scott was looking straight at her. She saw his face redden and felt herself blush.

The skis were easy to transport; the rack was still attached to the car's roof, but loading the luggage was a challenge. Benjie, in the front seat, had a bulging duffle bag on his knees. Another enormous duffle bag was crammed into the back so that Elizabeth and Scott were literally crushed against each other. To fit in, Scott had to place one arm around Elizabeth's shoulder. Surprisingly, Elizabeth did not feel awkward squashed against this stranger. Scott looked at her with soft brown eyes and smiled. She felt warm and comfortable. It was as if this was where she was meant to be. She was disappointed when the car stopped in front of Scott's dormitory, and they had to get out of the car.

They made a date to meet Scott and Benjie on the following Saturday.

The first week of the winter semester was going to be busy for everyone.

"I can hardly wait for next Saturday," Scott whispered in Elizabeth's ear.

"Me, too," she said. Spontaneously, Scott kissed her lightly on the cheek. She felt a warm glow, and in that same instant, Elizabeth knew. She knew without a doubt that Scott was the one.

Marie-France drove Elizabeth home, before driving Benjie to his parents' house in Gatineau. Elizabeth could not sleep. The little white lamp on the night table was still on when Marie-France tiptoed into the bedroom and put on her nightgown.

"Are you asleep?" Marie-France asked.

"No," said Elizabeth, and she turned over on her elbow. "Funny how life is — suddenly, without any warning, you meet someone and you know."

"That's what they call love at first sight," said Marie-France. Then she yawned and leaned over to turn off the lamp.

The end.

Printed in the USA
CPSIA information can be obtained
at www.ICGtesting.com
LVHW091451041223
765470LV00001B/108